D0523575

The Web of Light

Diana Cooper

The Web of Light

A Spiritual Adventure

Copyright © 2004 by Diana Cooper

First published in Great Britain in 2004 by Hodder and Stoughton
A division of Hodder Headline

The right of Diana Cooper to be identified as the Author of the Work has been
asserted by her in accordance with the Copyright, Designs and Patents Act 1988.

A Mobius Book

3 5 7 9 10 8 6 4 2

All rights reserved. No part of this publication may be reproduced, stored in a
retrieval system, or transmitted, in any form or by any means without the prior
written permission of the publisher, nor be otherwise circulated in any form of
binding or cover other than that in which it is published and without a similar
condition being imposed on the subsequent purchaser.

All characters in this publication are fictitious and any resemblance to real persons,
living or dead, is purely coincidental.

A CIP catalogue record for this title is available from the British Library

ISBN 0 340 83074 3

Typeset in 12/15pt Sabon by
Phoenix Typesetting, Auldgirth, Dumfriesshire

Printed and bound in Great Britain by
Clays Ltd, St Ives plc

Hodder and Stoughton
A division of Hodder Headline
338 Euston Road
London NW1 3BH

To Greg,
One of the wisest and most genuine
light-workers I know.

Author's Note

The Web of Light is the most exciting book I have ever written. As with *The Silent Stones* and *The Codes of Power*, I was sent on an adventure quest. This one started in the Timbavati, which adjoins the Kruger National Park. While I was there I read the following, 'It was not by chance that the White Lions were born in the Timbavati. A secret and ancient connection exists between the Great Sphinx of Egypt and the Timbavati. Between the paws of the sphinx are the back-to-back Lion Gods known as Akeru. They hold a clue! The Akeru guards a meridian on our globe, which the ancient Egyptians held sacred, and upon which the White Lions were born in our day.' – Linda Tucker, author of *Children of the Sun God*.

Intrigued, I sought more information about the White Lions and went to see some captive ones. They were truly special. As one of them looked deep into my eyes, I knew that they were important for the healing of that country. Later, my guide Kumeka gave me information about their awe-inspiring cosmic role for our planet and I realised that they are among the great beings who illuminate the web of light, which cocoons and protects Earth.

After the safari in South Africa, I swam with the

dolphins in Mozambique, and started to receive information about their purpose in the web of light. Weeks
later I flew to Hawaii and there I encountered angel
dolphins and learnt about their magnificent task, which
is to hold the wisdom of pure Atlantis in trust for
humanity. Here I saw whales, turtles and sharks and
was informed by my guidance about their planetary
origins and mission on Earth. I found this most
interesting.

I was given specific information about the pure times
of Atlantis and was led to books, which enlightened me
about that incredible civilisation. The angels of Atlantis
impressed on me that they wish to return the sacred
wisdom to humanity again and are seeking the help of
those lightworkers who are ready to work with them. If
you feel you can do this, please tune into them in meditation and they will impress on you your task.

While I was writing the book I travelled to Egypt and
explored the sacred mysteries of the pyramids and the
Sphinx, their galactic connections and their esoteric links
with Atlantis. I was told it is time for certain ancient keys
and codes to be revealed and have done this in *The Web
of Light*.

I also learnt the mystical and sacred truth about Jesus'
life and mission to bring Christ Consciousness to our
planet. I was guided to weave this illuminating information into the book and demonstrate how this cosmic
energy is returning to the planet in an unexpected way.
As I wrote, I did not know until the last page whether
dark or light would triumph.

The entire experience of writing *The Web of Light* was extraordinary. Just as I was completing it, I was surrounded by unicorns. I knew nothing about them but every day for a fortnight these shimmering ascended horses were near me, helping me and telling me that they too are part of the angelic hierarchy. I then flew to France to facilitate a teacher training course and, with the synchronicity I have learnt to expect, the fields round the hotel were full of beautiful white horses. The unicorns asked me to include information about them to help people and this I have done.

Finally I realised that the web has been torn through the centre of Africa, along the seam of gold, which was mined and pulled from the Earth. Gold represents enlightenment. This link of the web must be mended in order to heal that continent and the rest of the world. At present the dark forces can enter through this rift, causing war, disease and unrest. My guide, Kumeka, the Master of the eighth ray, told me that if enough people do the following with pure intent, we can help to heal the web and return enlightenment to the area. Look at a map of Africa, draw a gold line down the centre and picture the line of enlightenment intact again. Then place crystals on the map as follows.

On the Giza plateau at the top of the map a black obsidian.

On the source of the Nile a yellow citrine.

On the Great Zimbabwe a red garnet.

On the Timbavati a green malachite.

Over Durban a blue lapis.

See www.dianacooper.com to download this map and explore fascinating information.

Of course as you serve the planet in this way you automatically start to heal and strengthen your spine, which is your own rod of power.

I have interwoven all these experiences and spiritual understandings into *The Web of Light*, the latest quest undertaken by Marcus, Joanna and Helen. This has been the most fascinating book I have ever written, for the information pouring in to me was extraordinary and it resonated deeply.

This is an adventure story and can be read on many levels, but if you open up to the higher mystical truths that are revealed, your spiritual growth will be enriched and accelerated.

I do hope you enjoy it.

Diana

Chapter 1

Helen looked over the rail on the high deck of the *Nile Crown* at the tiny boats bobbing below them. In each craft two or three Arabs in jellabas, the long robes worn traditionally in Egypt, were standing or rather wobbling precariously as they held up clothes for sale to the tourists on the deck.

Tonight was gala night, a dressing-up evening for the holidaymakers on board and the Arabs knew it well. Grinning, they showed brightly coloured, one size fits all, dresses and shirts, attractively garish and, if they sensed the slightest interest, they threw it up in a bundle, wrapped in a polythene bag. There was laughter and encouragement all round as passengers tried on, over their bathing costumes or shorts, the sort of clothes they would never wear again. Then the money was thrown down to the trader, folded into rejected clothes. Everyone shrieked when a man missed a parcel and it landed in the water, to be fished out and the clothes dried in the sun, before winging their way up again to this boat or another.

Helen laughed, getting caught up in the excitement. 'Hey, Tony! Come and see!' she called to her new husband, who was lying on a chaise-longue, reading under a shade. He smiled, pleased Helen was so happy, put down his book and rose to join her.

'Look at that one!' She pointed to a black dress sporting a life-size peacock in sequinned technicolour. One look at her face told him that she would be wearing it to the gala dinner that night. He waved to the man, who almost fell into the murky water as he launched the dress into the air like a missile. With it came several other options he hoped might tempt them. On reflection Tony decided the wobbling was part of the act to soften them up!

Helen tried the dress on over her costume and felt great in it. The black looked good with her short fair hair and dark brown eyes. It was perfect for a fun night. Her eyes shone as she considered what she could get Tony into. She settled for a white jellaba with gold trimmings and he humoured her. 'You look like a Greek god!' joked a plump American woman, clicking at him with her camera.

'Or perhaps an Egyptian one,' added her companion. And Tony did look regal in it with his broad shoulders and grey hair. He was too square-jawed to be really handsome, yet he looked a successful businessman who was used to being in command and the robe suited him. Helen was glad he had retired and taken up writing, which allowed a gentler side of his character to emerge.

Tony had been her rock, supporting her in Machu Picchu, Peru, when her daughter Joanna had been injured as they tried to rescue the portal for the light. And in Australia he had been at the other end of the phone whenever he was needed, while she, Joanna and Marcus,

Joanna's partner, had faced danger and endured hardship as they sought the Codes of Power, undertaking a dangerous initiation to help raise the frequency of the planet.

Then on her return to England Tony had proposed. Helen flushed with joy at the memory, though the blush hardly showed on her suntanned cheeks. He had asked her over a candlelit dinner and the next day they had gone for a blessing to Kumeka House, with her daughter and Marcus. Here a special community of men, under the guidance of a wise mystic called Zoranda, lived in accordance with cosmic law and devoted their time to mind control and spiritual practices. It was a place of peace and perfect safety. When they brought the Scroll from Atlantis, an ancient manuscript containing esoteric information, back from India these men had given them sanctuary. Later they joined them at Machu Picchu to help them against the evil men of the Elite, the darkest brotherhood on the planet. Now she felt honoured to be their friend.

With a start Helen realised that Tony was eyeing her with his quizzical smile.

'Well?' he queried, standing to attention in his white robe and trendy sunglasses, awaiting her approval.

'Perfect.' She smiled. 'You've got to wear it!'

'I thought so!' Tony gave a jubilant wave of acceptance to the patient vendor waiting far below and found a few tatty notes in the pocket of his shorts to pay him.

No sooner had he thrown down the money than a small boat appeared manned by a young Egyptian who nosed into the middle of the floating merchants, right underneath where Helen and Tony were leaning on the rails. Wearing a traditional jellaba, the man stood out as being cleaner and neater than the others. He balanced in the boat, awkwardly as if unaccustomed to doing such a thing, and held up a blue dress. It caught Helen's attention and she paused, though she did not want another dress.

The other traders did not like it. They shouted angrily at him, waving their arms in 'get off our pitch' gestures.

Rocking dangerously, he ignored them and called to Helen, or it seemed to her that he was addressing her alone. 'Yes, missus, nice dress for you,' he shouted. His English was unexpectedly clear.

She shook her head and Tony turned to go but Helen put her hand on his arm to stay him. She was intrigued by this young man.

Some intuition urged her to tune into her psychic gift, given to her as a reward when she passed the initiation into the Codes of Power. She had been granted the ability to see into the hearts of others. She took a deep breath and stilled herself, opening her third eye, and saw something very rare. His heart was pure.

In the instant she paused he had folded the dress, shoved it into a bag and lobbed it to her. At the same moment one of the other boats struck his. Knocked off centre, he threw out his arms as he tried desperately to maintain his foothold, then fell backwards into the sluggish waters of the Nile.

Helen caught the package and held it tight as she tried

to make out what was happening in the commotion of splashes, shouts and yells. She thought one of the traders tried to hit the young man with a paddle but he ducked and disappeared. She watched anxiously for him, determined to give him some money for the dress, which she didn't want. But she did not see him again. He left without being paid. She frowned at the thought. Something was very wrong.

Back in their cabin, she pulled the garment from its bag, feeling guilty. What was she going to do with it anyway? As she opened it a piece of paper fluttered out of the folds. She picked it up and read: 'IMPORTANT. I have information for you. Meet me at the Sphinx at 8 a.m. on Tuesday. Be careful E.' It was written in an educated hand.

Her stomach flipped. Today was Thursday. Someone must know they were flying to Cairo on Monday night. Surely it couldn't start all over again. Not on her honeymoon! She was white under her tan.

Tony grabbed her by the arm and steered her out of the cabin to the bar for a medicinal brandy.

They looked at each other grimly as they took their first sip. At that moment his mobile rang.

Chapter 2

The car drew up in a puff of dust in front of the Great White Lodge and a tall, broad-shouldered man, dressed in white, stepped out into the searing heat.

Zoranda's head was shaved like a monk, yet he held himself with a noble, confident poise. He had never visited Cairo before and was filled with curiosity and a sense of anticipation, for he had been summoned to a meeting with the leaders of the Great White Brotherhood, an organisation embracing all the Great Mystery Schools in the world. He felt honoured at the invitation, for this was a secret enclave, one of vital importance to the future of the planet, and decisions were to be taken that could affect every living creature. But what was the meeting about?

During the flight and drive from the airport questions revolved in his mind. What did they want of him? Why Egypt? Why now? But he could not fathom the reason for the call. Throughout his life he had met some of the wisest people on the planet as an equal but now a worm of self-doubt entered his mind. He took a breath of the hot scented air and let it out very slowly to control a sudden feeling of tension. None of this showed, however, as he paid the driver and watched the car turn and drive away.

Zoranda noticed that the gates of the villa were purely ornamental. So too were the grilles on the windows, unusual in a residence of this size and opulence. The Great White Lodge was clearly protected by spiritual means alone, as was Kumeka House, the home of the Brotherhood of Light, which he had founded in England.

His glance took in the well-tended palm trees, emerald lawns and neatly raked paths. A circular turquoise pool graced the left-hand side of the house, where the soft spray of a fountain shimmered and floated, light as a bridal veil. He relaxed at last. This is beautiful, he thought.

Only one car stood outside the villa, that of the head of the Great White Brotherhood, a man whose light and wisdom was legendary in esoteric circles, a man of power and vision, yet who was invisible in the outer world. Few knew who he was or what he did.

Zoranda's quick eye observed an eagle circling overhead in the clear azure sky. He smiled. A sign from the universe, he thought, pleased.

He murmured a prayer, thanking the powers-that-be for the highest outcome to the meeting and for help in making the wisest possible decisions, then he picked up his small case and walked towards the marble steps leading to the great double doors that served as an entrance. As he approached, the doors opened and a man and a woman waited to greet him.

Suddenly the eagle catapulted from the sky on to a small bird, which shrieked and flapped as the great raptor rose with it in its talons. They all stared. Then something unbelievable happened, something he had never seen before. The eagle, seemingly deliberately, dropped its prey, which landed with a thud on the steps in front of Zoranda. There was a moment of stunned silence before the wounded creature struggled up and half dragged, half flapped its way painfully across the garden and out of sight. The predator soared away.

Zoranda frowned and goose-pimples rose on his arms. The man and woman both looked shocked and im- measurably grave. Zoranda deliberately put the shadow of fear from his mind and raised a hand in greeting to them, but he was aware of a prickling sensation at the back of his neck.

As he reached the top of the steps the man stepped forward to greet the newcomer into his home. 'Welcome, brother,' he said. In two words his voice conveyed such warmth that Zoranda felt enveloped in a tangible cocoon of love. This man was the head of the Great White Brotherhood, an ancient mystic order, which had served the light for hundreds of years. He was old in years yet he appeared youthful and glowed with an extraordinary radiance. His blue eyes were luminous, all-seeing, set in a finely chiselled face. He was universally known as the Master.

The woman was shorter, with dark skin and black eyes, but she too had a dignified and gracious manner and shook his hand firmly.

Another man walked into the hall. He was as tall as Zoranda and distinguished-looking, with grey hair and deep brown eyes. Like the Master and the woman who stood at his side, he was an illumined one. He represented the Order of the White Flame. Within a few minutes Zoranda was introduced to three other members of the board, who had travelled from all parts of the globe to Cairo for this extraordinary meeting. In total there were five men and one woman, some of the most highly evolved beings on the planet, all of whom had been tried and tested in this life and others, before being chosen to represent the Hierarchy of Light on Earth. Each of those who sat on the board of the Great White Brotherhood was of a different race and colour. They all lived an ordinary life in the outer world and served secretly in the inner one.

Their presences radiated a light so clear it was visible, even at times to the uninitiated. Many who glimpsed it gasped, and those who had murky auras often felt threatened by it. Zoranda, however, observed their light and felt immeasurably reassured as he shook each hand in turn.

When the introductions were over the head of the Great White Brotherhood touched his arm. 'May I show you to your room?' he offered, as if it were the most natural thing in the world that he should do so. Then he answered Zoranda's unspoken question. 'There is no one else in the house. Younger brothers who often serve us have been sent out on missions this afternoon. Total privacy is ensured and no lower thoughts or enquiring minds can reach into our deliberations.'

Whatever is it about? Zoranda wondered again. Yet nothing showed in his voice or expression. He merely nodded.

In the villa everything was unique and chosen for its spiritual radiance, for all objects emit the vibration of those who craft them. Goods that are mass-produced in sweatshops absorb and release into the ether the pain, frustration and bitterness of the worker. Those that are made with love pour harmony into the atmosphere.

His room was huge, simply but beautifully furnished with objects of the highest quality. Everything was hand-crafted and carefully placed. He picked up a wooden model of a lion and lioness; the male was stern and watchful, the female playfully rolling by his side. They were so delicately and intricately sculpted that he found himself stroking them as if they were living cats. They were carved with love and devotion, he reflected as he replaced them on a small table. They're truly beautiful.

Half an hour later, showered, changed and refreshed, he walked into the meeting chamber, a large airy white space. A large crystal was placed in each corner. One was rose quartz, one amethyst, the third white quartz and the fourth corner was graced by the biggest piece of lapis that Zoranda had ever seen. Each of them seemed to pulse with life force and he knew they had been chosen to raise the frequency of the room. In the centre stood a table with six chairs.

'There are twelve members on the board but today only six are able to be present,' the Master told him. 'There is an urgency to this mission, which is why we sent for you.'

Zoranda sat forward slightly, listening intently for messages spoken and unspoken. 'I am at your service.

What do you want of me?' His voice was soft and calm.

'Thank you. We wish you to oversee a situation.' The Master scrutinised him for a moment and Zoranda felt that his very soul was being probed. 'There will shortly be a cosmic moment, an event of great importance to humanity. It is an opportunity which the light wishes to utilise to raise the consciousness of all people and the vibration of the planet.'

Zoranda waited.

'We have examined the cosmic signs and the movement of the celestial bodies. We know that a divine symbol is to be sent to Earth very shortly. From our meditations into the universal consciousness we understand that this is of vital importance to opening the hearts and minds of the masses.'

The wise man paused for a moment and then continued, 'This can have an enormous impact on the health of humanity, for diseases such as cancer and AIDS must disappear when the heart opens.'

The bald man was startled. Of course, he realised, it makes perfect sense. Hurt and grief result in the closing of the heart, which in turn destroys the immune system. This allows cancer and AIDS and many other diseases to develop. Opening the heart to higher consciousness would offer a perfect healing. Zoranda smiled as he considered the awesome worldwide implications of this.

'There is another matter,' the Master went on. 'As you know, the sacred mystic teachings were distorted and rewritten by the holy fathers of the Christian Church. They had their reasons. They felt the populace was not ready for the truth. However this is no longer valid. Indeed it is time for the higher understandings to be revealed to the general public, for as I am sure you know we have entered a time of openness when secrets must come to the surface to be looked at without judgement.'

Zoranda nodded. He had studied the esoteric truths to which the great man referred.

'We ask three things of you. First, to divulge the mystery of Christ's message in a way that the uninitiated can understand and, second, to spread the great knowledge about the web of light.'

Zoranda felt his heart thumping but he waited in silence as he considered the web of light, a cocoon, like a spider's web, round the planet, which keeps it safe from attack by predatory planets. The threads of the web connect the portals and all sacred places and are fed and lit up by angels of light, beings from friendly planets and certain extraordinary cosmic energies. However, the web was already damaged in places, he knew, rendering Earth vulnerable to penetration by dark forces.

'We ask you to choose someone and teach him or her about these sacred truths, someone who has the courage to spread the information by writing and speaking about it.' The Master paused and looked at Zoranda with a question mark in his eyes.

Helen! thought Zoranda immediately. She could do it. She's courageous and she can speak out and write. He almost proffered her name. Then he remembered how much she had undergone since the Scroll was brought from Tibet. Would it be fair to ask her? Would she be pilloried and crucified just as Jesus was when He tried to spread the truth?

But he realised that six pairs of eyes were examining his heart and reading his mind. With a trace of reluctance, he murmured, 'Helen!'

All nodded. As keepers of the light they were aware of the extraordinary Scroll from Atlantis, which had been handed to Marcus and his girlfriend Joanna, Helen's daughter. In order to bring the attention of the world to the information it contained, the three of them had fought the dark forces. They had also travelled round the world following its instructions as they tried to reclaim the major portals of the planet for the light. And after that in Australia they had endured trials of initiation to obtain the Codes of Power for humanity. Zoranda also knew Helen wrote articles and had, a long time ago, written a book.

Is it right to ask more of her, especially as she is on her honeymoon? he asked himself, but after a fractional hesitation, he added, 'She's right here in Egypt.'

Again they all nodded and Zoranda realised they knew this and had intended him to nominate Helen.

He had a vivid flash of her as he had last seen her the previous week on her wedding day. Small and slim, her short fair hair glinted gold in the autumn sunshine and she had simply glowed with happiness as she looked up at Tony, her new husband. Zoranda guessed she was in her late fifties, though she did not look it and her deep blue dress managed to look vibrant, yet elegant. Helen was often quiet, which disguised her depth of wisdom, but on this day champagne and happiness revealed an exuberant side of her that he had not previously seen.

'We believe Helen is ready to undertake this.' The dark woman spoke and again he had the feeling that she was reading his thoughts.

'Would she be in danger?' he asked.

There was a fraction of a pause. 'Her spirit would not be in danger,' the woman replied.

Zoranda knew he must not let emotion cloud his judgement on anything. His life had been dedicated to the light. But this was not his life they were talking about. He felt unexpectedly protective of Helen.

'Why Helen?'

'The same reason that you thought of her. She's totally dedicated to her work for spirit no matter what. And her husband will support her.'

Zoranda nodded. A strange unfamiliar feeling swept through him and it felt uncomfortably like guilt.

'We believe the Evil Ones of the Elite know that Helen is in Egypt and may be looking for her. They know she has been used in the past as an agent to undertake special projects for the light. I imagine that after their débâcle with the Codes of Power in Australia, they are more determined than ever to thwart our attempts to raise the consciousness of the world.' The Master was speaking in a soft voice, the hallmark of all Essenes, the sacred sect to which he belonged. 'Of course, the Elite have access to cosmic information just as we do, so they know of the forecast event.'

What is the forecast event? Zoranda wanted to interject, knowing his third mission must be connected to it, but the Master continued, 'They realise it will give great power to the spiritual forces. They also believe it will unravel the great mystery of the Sphinx – and they want that secret for themselves.'

Suddenly Zoranda felt his palms sweating despite the air-conditioning. The secret of the Sphinx! A cosmic event about to happen! He must speak.

'What is forecast?' he queried.

'Ah!' said the Master. 'A being who symbolises the rebirth of the cosmic heart is to incarnate. Our third mission for you is to protect him.'

Zoranda felt his throat constrict but his eyes shone with an excitement he could not disguise.

The speaker continued, 'On no account must Helen go to the Sphinx, for they are watching it. Please speak to her immediately and ask her to come here for her own safety and so that she can be instructed in the sacred mysteries.'

'And her husband?'

'He may come here too.'

Thank goodness, thought Zoranda, feeling better. Aloud he said, 'Please tell me about the cosmic being and his connection to the Sphinx.'

'The cosmic symbol,' repeated the Master slowly as if revelling in the secret before he replied. 'Somewhere in South Africa a sacred white lion is to be born. The birth of this white cub is of vital significance as it is linked to the Christ and to the Sphinx.'

Zoranda suppressed a gasp and his mind wandered for

a moment before he realised that the Master was still speaking.

'The birth of the cub represents a cosmic opportunity to open the heart of humanity and bring peace. We must find it before the Elite does so.' He was looking directly at Zoranda. 'Helen must learn about the mystic connections of the web of light. The birth of the cub will give the dolphins permission to reveal their secrets. Yes, the white lion cub holds the keys, which will light up the web. The lion must live.' But even he did not yet know how vital this birth would be to the planet.

Zoranda frowned suddenly. The last thing the Dark Brotherhood of the planet wanted was peace on Earth. Much of their money and power came from the manipulation of wars everywhere. And they certainly did not want a cure for the major diseases. He was sure the pharmaceutical giants would do their utmost to stop this information reaching the masses.

Furthermore the Elite did not have to abide by the sacred laws of honour and truth as did those who were initiated into the various orders of the Great White Brotherhood.

His impassive face did not reveal his whirling thoughts.

'You wish me to go to South Africa to find the white lion cub?' he asked, but as the leader of the Great White Brotherhood's clear blue eyes pierced into him, he knew the answer.

The wise man opposite him shook his head.

'You want me to send Marcus and Joanna to South Africa, don't you?'

'Yes.'

The silence was intense. Would they be ready for such a task? Marcus, who had been given the Scroll of Atlantis by the dying monk and who had already proved his courage and tenacity? And Joanna, who had nearly died at Machu Picchu and again at Uluru? Was it right to ask them to lay their lives on the line again?

Zoranda met each gaze in turn. Then he said quietly, 'I'll contact them immediately.'

The woman who was seated next to him handed him a mobile. 'It is important that you phone Helen first. She must not go to the Sphinx or her life will be in danger.'

Chapter 3

Marcus and Joanna walked hand in hand through the beech woods as gold, orange and brown leaves swirled around them. 'I love England in October,' exclaimed Joanna, letting go of Marcus's hand and darting to chase a tumbling leaf, which twisted away, evading her grasp. She laughed, her whole face alight. 'I nearly caught it. I could do with a wish.'

As a child she used to run after falling leaves in the autumn and make a wish on each one she caught. At last, her long brown hair flying in the breeze and her cheeks pink with exertion, she snatched at an orange crinkled leaf with her outstretched hands and held it fast. 'Got it. Now what shall I wish for?' She looked at Marcus with her sparkling brown eyes. 'A new car for you or promotion for me?'

'Careful! You might get it,' her partner replied with a chuckle. His grey eyes twinkled back into hers. 'Why not play safe and wish for happiness?'

Joanna wrinkled her nose. 'We've got that. I've never been happier. Everything's going so well.' For a moment her expression sobered as she remembered their experiences in Australia. In England it was safe and that was wonderful as far as she was concerned.

Marcus was nearing the end of a contract for work and they were planning a holiday somewhere quiet. She wondered how Marcus would cope with that. He was a doer, filled with restless energy, who made adventure happen.

The words slipped from her mouth: 'I hope everything isn't going *too* well.' She was about to cancel the dangerous statement when Marcus's mobile rang.

For the rest of her life she remembered that moment, when the thin yellow sun was filtering through the beeches and lighting up Marcus's face. She saw his expression sharpen with surprise. 'Zoranda! Hello! What can I do for you?' His jaw tightened as he listened in concentrated silence and Joanna found her body frozen in an odd attitude as she waited. Two squirrels chased each other along a branch above them, shaking down a flurry of leaves. A thrush sang from some hidden thicket and a rabbit ran across a grassy clearing beyond the trees. She was oblivious.

'South Africa!' Those words she heard. 'When?'

She noticed that a leaf had landed on Marcus's brown hair and wanted to brush it off but did not. His face was inscrutable but she saw that his eyes were glittering with excitement and her stomach lurched.

'How important?' A long pause. Marcus nodded. 'Of course. We'll wait to hear from you.'

He clicked off and turned to Joanna.

'You heard that? Zoranda wants us to go to South Africa. It's something to do with the riddle of the Sphinx.'

19

He sounded as if he were trying to suppress the elation in his voice.

'The Sphinx!' exclaimed Joanna, then added, puzzled, 'He wants us to go to South Africa?'

Marcus nodded. 'He was phoning from Egypt and—'

Joanna interrupted. 'Egypt! What's he doing there? He was here last week at Mum's wedding.'

'Apparently he was summoned over there to a secret meeting.'

Joanna frowned and looked hard at Marcus. 'That's where Mum and Tony are! It's too much of a coincidence.'

'I know,' he agreed. He didn't want to tell her that they might be in danger, but she knew Marcus too well. He felt her tense and tried to pre-empt her questions. 'Yes, I know your mother and Tony are there on honeymoon but they'll be looked after.' Marcus hoped that was right. It was not quite what Zoranda had said.

'You're sure?'

Marcus nodded and she relaxed a little.

'Go on.'

'There's about to be a cosmic revelation to do with the riddle of the Sphinx. It's time for the sacred mystery to be unlocked.'

Joanna felt a tingle somewhere inside her stomach. 'What's it to do with South Africa and why does he want us to go there?'

'He says a ley line runs from the Sphinx down through Africa to the south. It's been disrupted and broken in many places, so the web of light is torn, which is part of the reason Africa is in such chaos and turmoil. It's vital to mend the section through the centre of Africa because it's of utmost importance for peace and healing everywhere.'

'And that's where we come in?' Joanna's voice was sharp. She had a gut suspicion there was danger involved.

'Well, yes. According to cosmic information, a white lion is to be born in the wild in South Africa.'

'A white lion!' she echoed in surprise. 'Not an albino?'

'No. A sacred white lion.'

'A divine animal,' Joanna found herself whispering. Her voice had softened. 'Pure white animals are sent at special times, aren't they, to bring an important message to mankind.'

'Yes! Zoranda says the white lion will carry the cosmic Christ energy and has the power to open people's hearts. It is being sent from the universe now as a portent of new awakenings in humanity's consciousness. This cub also holds the keys to the secret of Giza – you know, the true purpose of the Sphinx and pyramids.'

She nodded.

'And that's essential for the ascension of the planet. The lion must survive.'

Joanna started to feel stirrings of excitement in her heart. 'And we are to find the white lion cub?'

'Got it in one.'

'And the Elite?' She faltered. 'Do the Dark Ones know?'

Marcus nodded gravely. 'Almost certainly. They have access to occult information too.'

Joanna sighed. She hated the word occult, as it was

often misinterpreted as dark, whereas it simply meant hidden. She could feel tension crawling up her back and lodging at the nape of her neck. She shook her head as if to free it.

'How are we to connect with the lion cub? Where will it be?' There was an edge of sarcasm in her voice and Marcus knew she was afraid. He took her hand and held it tight.

'There's more than that. Zoranda says the Great White Brotherhood wants us to find the cub and protect it.'

Joanna gasped, 'The Great White Brotherhood!' In her wildest imaginings she had never thought she would be connected to such an august and awesome organisation.

Marcus nodded, 'It's unbelievable isn't it? Of course they want you to listen to the cub's message.' He smiled wryly. 'The gift you received for passing the initiation into the Codes of Power has proved a mixed blessing, hasn't it?'

She nodded slowly.

When they had passed the initiation ordeals, Helen, Marcus and Joanna had each been granted a spiritual gift to use with wisdom and integrity for the highest good of the planet.

Helen had received the gift of looking into people's hearts and seeing what truly lay within them. She had learned it was not an easy gift to carry.

Marcus's gift was to examine people's souls. He could see their soul journey and help them towards the next step but he found this an awesome responsibility and rarely used it.

Joanna had been thrilled to accept the gift of communication with the animal kingdom but, like Marcus and her mother, she found it a two-edged sword. Now clearly she was to be tested again.

Strangely, Marcus's words stirred her old fighting spirit which was lurking somewhere inside her. She had earned that gift and she knew she must use it. She gritted her jaw suddenly. Marcus noticed it and smiled. That was more like Joanna.

She simply could not imagine communicating with lions in the wild. She would have to learn to tune into their frequency, which might be very different from that of English animals. And how would she get near enough? There were so many questions to ask so she started at the beginning.

'How do we find the white cub? South Africa's a big place.'

'I know. We'll have to listen to our intuition and wait for divine synchronicity to guide us. It's never let us down yet.'

'That's true but it seems very vague.'

Marcus ignored that. 'There is something else. Zoranda said the Sphinx was connected to certain stars, which is where the lion comes from. Apparently it's known as a star beast. There are a group of astrologers working on the co-ordinates which should help us pinpoint its position.'

'That's more like it. Isn't that how the Wise Men found where Jesus was born? I thought they came to Bethlehem as a result of astrological calculations based on cosmic predictions. Then the star showed them the exact location.'

'Yes, that's what I understood too. I wonder if they'll send us a star?' Marcus mused. 'Anyway I'm sure they'll find a way.'

'Of course they will.'

Joanna looked down at her hand, which was still clutching the leaf she had caught. 'Now I know what I want to wish for.' She detached her hand from Marcus's and held the leaf with both hands. Then she closed her eyes and spoke aloud. 'I wish to find the white lion and reveal the riddle of the Sphinx.'

She opened her eyes again and added, with a sly grin to Marcus, 'Now I want to visit the zoo and practise connecting with lion consciousness.'

He groaned but secretly he was delighted.

Chapter 4

That evening as they dressed for the gala dinner, Helen
and Tony had the first disagreement of their married life.
It was more than an argument, almost a heated row.
Helen's intuition told her that 'Be careful' signified
danger, whether or not they responded to the note. Tony
was an academic with a tendency to bury his head in the
sand. Who else would switch off his phone when
someone might be trying to contact them? She felt unexpectedly irritated and needed to know what was going
on. So she suggested that they phone back the number
that had so startled them and caused Tony to cut off
means of communication. 'Then we might have some
idea what it's all about,' she declared, feeling braver after
a couple of drinks. 'We didn't recognise the number so
maybe it was that young man trying to contact us again.
He said he has some important information for us. If we
don't call back, we'll never know.'

Tony flipped. He did not want his wife mixed up in
cloak and dagger intrigue, let alone danger. He was determined all that was in the past.

'You must be mad,' he retorted in a cold, dismissive
voice, which she found totally alienating. 'There's no way
we're contacting anyone.'

Helen felt defensive and furious. I've made a terrible mistake marrying this man, she thought in sudden panic. Irrational with distress she lashed out verbally. 'I hope you're not going to try to stop me doing what I feel is right. Just remember that my work for the light comes first in my life.' She said it with such aggression that Tony stepped back, hurt to the quick.

He gathered himself to react with vitriol when Helen stopped him.

'Wait.' She sat down and took a deep breath, shaken at the way she had spoken. 'I'm sorry. What I said was inappropriate. I thought I'd dealt with my anger but I really let you press my buttons.' She drew a hand across her eyes and looked so frail that Tony immediately felt guilty.

'No, it was my fault,' he claimed.

'There's no blame,' replied Helen, calmer now. 'But we do have something to resolve. We were both reacting from fear.'

'I know.'

'And it's control issues. We need to watch that!' She smiled. Suddenly the tension dissolved and they were able to talk rationally and make up. Within ten minutes life seemed brighter again. She did reassure Tony that he came first in her life but even as she said it, she wondered if she was being honest with him or true to herself.

Nevertheless one thing emerged clearly from the conversation. Helen intended to go to the Sphinx to meet the young man. She explained to Tony that the young Egyptian's heart had been pure and she was sure he came with the best of intentions. 'I've rarely seen a heart so light,' she told him, running her hands through her hair. 'It amazed me. He is quite an extraordinary young man. He really is acting in our best interest but something was troubling him.'

Tony was bemused. Though he did not really understand Helen's gift, he honoured and trusted this woman he married. However, he did not want his honeymoon to be marred by accident or danger. Asserting his masculine energy, he placed the mobile in the bottom of his suitcase and declared he would not be answering any calls for the rest of their honeymoon.

Probably because of their quarrel and the subsequent make up, they had a hilarious evening at the gala dinner. The bizarre clothing many people were wearing broke down all barriers. Men wore white robes with strange headdresses, women shimmering sequinned clothes. The newly-weds chatted to lots of people, laughed at the comedy acts and danced. It was a fun evening and they had a thoroughly good time, so it was quite late when they went to bed. They walked across the wide foyer, past the little shop, which was closed now, and down the narrow corridor to their cabin. As they went they exchanged pleasantries with a charming couple called Ruth and Robin who, it transpired, had the cabin opposite theirs. As they opened their door they heard Ruth screech, followed by roars of laughter.

Knowing that the fun-loving Arabs often played practical jokes, Helen and Tony were both grinning as they entered their cabin. What they saw made Helen scream. A man was sitting on the bed staring at them! Tony pushed Helen behind him. His heart was thumping. She felt sick.

But when they put the light on they laughed shakily. It was a dummy in Tony's T-shirt and hat, and Helen's sunglasses, presumably dressed by the cabin attendants as a joke. From the laughter and squeals they heard from other cabins they knew that this harmless prank had been repeated everywhere.

Helen felt her knees shaking. That's stupid, she told herself. It's only a lark. But she could not help it. Strangely enough at that moment a firm resolution formed in her head. She would be at the Sphinx on Tuesday. No fear would stop her. She hoped to persuade Tony to go with her but she was going to be at the rendezvous whether Tony was with her or not.

Next morning was their last one on the cruise boat. They were to fly to Abu Simbel in a light plane to see the giant statues, then fly back and catch a train to Luxor.

In the minibus Helen felt jittery. She wished they had not come. She saw danger in every face and during take-off was convinced that the Egyptian on the flight was one of the Elite. She watched him minutely, jumping whenever he moved, but she did not articulate her fear to Tony. Instead she was irritable and snappy. Her husband understood and excused her mood because he knew she was nervous.

When the Egyptian fell asleep within half a minute of take-off, she relaxed and even laughed at herself. This trip at least was safe.

Looking out of the window at the dusty desert edged with jewel-blue waters below, Helen was entranced. 'It's like a gift from the gods,' she said softly. 'It's breath-takingly beautiful.'

And when they reached their destination, after walking in searing heat across rocky desert to the great temple, she was overawed. Even when she stretched up and stood on tiptoe she could not reach the knees of the gods. They were huge.

'You're just the size of a midge!' Tony teased with a grin as he photographed her against the wall of giants.

'Watch it! I'd chase you with my water bottle if it wasn't too hot to run.' She laughed back, feeling more like a teenager than a mature woman of nearly sixty.

'Yes, it's unbelievably hot. I can't imagine how the ancient Egyptians built a civilisation in this heat,' agreed Tony. 'Let alone sculpted these statues.'

'They were highly advanced peoples,' said Helen. 'And I suppose they had slaves, which isn't so evolved.'

'No,' he said soberly. 'But with or without slaves it's an amazing piece of work. And to think it was moved in recent years.'

Originally sited where a dam was to be built, the great temple with all its vast statues had been moved to higher ground. It was an enormous project, which involved international co-operation and teamwork.

'It's incredible, isn't it. Perhaps the Pharoahs were influencing humans from the other side to get everyone working together!'

'I hope so.'

'If the world could unite to save this temple, surely we can get it together for humanity,' Helen declared, wiping sweat from her face as she scanned the incredible structure. 'Oh look!' She pointed out a beige-coloured lizard which was as still as a statue itself and was scarcely discernible against the rock face.

'Wow, that was the most fascinating place,' she commented an hour later, as she settled back in her seat on the plane. 'I could have done with longer there though.'

'Me too. Tell you what. I'll bring you back on our twenty-fifth wedding anniversary!'

'Don't be silly. We'll be too old to climb down to the temple then!' she exclaimed with a half giggle.

'Nonsense. First, now that we've got each other we'll get younger all the time and, second, they'll have a moving pavement or little train there by that time.'

'Yes,' she agreed. 'You're probably right.'

Three hours later they were on the train to Luxor, waiting for it to draw out of the station. Tony had his head in a book and Helen was delving in her bag for a tissue when suddenly she glanced up. A young man was hurrying past the window. He looked in as he passed as if he were searching for someone, but she knew he had not seen them.

'Quick, look! It's him!' she exclaimed, but he had gone by the time Tony glanced up.

'Who?'

'The man who threw the warning note up to me on the boat! I'm sure it was him!'

'The Arab who wanted you to meet him at the Sphinx?' Tony's voice was sharp.

Helen ignored it and stood up to peer out of the next window but he'd gone. 'I'm sure it was him!' she repeated, sitting down, an anxious look on her face. 'I wonder if he was looking for us.'

Helen was right about most of it. The young man, whose name was Edward, had not seen them and he had desperately hoped to find them. However, he was not Egyptian but a dark-haired Englishman, dressed in Arab clothes. Sent by the Master on an important mission, Edward had been mugged by agents of the Elite, who had stolen important papers from him. He feared for Helen's life and since that time he had been trying to warn her that the Elite were after her.

He leaped on to the train at the last minute. At Luxor he took a taxi to the airport to catch a flight to Cairo. There a car took him straight to the villa on the outskirts of Cairo where the Master and Zoranda were waiting. Edward had to face their reaction to the terrible news that the papers had been stolen from him. To add to that he had asked Helen to meet him at the Sphinx, despite knowing she was in danger and the Elite were watching her. Worse, he could not contact her to warn her.

He did not know that Zoranda had already left several messages on Tony's mobile but there was no response from him. Danger was looming for Helen.

Chapter 5

Edward was slightly built with a lithe, whippy body, brown eyes, beaky nose and dark complexion. He was English though he had spent part of his childhood in Egypt, where he had learned Arabic and was often taken for Egyptian.

As a child Edward was a dreamer who saw the spirit world. When he was five the boy was contacted by his father's grandmother, so he told his dad about her. She had died many years before the child was born but, as her spirit stood in front of him, he described her hair, her clothes and the pet name she used for her grandson. Young Edward, with a faraway look in his eyes, had said, 'Daddy, she's giving you a white rose. She says thank you for the roses.' Edward's father went white. His beloved grandmother had died when he was thirteen and he placed white roses on her grave whenever he visited it, though he had never told anyone. The man could not cope with such strange revelations from beyond the veil. He made it known that such 'imagination' was not acceptable. From that moment comments of a bizarre and unnatural nature were outlawed and as he grew up Edward learned not to speak of the spirit world but he remained aware that the visible world is only a small part of reality.

His parents had been married for three years when they adopted Bede. He was the child of a black father and white mother, which had raised eyebrows among their friends, especially as they were living in commuter-belt Surrey at that time, long before they were posted to Egypt. Their natural son, Edward, was born three years later. The latter was a gentle child who had always been able to pour oil on to troubled waters and had an innate sense of goodness and kindness. This was fortunate for the family as Bede did not. Yet, despite all provocation from the hell-bent Bede, his parents never consciously favoured their natural son.

Once, when Edward was four, Bede was particularly nasty to him and their mother was in despair. Edward piped up, 'Don't worry, Mummy. I chose to be his brother before I was born. I'm here to help him.' That was before weird statements were banned.

She had turned away with a frown, which he did not understand. In fact there was a lot about his family he did not comprehend, secrets lurking below the surface. Over the years he learned to keep his own counsel.

When he was eighteen Bede went to visit his Aunt Monica and Uncle Peter in South Africa. His mother did not want him to go. Her deepest fear was that she would lose him and she cried for days after he left. 'He'll never come back. I just know it. It's not fair after I brought him up,' she wailed and was inconsolable at the loss of her difficult elder son.

Edward's father decided his younger son was destined to become a lawyer but the youth had other ideas. When it was time for him to go to university, he refused politely. 'No,' he said to his appalled father. 'University stuffs your mind with other people's information. There's no room for original thinking or creativity. Sometimes it takes years to clear all that rubbish out so that you can be yourself again. I don't want to live my life that way.'

His father did not understand and thought a year out would change his mind.

So Edward too was despatched to South Africa to stay with his Aunt Monica and Uncle Peter at the safari lodge they ran. He looked forward to seeing his brother, who had been working there for three years and had taken to the place as if it were his soul home. To Edward's delight, Bede looked a different person, happy, fulfilled, joyous even, quite unlike the morose boy Edward had grown up with in England.

The younger brother reflected on how distressed his mother had been about Bede coming to Africa. It's as if she knew he would never return, he thought, and was struck by a shocking realisation. She didn't want to let him go even though she thought he would be happier here. Bede had always wanted to go back to the bush, ever since the family had holidayed there with his aunt and uncle years before.

That's why she was different with Edward, quite happy to let him visit his aunt and uncle. She knew he would return home. Indeed Edward had only stayed in South Africa a few months. Then he came back to England, joining the brotherhood at Kumeka House for a probationary period, where he dedicated his life to mind control, spiritual practices and helping the community. There, for the first time in his life, Edward felt truly fulfilled and five years passed in a flash.

Six months ago a position had become available at the Great White Lodge in Cairo for a young man to work and study there. Zoranda, who was in charge of Kumeka House, could see Edward's potential, so he put his name forward and he was duly accepted. Because he spoke Arabic and had dark eyes and hair, Edward could readily merge into the background and was sometimes sent on delicate missions. A few days ago he had been sent to Aswan, to collect an important package, which he was to bring back to the Master, the head of the Great White Brotherhood himself.

The packet consisted of a large envelope, sealed with tape, and Edward received it from the intermediary without problem. The trouble came later. On his way back to the station, because he was early, he stopped at a café. To keep the envelope safe he sat on it then placed his overnight case on the floor between his legs. While he was drinking his coffee he overheard a conversation, which turned him to stone.

Two men with unpleasant-smelling brown-black auras were discussing a white woman. They were careless in their talk and from their description he knew it could only be Helen.

He had often met Marcus and Joanna at Kumeka House in England and had heard about their experiences with the Scroll. Naturally he had heard them talk of Helen and had even seen pictures of her, though he had never met her. Fate seemed to decide he should be away whenever she visited the brotherhood. So when Marcus e-mailed to say that Helen was to be married and would be coming to Egypt for her honeymoon, Edward responded at once that he would love to meet her and her husband and offered his services to show them the sights. He was aware that Helen was on the *Nile Crown* because Marcus mailed him their itinerary and the number of Helen's new mobile phone, which Joanna had bought her. Typically, she left it at home when she went to Egypt.

As he listened it became clear that one of the men was a vicious thug who worked for one of the bosses of the Elite. He had been lurking at Luxor airport on some piece of skulduggery when he had spotted Helen and her husband coming off the plane. The Elite made sure their agents regularly saw photos of the enemy.

'Soon as I saw her I recognised her from her mug shot,' he leered to his companion, showing broken yellow teeth as his mouth opened. 'I've heard Sturov hates her guts.'

The man, universally known as the Shark, was not one of the brightest of men, but he would do anything if the money was right and he was intelligent enough to keep an eye on Helen's movements. To his disappointment Helen and her husband had acted like any tourists and taken a taxi to the cruise ship, the *Nile Crown*. Nevertheless he told his boss what he had seen and it caused a satisfying stir. The Elite presumed that the White Brotherhood had recruited Helen, so they decided to pay the Shark to watch her.

Those who headed the Dark Brotherhood were aware that there was a major event expected. They knew it was linked to the riddle of the Sphinx and that the result would release great power. They equated power with money, corruption and influence over the masses. Whatever happened they intended to keep tabs on Helen this time. She had thwarted them before and lessened their evil grip on mass consciousness.

The Shark did not know this but he was delighted to be paid to shadow the woman, which was why he was at Aswan, when the *Nile Crown* docked there. Here he had met up with one of his brothers in the café where Edward was awaiting his train and told him of his luck. The brother had a toothy smile and vicious black heart. His nickname was the Crocodile. The pair had been hated and feared as boys at school, vicious bullies. That was where they received their names, Shark and Crocodile, labels that pleased them immensely. And now their eyes were glinting like those of creatures about to bite someone's leg off.

The conversation overheard by Edward was scary. They reckoned Helen must be very important and decided that she must be seeking information or carrying some special documents. When they got hold of it, whatever it was, they would sell it to the highest bidder.

Edward had heard about the fate of the agents who tried to double-cross the Elite at Uluru and for a fleeting second felt sorry for the murky pair.

'And her?' asked the Crocodile, meaning Helen.

The Shark made a grating sound and throat-cutting

gesture. He grinned widely and Edward's blood ran cold. Murder Helen! Despite the heat of the day, icy shivers ran down his spine and a sick dread filled his stomach. His head whirled.

He ducked his head as the brothers scraped back their chairs and stood up. Both were smiling. The Shark rubbed his unshaven chin with one hand and touched the knife he kept in his belt with the other. He had seen Edward sit on the envelope. Men only did that if they were trying to keep safe something valuable. He smirked and whispered something to the Crocodile, who nodded.

The Crocodile nudged Edward as he passed his table so that, glancing up, he found himself looking into a pair of faintly yellow, reptilian eyes. At the same moment the Croc's hand chopped the back of his neck. Everything swam out of focus, then his head hit the table with a thud and his coffee spilled over his clothes. He was not aware of it. The café owner thought he was drunk and shrugged. Moments later, when he came to, his movements were unco-ordinated and he felt terrible. The package was gone.

In the shocked moments after that, Edward was in total panic. The packet! Helen in danger! As soon as his wobbling legs would carry him he ran outside to search for the men but they had disappeared like rats down a drain. With shaking fingers he tried to phone the Great White Lodge, although he knew that no one would answer the phones because of the special meeting there. But he had to try. He left a message, unable to disguise the tremor in his voice. Then he tried to phone the number Marcus had given him for Helen but, still on her dressing-table in England, her mobile was switched off.

Heart thumping, hands slippery, he tried to think through the situation. What was the best course of action? He could do nothing about the packet for the present. He decided to try to warn Helen. He must get her to Cairo where she could be protected by the brother-hood. It was with a flood of relief he remembered that Zoranda would be arriving in Egypt that day.

That was when he wrote Helen a warning note and set off to find the *Nile Crown*, which he knew was berthed at Aswan. Somehow, the powers of light would help him find her. He had to trust that.

As Edward stood on the shore he saw Helen on deck watching the Arab traders selling their wares. A man appeared beside her, who he assumed was Tony, and they engaged in a purchase. In extremis people act strangely and Edward, despite his training, succumbed to impulse. Without a second's thought he bought some dresses from a nearby stall, threw a ridiculous number of dollars at a dozing man to borrow his boat and intrepidly rowed out to the Nile cruiser where, wobbling precariously, he called to Helen in an assumed Egyptian accent. Then Edward threw the dress and the warning note up to her. He did not see what happened after that, for his boat was rammed and tipped over, knocking him backwards into the turgid water. An oar, wielded by an angry trader, hit him on the shoulder, but ignoring the pain he ducked down and swam underwater until he was round the side of the *Nile Crown*. He knew that the Shark or the Croc would be watching from somewhere. He hoped they had not been observing too closely or his days might be numbered.

Edward decided to spend another night at Aswan. He must speak to Helen. So he rebooked his hotel, then changed into European clothes and wandered on to the *Nile Crown* to seek her. No one stopped him as he looked in vain for her on deck and in the lounge. When he became aware that a purser was looking at him questioningly, he slipped off the boat.

Next morning he glimpsed her with Tony as they got into the minibus and were taken to the plane to fly to Abu Simbel but he had no opportunity to speak to her. It was a pity he had not seen them on the train to Luxor. He was sure they were on the same train as he was and had walked all the way down the platform looking for them.

And now he had to tell Zoranda and the Master that the packet had been stolen and about the conversation he had overheard in the café. He had to inform them that Helen had been seen arriving in Egypt by the Elite and was in danger. He also had to explain his decision to ask her to meet him at the Sphinx on Tuesday, when they arrived in Cairo. He should not have done that. His hands were damp with sweat. He must speak to her. On impulse or desperation, he was not sure which, he phoned Marcus in England to say that he wanted to contact Helen but her mobile was constantly switched off. Marcus had laughed and said that was typical of

Joanna's mother and she had probably left it at home. He didn't know how right he was. He gave Edward Tony's number but warned him that Tony did not seem to be answering his either. Edward groaned to himself.

Marcus then mentioned that he and Joanna were going to South Africa for a holiday. They wanted to go on safari in the Kruger Park.

Naturally Edward said that his aunt and uncle ran a small safari lodge in the Timbavati and that his brother Bede was there. He pressed Marcus and Joanna to stay with them and assured them of a warm welcome. Such was the measure of the man that, despite his own troubles, he insisted that Marcus wrote down the contact details and promised he would phone his aunt and uncle to tell them of their impending visit.

After the call Edward felt much better. He had Helen's itinerary so at least he would know where she was, and for a few minutes it had distracted him from his problem, but he could not shake off the dreadful feeling he was sending her into the lion's den.

As the taxi turned into the gates of the Great White Lodge, his heart started to thump wildly. He employed every technique he knew to keep calm. He slowed his breathing and focused his mind on a positive mantra, refusing to allow any other thoughts to enter. It worked.

As the car stopped by the white marble steps that led to the double front door, he thanked the driver and stepped out in an aura of peaceful gold. The Master noted this with satisfaction, as did Zoranda. They were watching his arrival from the window of a cool room, filled with green plants, which served as a meeting room, and were waiting for him as he entered.

Chapter 6

To Edward's considerable relief, Zoranda and the Master greeted him genially. They shook his hand and asked him how he felt after his ordeal. There were no recriminations.

They did not mention the stolen packet that he was berating himself about. They were behaving in the way of highly evolved beings, with compassion and self-responsibility.

Edward did not know that, when they were given his message informing them that the packet had been stolen, they had responded with shock but no anger.

'The boy is pure and good, just inexperienced,' said Zoranda.

The Master agreed. 'It would have been better to send someone used to the hidden possibilities of the darkness. Edward's light is bright so evil men would automatically be drawn to put it out.'

'It is our responsibility for sending him.'

'Indeed. That young man has faithfully served the light in many lifetimes. We must restore his confidence,' the Master answered quietly and added, 'I believe the papers are already in the hands of the Elite.'

'I agree. The information in the document will lead them precisely to the white lion cub when it is born.'

'Yes, we can discover from astrology the general area where the cub is to be born but they will now be able to determine its exact location.'

'We must meditate for guidance,' stated Zoranda, and together the two men of the light sat in perfect harmony and raised their frequency so high that they became invisible. They tuned into the great pool of universal knowledge and received much information. Now they waited to talk to Edward.

First they reassured him that he had done his best. The last thing they wanted was to take away his confidence. No person of good intention ever does that. At last the Master looked at him with a gentle expression. 'Is there anything you would like to ask?'

Naturally Edward had never asked what the document was about, assuming he would be told if it was ever appropriate. Now he dared to pose the question.

The Master smiled. 'I wondered when you would ask. I believe the papers contain a prediction by a Magi of the Great White Brotherhood, made immediately after the death of Jesus Christ, about the return of the Christ consciousness to Earth. It is to be heralded by the birth of a pure white lion cub, symbolising Christ who was known as the lion of Judah.'

Edward gasped in surprise.

'I understand the document written so long ago rightly forecasts that the web of light around the planet would become torn in several places, especially over Africa, and it contains precise instructions about how this part of the web can be repaired. This will enable peace, stability, integrity and healing to return to Africa.'

'The very last thing the Elite want,' Zoranda interjected.

'The very last thing!' the Master echoed, pursing his lips in thought and remaining silent for a moment. 'They will want control over the web of light but they certainly don't want it repaired. So they will use what suits them and suppress the rest of the information.'

All three were aware that the forces of darkness thrive on war and disease, which keep everyone disempowered and evil men in control.

'However,' continued the Master, 'the document and its translation will be written in the language of light and the Elite may not be able to comprehend it.'

'Please can you explain that?' Edward's brow was furrowed in concentration. He had not expected esoteric secrets to be divulged to him and wanted to make sure he understood everything.

'Yes. Many of the keys contained in the papers will be about such matters as drawing in the energy needed to repair the web, which must be done by raising the consciousness as high as possible. There may be instructions to chant sacred sounds, which connect with specific galaxies. I also believe acts of kindness or compassion will unlock portals or energise symbols and beings of light.'

'And those are things that the darkness cannot do?' the young disciple queried.

'That's right. So they have the information but may not be able to make the connections. Also with the web broken our planet is unprotected, so the Elite can call in energy from dark planets.'

Edward felt a surge of anxiety, which he breathed away with a golden breath.

The Master continued, 'But they cannot call in the help they might need from the light planets such as Orion, Sirius, Arcturus or the Pleiades.'

The young disciple focused on the positive. 'What sort of help might the Elite ever need from the light?'

'Take healing. Both darkness and light can access healing powers but that from the dark powers does not last.'

'Why would the dark powers want to heal anyone?' queried Marcus.

'Oh, for instance, if one of their own is injured or for self-aggrandisement. The power also draws in disciples who look up to the healer. And remember, if a light-worker channels healing, he is detached from it, knowing it comes from the divine, but if a dark person heals, he can put cords into the sick person, attaching him so that he can control his victim emotionally and psychically.'

'That's horrible!' exclaimed Edward, shocked.

The Master ignored his comment and went on quietly, 'Look at ageing. A young person with a dark heart may appear beautiful and enticing but as he grows older he shrivels and becomes ugly! Only love can transform this.'

Edward nodded thoughtfully and wondered what

would happen to Sturov! He noticed that the Master's face, though lined, glowed as he talked.

'More important still, an evil one can't love. He can only control others, which is a substitute for love. Yet every human being has a desire for love, however deeply unconscious it may be, yes, even Sturov himself. If a dark heart is touched by pure innocence, it can suddenly experience love. Once that happens it is hard to close the door against the floodgate of emotions that are released. Such a person will need to call on the light for help and then his heart must inevitably open to love again, however slowly.' He paused and glanced at the young man. 'Those are some of the factors that bind the dark.'

'I see.' Edward had a new picture of the limitations on the powers of darkness. 'So that's why no one is beyond redemption?'

The Master and Zoranda nodded.

Edward felt a rush of hope. Perhaps there was something he could do now, something to change the situation.

'Is there any chance I can retrieve the packet?' he asked eagerly. 'I'll do anything. I offer my life.'

'I hope that will not be necessary,' the Master responded gravely.

Both Zoranda and Edward noted his use of the words 'I hope.'

Edward remembered that the monk had brought the document from Tibet to be handed over at Aswan. 'Could I go to Tibet to get another copy?' he asked, but as the question left his mouth he knew it was a stupid suggestion, one unworthy of a true disciple. His insides cringed.

'No. Nor can we get another translation. The archives of the Great White Brotherhood in Tibet are closely protected with physical and psychic seals, so that the Chinese cannot find and destroy them. It was a great risk to remove the protection so that the document could be accessed in the first place. We cannot ask for it to be done again.'

'Is there a copy in the Great White Brotherhood archives in India?' Again Edward was aware that the answer had to be 'No'. Otherwise they would have accessed that copy originally.

As expected the Master shook his head.

The Great White Brotherhood maintained vast libraries of sacred records in Egypt, India and Tibet, scribing the true history of the lives and teachings of the great masters and avatars as far back as pre-Pharaoh times. In the third, fourth and fifth centuries the Christian Church fathers ordered the destruction of many libraries, which contained records about the life and teachings of Jesus, because they did not accord with the information they wished to dispense. Thousands of precious books were burned. However, many old documents, carefully guarded, are still preserved waiting for humanity to be ready to accept the knowledge they contain.

'Would the Rosicrucian records contain information that could help?' Zoranda wondered aloud, for he knew that the Rosicrucians also maintain sacred records in trust for the world.

But the Master shook his head. 'We considered all this before we requested the records from Tibet.'

Edward sighed, the faintest exhalation of breath, as his last hope faded.

The Master touched the young man on the shoulder, an avuncular gesture. 'We must remember, Edward, that everything has a higher purpose. The darkness always serves the light. I am sure that what has happened will ultimately serve the greater good in ways that we have no concept of. I suggest the three of us meditate together now to access further information.'

Before they closed their eyes, the Master glanced at Zoranda, who nodded. The two great and wise masters were to use their energy to raise the consciousness of this young man, pure but inexperienced in this life, to confirm the information they had received from the cosmic knowledge. This would boost his shattered sense of self-worth, for they had noted that Edward had worked hard to master his energy bodies, yet he still blamed himself. Guilt and shame are detrimental to anyone's spiritual growth.

The three men sat together in meditation, two as holders of the light, one to reach into the holy records. When they eventually opened their eyes the two older men glanced at Edward.

Zoranda asked, 'Did you receive guidance during your attunement?'

'I was shown that one of the lines of the web of light runs through specific sacred sites in Africa. These sites have moved out of alignment with the source of cosmic energy that should maintain them in harmony,' Edward replied. 'That is one reason why the web is broken over Africa.'

'Excellent! Go on.'

'The sites I saw have direct links to the stars, Sirius and Orion mainly. These constellations transmit energy to Earth and particularly to Africa. I was shown Africa is the land of the lion heart. The land of people carrying the lion qualities of leadership, bravery and inner strength.'

'Very good!'

'I was shown that the spoke of the web of light I mentioned travels from the Sphinx, through the source of the Nile down the centre of Africa to South Africa.'

The two older men sat in receptive silence, so Edward continued, 'The Pharaohs were embodiments of Horus, the solar lion god, and were able to work in harmony with the great cats because they too had lion hearts.'

'And the Sphinx? Were you offered any guidance about the Sphinx?'

Edward hesitated. 'Well, only that it does not represent a specific animal, but all animals. It stands for purity. I was shown that it is precisely placed to guard the pyramids and the planet itself. It is a watcher of the planet.' He sounded slightly confused. 'I don't understand how a statue can be a watcher.'

Zoranda reminded him in his quiet voice: 'Remember the Sphinx was constructed as an earthly symbol of the Leo constellation thousands of years before scientists currently date it. It represents the God of that time.'

The Master added, 'It was created, with the help of

galactic beings from other star systems, by a highly advanced civilisation. This coexisted with the Stone Age at the commencement of the Age of Leo.'

'Oh, I didn't know that.'

Zoranda nodded thoughtfully. 'More than ten thousand years BC, before the fall of Atlantis.'

The Master continued with the story: 'That was when the lions came to Earth from Orion. The Masters of Orion helped to construct the great pyramids, which had star shafts targeted at Orion's Belt and Sirius, through which they drew in galactic messages. The light was then pulsed down through the centre of Africa via the vein of gold.'

'The seam of gold that runs through Africa?'

'Yes. As you know gold is the metal of enlightenment. Physically it is beautiful and much prized for its qualities, but metaphysically it carries the highest light on the planet. That is why it was strategically placed on Earth by the great Masters in consultation with the Archangels and Lady Gaia when the planet was formed.'

'I see! Then the gold rush brought in millions of greedy and desperate people literally to pull this light from the Earth,' Edward commented. 'No wonder Africa's in a mess. Its light has been taken away.'

The Master smiled. 'Indeed. Gold is synonymous with light. So is the lion. Both represent enlightenment.'

They pondered that for a moment.

'We must find a way of realigning the sites, so that the higher light can flow into Africa again.' Edward was feeling more confident now. 'But what will the Elite do to stop that happening?'

'That is the question,' agreed the Master. 'A dark plot is afoot. We must find Helen and bring her here to safety so that her mission can start immediately. The world needs to know the truth. Edward, make sure she does not go to the Sphinx.'

Edward's stomach plunged as he confessed his proposed rendezvous with Helen at the Sphinx and his inability to contact her to change the meeting place. The wise men looked at him in grave silence. They did not judge. Edward did that far more harshly for himself than they could ever have done.

Chapter 7

In an expensive hotel suite in Cairo a tall dark-haired man, immaculately dressed, was holding the stolen document in his hand. He had read the translation and could be forgiven for gloating, for he had just been handed the key to immense riches. In his estimation, as long as he held this information, the light could no longer hope to heal Africa. He could continue to foment war and sickness, promote corrupt leaders and enjoy the rewards of power. He indulged himself in a moment of self-congratulation.

The man was Sturov, head of the dark band of the Elite, a man personally responsible for stirring religion against religion, country against country and leader against leader. He was one of the most evil men on the planet.

He had almost been vanquished at Machu Picchu by the power of Zoranda and his disciples working with the shamans of South America and, of course, Marcus, Joanna and Helen. He held a deep, bitter and personal grudge against each one of them.

After his escape he spent many months in a semi coma, for his strength had been sapped. But now, thanks to the eruption of war in many parts of the world, he was feeling better, energised by the fear of those whose lives he disrupted, those who were controlled by his calculations. He was excited by the lucrative spoils of war and the profits from medicine and drugs. He gained financially from every form of unhappiness and had a finger in every pie.

As he glanced again at the document he laughed aloud and said disdainfully, 'They think they can heal the world. They think they are stronger than I, Sturov!'

He looked with contempt at the two miserable specimens of manhood who stood in front of him: two Arabs with broken teeth and crafty expressions. These animals with juvenile macho names, the Croc and the Shark, had stolen the papers so easily from the force of light. 'Well done, men!' he said smoothly, offering them a sum of money, which was insignificant to him and overwhelmingly huge to them. They accepted it with pathetic eagerness, all thoughts of a higher bidder evaporating. 'On one condition,' he added, smiling expansively, seeing that they were firmly hooked to the bait. Their eyes slithered away but they nodded.

Sturov's mind darted to Helen. He had once seen her wise and innocent aura. Curse the woman! A saturnine expression flitted across his face and his eyes glittered with bitter mirth as he named the deal. 'Continue to watch the English woman. Never let her out of your sight. One of you return tomorrow and receive instructions, while the other stays near her. Half the money today. The other half a week from now.'

A plan was beginning to form in his mind. A plot that

could well ignite another lucrative war. Luckily he happened to have a cargo of weapons, just waiting for a purchaser. If his plan worked it might well kill that woman and probably those two animals in front of him at the same time. He turned away to hide a smile of satisfaction as they strutted out of the room.

When the Shark and the Croc left his office, Sturov had it sprayed with air freshener. He prided himself on his fastidiousness. He rarely came into contact with such low life but for this document it was worth it.

Now he could destroy the best plans of the light and plunge the world into chaos. He gloated at the thought of the continuing AIDS and cancer epidemics and the profits he siphoned off. Bringing in and anchoring the light of the cosmic heart in Africa could well have healed them all! That was a close one. But now that he had this information he could capture the lion cub and make sure the sacred places that received the higher pulses of light could not operate.

His scientists would continue to persuade governments to add more chemicals to food and water supplies, and produce more sterile GM crops, always letting them feel it was in their best interests. His team would manipulate poor deluded countries run by men of limited intelligence and no vision to release 'controlled' germ warfare. They would stir civil war and all this would maintain the ill health of the subhuman species that called itself men and women. The world would stay in pain and disruption and he, Sturov, would remain the superpower over them all. He had cause to feel good.

He called for a bath of pure water imported from an unpolluted spring to be prepared for him, in case those disgusting creatures had contaminated him.

'That planetary alignment is an infernal nuisance,' he growled to himself. 'Means I can't touch the cub until it's born.' A trifling sum would have ensured a bullet in the mother and the cub would never draw breath. But there were some things he could not interfere with and a cosmic birth was one of them. He shrugged and thought, No one can stop it dying soon after it's born. And his lips tortured themselves into a smile.

Then he picked up the phone and issued a series of orders. Finally he drawled, 'And get me a first-class ticket for Johannesburg on Friday week.'

Plenty of time to relax a little and organise matters before the cub is born, he thought with satisfaction. An easy death to organise.

Chapter 8

Neither Marcus nor Joanna slept much on the flight from Heathrow to Johannesburg. They were both charged with energy by the thought of what lay ahead and amazed by the synchronicities, which had brought them here so quickly.

After Zoranda's phone call and his mention of the white lion cub, they had visited London Zoo and Joanna had felt rising excitement as she connected with the lions there. She and Marcus had stood outside the enclosure for a long, cold time while she projected messages of love and respect to them. She reminded them that they were the kings of the animal kingdom. A lioness looked up from her sleep and glared. Joanna was sure the animal said, 'Go away. You can't possibly understand,' with such anger that she stepped back, startled.

Regaining her composure, she continued to project a message of peace. At last the mighty lion himself looked up, straight at her. Joanna felt a twinge of alarm. As their eyes locked across the distance, she received these words direct into her mind: 'We know. Thank you!' Then he turned his head and closed his eyes again. Joanna told Marcus what had happened.

He was delighted. 'That means you can connect with

them. With practice maybe you'll be able to receive messages from the wild lions, maybe even the white lion cub!'

Joanna was not sure she wanted to go that near a lion, even in a safari vehicle. As for connecting with a lion cub, even a sacred one, with its wild mother near – the thought filled her with horror but she wisely kept quiet.

One of the synchronicities that had propelled them to the Timbavati was Edward's phone call from Egypt to ask for Tony's mobile number as he could not contact Helen. When Marcus had mentioned that he and Joanna were going to South Africa, Edward had pressed him to get in touch with his aunt and uncle who ran a safari lodge in the heart of the Timbavati. 'My brother, Bede, is working there too,' he told him. 'They'd love to see you.'

After their conversation Edward had evidently phoned his aunt who had e-mailed Marcus and invited him and Joanna to stay, refusing to take no for an answer. They sensed that a divine hand was smoothing their path. Everything seemed to be falling nicely into place.

Their only concern was that they could not contact Helen or Tony. 'It's just not like Tony to turn off his mobile,' Joanna kept saying.

'Well, it is their honeymoon,' Marcus tried to reassure her, but he too felt a twinge of unease. Edward had sounded jumpy, evasive even when he talked about Helen. Ever since his phone call, they had been concerned about her.

They arrived feeling slightly jaded at Johannesburg

airport, ready to catch a small plane to Hoedspruit airport, where Edward's brother Bede met them in his land ranger.

Bede was tall, broad-shouldered and handsome. His skin was dusky rather than black. He had a wide African face with eyelashes to die for bordering his dark brown eyes, but his other features were distinctly European. It's strange, thought Joanna, eyeing him frankly, I know he was adopted, but he looks a bit like Edward. I suppose that families grow to look alike. But she forgot the thought as she raised her face to the sun, smiled at the glassy blue sky and absorbed the heat and the smell of Africa. She crossed the tarmac road and stood under the straggliest tree she had ever seen, littered with twigs from the untidy nests of weaver birds. The tree reminded her of a gangly youth covered in acne and dandruff. The white thorns on an acacia bush beside it were the longest and most vicious she had ever seen, as lethal as any dagger, she thought, with a shiver at the unbidden comparison.

She stretched her arms and took a deep breath before she realised that Bede and Marcus had loaded their bags into the car and were looking at her.

Bede was charming and chatty as he drove them along the dusty road, protected by a wire fence, well set back. Beyond it the trees were so desiccated they were like kindling waiting to be incinerated. He pointed out a group of monkeys playing in the trees, then several giraffes whose tall necks were disguised as branches. Marcus and Joanna were enchanted to see the creatures prance off with their curious swaying gait.

The air smelled of peppery dust with an exciting whiff of distant game. Under one of the rare roadside trees in full leaf a black woman wearing a red turban lay face down, with her bare stomach on the earth for coolness.

When they entered the Timbavati reserve Bede pulled the car off the road to let them watch an elephant noisily shredding a thorny acacia. Joanna had a delightfully scary feeling as if she could reach out and touch it. It was wrapping its snake-like trunk round bundles of dead twigs and shoving them into its mouth. Just as the visitors were deciding that the huge beast actually preferred dry twigs to eat, it grabbed a bundle of greenery for pudding. Then it walked disdainfully towards them as if to say, 'Move out of my way,' which they did with alacrity.

It was strange but despite Bede's jovial manner and her fascination with all that he pointed out to them there was something Joanna did not quite trust about him. She tried in vain to put her finger on it. It left her with a feeling of disquiet.

His aunt, Monica, was quite different. She came running out of the lodge to greet them and made them feel immediately welcome. Tall and fair, with a willowy figure, soft blue eyes and narrow face, she looked physically tough, yet there was something appealingly fragile and vulnerable about her.

Bede took their cases to their room while his aunt pointed out the dining area, the bar and swimming pool. Beyond the pool the barbeque was installed and next to it stood a huge table with benches on either side. This area was enclosed and illusorily protected by a wooden fence. 'Those naughty elephants do terrible damage if they get in,' Monica confided. 'Sometimes they drop their turds in the swimming pool. And they are always knocking over our trees.'

Joanna was not sure she liked the idea of elephants wandering round inside the hotel garden. She took Marcus's hand for a touch of reassurance as Monica pointed out the water hole at the end of the sloping garden.

'There're always game coming here for a drink, especially at night. You can sit on these seats and get a wonderful view.' She indicated some strategically placed benches and chairs, carefully shaded in daytime by large umbrellas, which overlooked the water hole. They were near enough to see and far enough away for safety. It looked idyllic.

By the time Monica had shown them to their rooms and given them a cold drink, Joanna had told her of their fascination with the white lion, though not about the birth of the sacred white cub. Monica was not surprised as many of their visitors wanted to know about them. 'Just don't visit the white lion farm,' she responded. 'They breed them in captivity to sell to hunters. It's appalling.' Her eyes flashed and Joanna and Marcus soon learned that she passionately hated the trade in lions, especially the specifically bred white ones, which fetched a premium when they were shot.

Monica knew of her nephew, Edward's, devotion to mysticism and that these friends of his had met him at

Kumeka House, which was a great spiritual centre, for she was somewhat inclined that way herself. 'I know someone you'd be interested to meet.' She smiled. 'I'll try to get hold of him.' Because she knew everyone and everything about the area, she made a few strategic phone calls after lunch and arranged for them to meet a shaman, a sangoma or Wise One who could communicate with the lions. 'Apparently he has his feet in both worlds,' Monica told them. 'He's been educated and even worked in an office for a time but he came back to rejoin his tribe when his father died. Some people say he can shape-shift into a lion,' she added with an embarrassed flush and slight squirm of her thin shoulders. 'Not that I believe that,' she added hastily, for her understanding of the inner worlds did not extend that far.

Remembering their extraordinary experiences in Australia with the Aborigine karadji or shaman, Marcus and Joanna found themselves reassuring her that strange things happen all the time. She nodded and her pupils were huge with interest and curiosity.

The following evening Bede drove them into the bush to meet him.

The elderly African shaman, in faded clothes and battered hat, greeted them with a handshake and, when they explained about their interest in the white lions, he appeared pleased but not surprised. They sat in silence for a few minutes, staring into the flames of the small, well-tended fire, under the black star-spangled sky, breathing in the smell of wood smoke and Africa.

Then the wise man started to speak in a deep slow

voice. 'Lions and all cats are psychic. They can see into realms and dimensions that most humans have no concept of. Centuries ago the cat family volunteered to come to Earth to help humans.'

'Wow!' murmured Joanna.

'Do you know that most families think they are looking after their domestic cats when in fact their cats are looking after and protecting them?' He looked up at them and chuckled, his eyes glinting with humour. Then he sobered and continued, 'The lion, the great king of the beasts, was known as a star creature because our ancestors knew that it came down to Earth from the stars.'

'Which star did they come from?' Joanna dared to interrupt.

The man's dark eyes sparkled suddenly in the reflection of the firelight. He looked up into the star-splattered dome above them and pointed to a row of three stars. 'The cats come from Orion.' He watched her as she craned to look at the sky and seemed to be satisfied by her sense of wonder. He continued, 'Originally the lions' mission was to protect humanity from evil entities and invasion from an unfriendly planet.'

'Really?' Marcus sounded surprised.

The old man nodded. 'At first people were grateful and honoured the great cats. A brave man was known as having a lion heart. Mighty rulers who had conquered fear worked with them. Such men never tried to subdue them but walked in alignment with them. That was in ancient times when people lived in harmony with animals and nature.'

'Why did witches have cats?' asked Joanna.

'Witches! You mean the wise women and healers?'

She nodded.

'Cats aren't just psychic. They have power and they added their power to that of the herbs and sacred incantations. And to dark spells too of course.'

Joanna shivered. 'Why black cats?'

'Black is the colour of night, when magic is most potent. It is the colour of mystery, of secrets. It contains all knowledge. Black cats are special.'

'Why did humans and animals stop working together? When did it change?' Joanna wrinkled up her forehead as she considered her own question.

'Well, you see, eventually humans developed fire, then weapons, then technology. Then they decided that they had priority in the nature kingdom.' The African paused and glanced from Joanna to Marcus, checking that they were paying full attention to his words. Satisfied, he grunted and continued, 'Now listen to this, for it is very important. At that time, in their greatness of spirit, the lion kingdom handed over the crown to humans. It was a gift not a right. A gift, mark you! But humans conveniently forgot this. They accepted the offer to rule the planet, then misused the power. In many parts of the world they took the land for themselves and drove lions and other animals out. However here in Africa the great beast maintained its majesty. It continued to work selflessly to protect our Earth and the people.' He sighed and his great chest heaved. Somewhere in the distance an owl screeched.

The old man carried on, 'Totally oblivious of the sacrifice made by the lions, still trying to prove their superiority, people with sick hearts hunted and killed them as trophies. With contempt for the royal creature of the stars they pegged out their pelts and even mounted their heads to gloat over.' He roared suddenly. 'Do people really imagine they can kill a lion without the permission of the beast itself? The king walks forward as a sacrifice. It offers itself in the hope that its death will touch the hearts of its murderers.'

Both Marcus and Joanna jumped at the vehemence of his words. They took a moment to digest them. 'I see,' murmured the girl at last, while Marcus nodded.

The shaman went on, 'Now in the plains of Africa where lions used to walk free, many of them are being bred in lion farms and sold specifically to be hunted. Often they are shot in a safe enclosure so that a lily-livered human can boast he has killed the king of beasts.' His chest quivered in indignation and frustration.

Joanna found herself wondering what karma such degenerate people accrued.

There was a silence as the wise African calmed himself. 'You have heard of the new enlightened children being born? You call them indigo and crystal children, I think?'

Marcus nodded.

Joanna said, 'I think they are called indigo children because they have dark blue in their aura, which is the colour of advanced spiritual development.'

'And the crystal children have clear auras and are very psychic,' finished Marcus.

The older man inclined his head, pleased at their knowledge. 'The indigo and crystal children have often been cats. They have incarnated now to spread spiritual enlightenment.'

Before Joanna could frame the questions burning on her lips the wise man had changed tack again and was talking about the white lion.

'Some years ago in that exact place' – he was pointing with his hand to a slight hollow – 'I saw a fully grown white lion. It was the pinnacle of my life.' He paused as if he were far away, reliving that moment. 'He stood there and looked at me. His eyes were clear golden blue, or it may have been a reflection of the sun. The white lion transmitted these words telepathically into my mind. "The golden lion represents the sun on Earth. When the lions withdraw from the planet the sun of happiness will go out. But there is hope. The white lion represents the cosmic heart. I come to remind all of the love that is possible on Earth. White lions have allowed themselves to be bred in captivity to keep hope alive. There will be another chance for humanity. In years to come another white lion will be born in the wild, carrying a twin flame of peace and love. If this is ignored, it will be a long time before another messenger ventures from the stars into this devilish world." And with that he was gone in a flash. To be honest, for a moment I thought I imagined him but my heart was pounding. I was crying and singing at the same time.

'Since that day I believe we have plunged Earth deeper into darkness. When I look now into the eyes of a lion I can only say, "I am holding faith. I acknowledge you as king of the beasts, as the sun king. Together we will hold the light for all the ignorant masses on Earth." '

Joanna noticed that the sangoma had tears in his eyes. In her mind she could see the proud white lion delivering his message, and she shivered. 'I'm sure he'll return soon,' she murmured, touching the man's arm lightly. 'We'll hold faith with you.'

He smiled down at her through his tears.

Together they looked up at the belt of Orion, the constellation from whence the mighty lions originated, and offered a prayer for forgiveness and hope.

Chapter 9

When Helen woke with a start it was still dark and her body was ice-cold and shaking. She must have had a nightmare. For a moment she tried to recall where she was. Oh, yes. In a hotel in Cairo and Tony was asleep next to her. She was just going to turn over and cuddle up to him when she remembered that this was Tuesday. Today she intended to meet the Egyptian at the Sphinx, the man who had thrown the note up to her on the deck of the *Nile Crown*. She was going to meet him despite Tony's vehement objections. A sick dread surged into her stomach.

She had tried all her persuasive powers to change his mind in vain. He would not accompany her and still insisted she must not go to the Sphinx. He was utterly intransigent. She lay, rigid with tension for a few moments, staring into the gloom. I don't have to go, she reminded herself, glancing at Tony. She could just make out that he was sprawled on his stomach and knew from his breathing that he was in another world. For a treacherous instant she longed to change her mind, to follow her first instinct and snuggle into the warmth and safety of his arms. As honeymooners should! she thought. But she tightened her jaw and closed her mind to the possibility. I've got to do it. That man's heart was pure, so it must be important, she told herself firmly. I'll have to face any danger and Tony's opposition. I know I must meet him.

She let out a sudden cold breath. Tony was totally against her meeting this stranger. He feared nameless problems and danger, and she knew from experience that he had a keen nose for trouble. Her toes curled tight at the thought of what might lie ahead and of facing his anger when she returned, if she returned.

Enough of that negativity, Helen, she chided herself, but her teeth were chattering as she inched out of bed and gathered up the clothes she had laid out on the floor the night before.

She crept into the bathroom and dressed without putting on the light, then, holding her breath, tiptoed across the room to the door. Had she got everything – money, sunglasses, sun cream, hat? She ran a quick checklist through her mind. Too late anyway.

Tony gave a snuffling breath and stirred. She froze but he settled again and she pulled open the door, hoping the light would not wake him. The door shut with a bang that she could not avoid and she found herself running down the corridor. At last she dared to glance at her watch and saw that it was ten past six. Before she went to sleep she had impressed her subconscious mind to wake her at six. Perfect timing! So far so good.

She exited the bedroom block and walked fast through the spacious flower-filled gardens towards reception, hugging her arms to her chest against the chill. She had not expected Cairo to be so cold in the early morning. The sick feeling in her stomach intensified and waves of anxiety kept sweeping through her. She scarcely glanced at the vast octagonal swimming pool, the waters as still as a turquoise silk carpet. But the aroma of coffee wafting from the dining room stopped her in her tracks, lowering her resistance. She had not intended to stop for anything, but the smell proved too enticing. It's twenty minutes before my taxi's due and Tony's fast asleep, she persuaded herself. Just a quick coffee and a croissant and I'll feel better. Perhaps something hot in her stomach would take away the nauseous feeling. As it was she was going to be hours too early but the risk of waking Tony would have been much greater if she had left it later.

Even at that early hour the dining room was quite full and she hid herself in a corner behind a group of bright-eyed tourists, who loudly anticipated a heavy day of sightseeing ahead.

Every second she expected to see Tony storming in to look for her. She had no doubt he would be furious, a rage fuelled by fear for her safety. When he found her bed empty he would realise immediately that she had gone to meet the mysterious E at the Sphinx. Suddenly her hand shook uncontrollably, and she spilled her coffee.

This is no good, Helen, she told herself sternly. Get a grip! She forced her breathing to calm and made herself finish her croissant, then walk slowly to reception, where she enquired if her taxi had arrived.

'Five minutes,' the receptionist said, with a toothpaste grin beneath his wide moustache. Dread and butterfly nerves forced her to visit the ladies. Still no taxi! It arrived fifteen tension-filled minutes late.

This is terrible, she kept thinking. He's my husband, for goodness sake. I shouldn't be trying to evade him or be scared of him catching me before I go. I feel as if I'm a teenager.

As soon as she was safely ensconced in the taxi, the butterflies subsided, but the dread remained and she knew that her fear that Tony would stop her was masking a deeper terror. Now the words written on the note kept whirling in her mind: 'Be careful!' What was the information E had for her? Why the warning? What was the danger? She recognised the feeling of doom. She'd had it before, of course, and it inevitably preceded terrible danger.

I must gather my energy. It's scattered by fear, she told herself and tried to focus on her breathing. However the chatty driver, an Egyptian caricature with his thick moustache, bulbous nose and fleshy lips, insisted on asking her where she came from and pointing out every mosque or landmark on their way. Normally friendly, she now felt she would scream if he did not shut up but her reticence encouraged him to become positively loquacious. And when he was not addressing her, he was commenting on the defects of the other drivers.

At last they left the oasis of Cairo and entered the bare desert. The Giza plateau loomed ahead and suddenly Helen could see the pyramids silhouetted against a rose-apricot sky, more spectacular than she had ever envisaged.

'I want to go to the Sphinx,' she reminded the driver.

'Pyramids first. Everyone go to pyramids first,' he replied.

'No! To the Sphinx!' she commanded with such ferocity that he shuddered slightly and allowed the wilful English lady tourist her way, swerving to the left in a cloud of beige dust.

'Camels,' he pointed out as a distraction from her anger and Helen watched a string of three bored and bad-tempered-looking camels being led to a propitious place, from which the owners could harass tourists to have a ride. Another time Helen would have smiled but now her mind was filled with a combination of disquiet and anticipation.

When she saw the Sphinx Helen forgot her fears for a moment. It was spectacular, bigger, more impressive, much more imposing than she had imagined. It sat staring into the distance, looking out into space, guarding the esoteric secrets of the plateau. Helen was entranced, yet when the driver pulled up she shrank into her seat for a moment, scared of entering the world of tourists in white hats with cameras slung over their shoulders, and scruffy Arab traders jostling for attention.

Her heart was thumping loudly. Would she recognise the young man she was to meet? What would he tell her? Was she right about his pure heart? Sudden doubt assailed her so she took a deep breath as she emerged from the car. 'Please wait,' she commanded the driver and he nodded. Of course he would. He had not yet been paid.

She looked in all directions for signs of the young man. She was early, as always. Trying to make herself inconspicuous, she examined cheap trinkets piled up on a table. She would not approach the Sphinx yet. She would remain cautious and alert. She did not know that fate in the form of two evil brothers was closing in on her.

The Shark and the Crocodile had watched Helen's every movement since their meeting with Sturov. The hotel receptionist was distantly connected to them through friends of friends and the taxi driver who collected Helen from the hotel was their cousin. The two brothers had arrived at the Sphinx very early that morning. Their instructions were clear and simple. They were to offer Helen the opportunity of going into the cordoned area of the statue to touch its paws. Of course she would not be able to resist such a chance. They were to photograph her inside the forbidden area and Sturov himself had arranged for them to be given a high quality digital camera for this task. They did not know it was packed with explosives, which would be detonated by an agent at the most strategic moment. The brothers had already bribed certain guards, whose paltry wages made them most receptive to offers so that they were more than willing to negotiate to bend the regulations.

Neither of the brothers stopped to wonder why they were being paid to arrange for this English woman to touch the Sphinx. Nor did they consider why Sturov, the Big Boss, would bother with something so trivial. They were blinded by greed. Once they had been paid for the photographs, they would carry Helen off, which would be simple with the taxi driver in their pay. They could extort information from her at their leisure, which would inevitably mean more money coming to them. They hugged each other jubilantly. Confidence and cunning oozed from their greasy pores.

Naturally they had seen Helen's taxi arrive. The two brothers grinned at each other. 'Stupid bitch, coming alone. No good Egyptian wife would do that!' She was really making it easy for them. They did not know that she was supposed to be meeting Edward at the Sphinx, Edward the young man the Croc had mugged in the café at Aswan. They only knew that all tourists came here some time, so the visit was inevitable. And if they had known of her proposed rendezvous with a youth they regarded as naïve, they would have shrugged and laughed. They felt invincible.

As Helen very slowly approached the great statue looking for Edward, the two brothers eased themselves through the crowds until one was on either side of her.

'Good morning. You English?' The Crocodile flashed his teeth at her.

She smiled tersely and said, 'Yes,' as one does.

'From where in England?'

'London,' she replied. She had long ago learned that it was always best to say London. She did not like the feel or look of them and turned away but they were like leeches, always at her side.

She stopped to examine a small pyramid on a stall. She

looked at it for a long time, while the two men gave her
advice and even bargained with the stallholder for her.
She was beginning to feel desperate. How could she get
rid of them? Now she had a tatty wooden pyramid she
didn't even want.

The energy of the Sphinx felt very powerful. She was
longing to get nearer to it but it was strange how her head
was buzzing. And she must find E.

'I'm waiting for a friend,' she said to the men. 'Please
leave me.'

'Oh, we'll wait with you. We just want to practise our
English.'

'Go away!' she wanted to scream.

'We have a pass into the Sphinx. We can take you to
touch it. Very special for you because you are a nice lady,'
offered the Shark.

'No, thank you.' She searched desperately for E. She
wished she could remember what he looked like. She'd
never find him in this crowd.

She felt slightly dizzy and couldn't think straight. It
must be the heat. The sun was high and a dog was already
slumped in a thin strip of shade.

Almost against her will she was being drawn towards
the mighty stone animal.

'I will take photo of you touching the Sphinx!' said the
Crocodile. It was a statement not a question. They did not
know that Helen always liked to be good and law-abiding.

She was horrified. 'You can't do that!' she exclaimed.

'Oh, yes. Easy. I have pass and guard is my friend.'
They were at the rope.

The well-bribed guard smiled and nodded expansively. 'Okay. Okay. Very special. You go.' He almost pushed Helen and the two men through the barrier.

'You touch Sphinx. I take photo,' said the Crocodile with a grin.

At a distance Sturov's agent fingered the detonator. This was going like a dream.

Suddenly Helen heard her name called. Tony, red-faced with exertion, was racing towards her and beside him was a young man, who looked vaguely familiar. 'Helen. Helen,' they were shouting. Something cleared in Helen's head. Instantly she sprang from the Sphinx and ran towards Tony.

The Crocodile took most of the blast. His body was blown up on to the statue where his mangled remains were spreadeagled over the Pharoah's head. Behind him the Shark and the guard took the rest of it, so that the plinth was minimally damaged and the Sphinx not at all.

Helen was blown off her feet. Tony and Edward grabbed her and half dragged, half carried her to their taxi, pushing her into the back. She was white, shocked, shaking and scratched but otherwise unharmed. There was turmoil and panic at the statue. Some were rushing towards it to gape at the horror. Others were hurrying to their vehicles to flee from danger. Their taxi drove them away in a confusion of cars, screaming people, flashing lights and sirens.

As Helen predicted, Tony was furious.

Chapter 10

'It was lucky you arrived just then,' muttered Helen as soon as she could stop her teeth from chattering. She had buried her face in Tony's shoulder as if to shield herself from the horror of what had just happened as well as from his anger.

'Lucky!' exclaimed Tony with bitter sarcasm. 'You specialise in explosions, don't you?' He was thinking of another occasion when Helen and Joanna had almost been killed when a car exploded, thanks to Sturov. A volcano erupted inside him. 'You stupid woman! Whatever possessed you?' he shouted suddenly.

She had never heard anyone so enraged and she shrivelled deeper into shock.

The car lurched and bumped along the road, nose to tail with the escaping convoy. Without waiting for a reply, Tony twisted his head to see what was happening at the statue.

Grey smoke rose from the area in front of the Sphinx where Helen had been standing. All he could see was a writhing mass of people and a dark, dripping stain on the statue itself. In the midst of chaos there was a sharp bang and Tony ducked automatically. People started screaming as they fled dementedly from the scene, Arabs holding up their robes so that they could run faster, tourists losing hats and packages in their panic.

Tony could no longer see anything through the scuffed-up dust. He wanted to yell at the taxi driver to go faster. As that was a physical impossibility in the crush of cars and people, he tensed his fists into a ball and gripped Helen tighter. Sweat was dripping down the back of the driver's neck, staining his T-shirt.

Sitting on Helen's other side, Edward maintained his calm. He gently placed a hand on her back and focused all his attention on helping this woman, whom he had inadvertently placed in such danger.

'Sorry,' Helen murmured into Tony's shoulder.

At the muffled sound Tony pulled her head back and saw that her face was pale, her eyes wide with shock and her pupils dilated. The apoplectic rage, which had been coursing through him since he realised that she had gone to the Sphinx to meet the unknown man, evaporated instantly into terrible fear for her.

The taxi driver had seen her condition when she was hustled into his taxi. He said, 'Shall we go to hospital?'

'No,' replied Tony and Edward instantly and rather too sharply.

'Thank you but it's all right,' added Tony more politely. 'I think she had a bit of a shock. She was near the explosion.'

The taxi driver knew that, but judged from their faces that he had better not ask any questions.

Suddenly Helen exclaimed, 'Oh, I never paid my taxi driver. Oh dear!' She hated to let anyone down.

Edward said quietly, 'He'll probably go to your hotel to find you. You can leave the money for him at reception. I suggest we call there now and you can pack and check out. Then I'll take you to the Great White Lodge if that's all right with you. You'll be safe there.'

'Do you think the police will find out it was me touching the Sphinx?' Still shocked, Helen was concerned that she might be in trouble for being inside the barrier.

'Why? Why did they do it? Why do they want to hurt me?' she whimpered, so that the driver could not hear.

'You've beaten them twice – first at Machu Picchu and then at Uluru. Sturov feels humiliated,' Tony replied.

'Love forgives and lets go,' added Edward. 'Darkness bears grudges.'

Helen shivered and Edward was sorry he had spoken and tried to reassure her. 'They aren't interested in you when you're going about your daily life. You're safe then. It's only when they think you're trying to stop their machinations that they feel threatened by you.'

'But I'm not doing anything. I'm on my honeymoon,' Helen responded in a bewildered, almost plaintive voice.

Edward realised that she did not know about the impending birth of the white lion and the thrust forward that the light intended to make to seal the rift in Africa and re-energise the web of light – or how they wished to use her skills to help them. This was not the time or place to tell her. 'Just rest,' he murmured soothingly. 'It'll be all right.'

'Who are you . . . ?' she started to say but a wave of nausea swept over her and she could not continue.

79

Tony's anger had evaporated, leaving him feeling slightly unwell and very depleted. He gathered his energy together. 'Don't worry, Helen,' he murmured. 'I'll make sure you're safe. I'll go to our room and pack our things, then check us out of the hotel. You wait in the taxi. Edward's right. We'll be safe at the Great White Lodge. I'm sure it's protected spiritually there, just as Kumeka House was.'

Edward assured him that the pure light inside the Lodge rendered it invisible to the dark forces. Privately he had misgivings. The fear emanating from Tony and Helen now could make a hole in the surrounding armour of light and let danger in. He just had to trust that Zoranda and the Master would be able to seal it.

The driver drummed his stubby fingers on the steering wheel as they waited for Tony to check them out of the hotel. In the back of the taxi Helen slumped with her eyes closed, seemingly asleep, while Edward entered the Silence and mentally started to weave a web of peace around her. It seemed to help. By the time Tony returned with their cases, some colour had returned to her cheeks and she opened her eyes and smiled at him.

By now she was aware that the young man accompanying Tony was the youth she was intending to meet at the Sphinx. She also realised that Edward was not Arab but English. She was ready to ask questions. 'Tony, how come you and Edward came together to find me?'

Tony replied, 'When I woke and saw your bed empty, I knew instantly where you had gone. I thought I was going to have a heart attack! I had to sit on the edge of the bed and do some deep breathing to recover.' He saw his wife's look of anguished concern as she reached for him. He put out his hand to her and they clasped each other. They were silent for a few minutes until Tony continued, 'It seems strange now but the first thing I did was to unearth my mobile from the suitcase. I thought perhaps you would phone me. It was irrational as you knew it was turned off but I wasn't thinking straight. Anyway as soon as I turned it on there were all these messages from Edward. I phoned him immediately. At first he was relieved, thinking I was responding to his calls and he could prevent you from going to the Sphinx, but when he heard you had already left he told me he had been trying to warn you not to go. He said the Elite were watching for you there. Oh yes, and that it was he who threw up the original message and then to his horror he'd learnt that the Elite would be visiting the Sphinx. Because he had not been able to contact you he was waiting for a taxi to take him there to meet you. It arrived while we were still on the phone and he said he would pick me up at the hotel on the way past. It seemed sensible and that's why we arrived when we did!'

Helen winced and squeezed her husband's hand. He continued, 'And there were messages from Joanna and Marcus. They've gone to South Africa.'

'South Africa!' Helen exclaimed.

Tony looked at Edward who explained his connection with Marcus through Kumeka House.

'Oh, that's who you are!' breathed Helen. 'Edward! Of course, Marcus often talked of you and I've seen a photo of you. I kept thinking you looked familiar and that explains it.'

He smiled and she continued, 'I said it was strange we'd never met and now we meet here of all places!'

Edward nodded. 'Life is full of surprises!' he remarked. 'And here's something that will interest you.'

He told her about the prediction that a white lion cub would be born, what it meant for the planet and Marcus and Joanna's quest to save it from Sturov and the dark forces. Helen listened with horror. So the battle between light and dark was starting again just when she thought there was to be a lull. It was inevitable that Marcus and Joanna would be in danger. She shivered inwardly. It was so much worse for your children to be at risk than yourself. I must send a bubble of protection to them, she decided, but her mind was still buzzing strangely as it had done at the Sphinx. She could not concentrate. She found she could not help them.

Half an hour later the taxi dropped them at the Great White Lodge and the driver roared away with a lot on his mind.

Helen and Tony were given hot sweet tea and hands-on healing by some of the residents of the Great White Lodge. Edward was just wondering whether to give Helen information about the Sphinx and tell her what was required of her, when he heard Zoranda's voice in the hall. Helen picked it up too and her eyes opened wide with astonishment, believing she must have misheard. 'Zoranda!' she exclaimed, sitting up as the big bald man walked into the room, smiling with delight to see her and Tony but deeply concerned about the event at the Sphinx. He too was aware that the disturbed energy of the newcomers had blasted a hole in the protection around the Great White Lodge. Ten minutes later he excused himself from the room and sought out the Master. Together they sent out invocations and prayers to seal the dome of light around the entire building once more.

They knew only too well that burglaries and intrusions are invited in by the energy within a home, so they continued until they were certain that their light would be strong enough to hold the situation. It was as well they did.

Zoranda returned some time later to the reception room where the guests and residents were grouped. He wanted to know about Helen's experience and she told the story again. This time she mentioned the strange buzzing sensation in her head when the two men surrounded her, so strong that she could hardly think straight. He looked grave.

'By the time Atlantis had been taken over by the dark priesthood, they were implanting conditioning boxes into people. Through these the Evil Ones could control the masses. One of their powers was to buzz people's minds, so that they lost clarity. Without the ability to think for themselves, they became automatons, putty in the hands of the controllers.'

'Is that why I let those two men take me up to the

Sphinx? It's so unlike me. Do you think I have a conditioning box from Atlantis in my aura, which they've reactivated?' asked Helen in horror.

'No! I don't think you had one placed in you when you were in Atlantis. You had too pure an energy then and were protected within the Cathedral of the Sacred Heights. It's worse than that. Sturov was one of the black masters who was subjugating people before the fall of Atlantis. I suspect he remembers how to place a conditioning box in your energy fields and managed to do this psychically in the last couple of days.'

'Surely Helen's energy fields aren't open to such manipulation!' exclaimed Tony in distress and anger.

Zoranda spoke quietly and without judgement. Edward never took his eyes from the wise man's face. Nor did Helen. 'I imagine, Helen, you must have been very afraid when you received the letter from Edward warning you to be careful and to meet him at the Sphinx?'

Helen nodded.

'And even more so when you decided to go despite Tony's total disapproval?'

'I was,' she admitted. 'Actually I was terrified of danger at the Sphinx and also of Tony's anger. I was scared of what my going would do to our marriage. I felt it might be over when it had hardly begun but I had to go.' She felt her lips quiver and Tony put an arm round her shoulders.

'Your fear opened up your energy fields and allowed the dark forces in. We have to be so careful. Sturov will stop at nothing to quench the light.'

'Why didn't he use this tool before, for instance on Joanna when she was injured at Machu Picchu?'

Zoranda recalled only too well when Joanna was stabbed as the shamans tried to reclaim the portal of Machu Picchu for the light. 'She was physically injured but her thoughts were not of revenge but of healing and forgiveness. Also she was surrounded by people who were holding her in the light. You were acting alone, Helen, and in emotional turmoil. That is why you were vulnerable.' She winced and he spoke more slowly and calmly as if to soothe her. 'Remember you have work to do. It is because your energy is so high that the darkness is trying to stop you. We have not told you yet, but you have an important part to play for the next wave of light going out to the planet.'

Helen did not know which was stronger, shame that she had inadequate control over her energy fields and had let darkness manipulate her, or delight that she had been chosen for special work.

True to character her doubts surfaced now and had to be expressed. 'Can they still buzz my mind? Can the conditioning box be removed? Can you trust me to do the work?' She hesitated. 'And if you can, what is it?' Suddenly she smiled. Deep inside she knew Zoranda would never have mentioned the work if she was not good enough to do it.

He laughed at her expression.

So did Tony. 'Helen, you are incorrigible!' Her husband chuckled and kissed her on the cheek.

Zoranda spoke in his deep quiet voice. 'At this moment

they can buzz your mind but we will remove the conditioning box and then their hold over you will be gone. We will cut it out psychically with the power of our minds, by visualising it being removed. We'll do it tomorrow when you are feeling stronger. This is a warning to all of us about the dangers of letting anger, fear or any negative emotion take hold of us.' His clear blue, all-seeing eyes met hers and then moved round the room from face to face. 'None of us can afford to relax our self-vigilance.'

He rose. There was a television in the reception room at the Great White Lodge, though it was rarely watched or plugged in. They knew that the dark forces could transmit low-frequency energy even through turned-off sets, to lower the resistance of the masses and manipulate their energy fields. Zoranda explained that he would like to watch the news and obtained general consent. When he pressed a button, a door swung open revealing a screen. The news was just starting and the explosion at the Sphinx made the headlines. Within seconds they were all staring aghast at pictures of what had occurred, taken by a rather good amateur video enthusiast. The Crocodile was bringing the camera up to his eye. Tony and Edward were clearly seen running towards the Sphinx, though Helen in sunglasses and sunhat was somewhat less recognisable. Helen felt faint as she saw herself escaping just in time and being blasted into Tony's arms. Then the camera focused on the nauseating sight of the Croc's bloody corpse and the injured bodies of his brother and the guard.

The frenetic scene was presented in vivid technicolour as the cameraman relentlessly focused on horrified faces and devastation; and Helen was back there smelling the fear and sweat, feeling the burning sun and strange buzzing in her head. On the screen someone helped the Shark to sit up and he screamed as he saw his brother.

Then there was a crack from somewhere in the crowd and the unholy wails of the Shark were silenced.

The crack we heard was a shot! thought Tony. That was what caused the panic.

No one moved or spoke. They felt sick. Nor did anyone ask who had fired the shot. They knew it must have been the operative who detonated the camera bomb. The Shark had paid heavily for his inside knowledge or his perfidy.

Zoranda decided to wait until the following day to tell Helen of the mission he had in mind for her.

They did not know that the agent who detonated the bomb, by dint of good positioning, a cool head and great agility, had managed to reach his car and trail the taxi containing Edward, Tony and Helen to the Great White Lodge. This was before the Master and Zoranda had time to place the house in a bubble of protection so he was pleased to report Helen's whereabouts back to Sturov.

Nor did they know that the taxi driver, in a police car, was directing the forces of law and order to the Great White Lodge. 'This is where I took them,' he declared. 'It was one of the houses down here. I'll know it when I see it. I said to my wife there was something strange about those people. Why didn't they want the woman to go to hospital? And why did they move from the hotel? They said they'd be safer at the lodge.'

As they cruised up and down the road, peering at the beautiful villas beyond their firmly shut gates, the taxi driver was getting increasingly hot, bothered and loquacious. 'Hey, it was down here. I know it. Near the end. Beautiful place with white gates. That made it unusual. It's got to be here.'

He became more and more disgruntled and embarrassed as they drove down the road three times and he could not recognise the Great White Lodge. He could not know that the great powers of light had placed a dome over the building, which rendered it invisible to those of lower vibration.

Chapter 11

The sound of an elephant crashing through trees in the dark sounded alarmingly near to Joanna, who had always been nervous of big animals, despite her love of them. She was glad it was on the other side of the wooden fence, which enclosed the barbeque area at the safari lodge.

Bede read her thoughts. 'It could knock the fence down as easily as you could destroy a spider's web if it wished to,' he remarked.

Joanna felt suddenly small and vulnerable. She had felt protected by the brilliant fire, which illuminated the huge table at which they were sitting under the stars. The conversation with Bede's family and their other visitors had been so captivating that she had forgotten the rigours of the bush at night.

Bede suggested that they stand on their chairs and peep over the fence. They agreed with alacrity and Joanna was horrified to see the enormous black silhouette of an elephant barely ten feet from them. It was decimating a tree with determined efficiency.

Bede laughed at the look on her face. 'Come,' he whispered. 'All of you bring your torches.'

His Aunt Monica said, 'Those naughty elephants. They do so much damage but remember they are wild creatures.'

Clutching torches, Joanna and Marcus, together with two of the visitors, Jo'burg businessmen enjoying a break, crept behind Bede past the swimming pool to the entrance porch. It was really a roofed platform, which served as a reception area, with a small room and shop built on one side. The two steps up to it acted as the nominal boundary to separate the hotel from the bush.

'Look!' Bede shone his torch and from this angle they could make out two of the great pachyderms chomping up the trees in the front garden. To Joanna's consternation Bede decided to be macho and chase the elephants away while shouting and waving his arms. Joanna held on to Marcus's hand tightly just in case he had any thoughts of similar bravado but the giant creatures lumbered off with their little tails between their legs and their big ears flapping. She was sure she heard them calling, 'Just you wait!' as they retreated and knew their sensibilities were outraged. She wanted to talk to them, to pacify and re-empower them but there was no chance. Bede returned looking smug.

Later that night, however, the intelligent creatures exacted revenge in their own way.

After dinner Joanna and Marcus relaxed on a bench, carefully sited to overlook the water hole. At the safari lodge there was no electricity, so flares lit up the gardens, which were also intended to act as a deterrent to wild animals. Nevertheless Joanna had privately sized up how far it was to the safety of their bungalow.

They could see the Milky Way stretching like a silver stream across the sky. 'That's Orion's belt, isn't it?' Marcus asked, pointing to the distinctive three stars in a row.

Bede joined them and was able to show them the Pleiades and Mars. 'Strange, isn't it. I imagine there's a whole world out there we know nothing about,' he was saying. Then he stiffened suddenly. 'Sh! Look!' He touched Joanna's arm as a giraffe, the size of a tall tree, stepped from the shelter of the bushes and nervously approached the water hole. Bede whispered that a giraffe was at its most vulnerable when it was drinking. They watched it spread out its legs and lower its neck until it could reach the water.

Joanna found she was holding her breath, hoping it would be safe. As it quickly regained its feet and tottered away out of sight, she let out a sigh of relief. 'That was beautiful,' she murmured, hoping more animals would appear, but nothing rewarded their vigil.

They were about to turn in for an early night when a shadowy form slipped up to them, making them start. It was the lion shaman. After a few words of greeting he sat on a chair enjoying the night with them in silence.

At length he pointed to the brightest star they could see. 'This is Sirius,' he said. 'Many on Earth now come from Sirius. Important for Africa.'

'Come from Sirius! What do you mean?' questioned Marcus.

'Important for Africa?' queried Joanna.

The shaman nodded vigorously. 'All stars and planets affect us but especially that one right now.' He ruminated for a moment, then added in a reverent voice, 'And Orion.'

They waited in questioning silence for him to continue. He soon spoke in his deep rumbling voice. 'Long time ago there was a great continent. You call it Atlantis.'

They nodded to indicate that they knew of it.

'They were a very advanced civilisation and their priests could connect with the stars. Not in the way we can now.' He shook his head. 'No. No. They could communicate with the beings on the other planets.'

'Beings on the other planets?' echoed Marcus.

He nodded. 'Different beings live on the stars or galaxies. Not as you and I live in a physical shell of course, but as spirits, in etheric bodies. Each star is a place for a particular kind of learning. Our planet Earth is a unique school to learn about a physical body, emotions, sexuality and free will. Spirits from other planets enrol here to learn about these things. And of course an entry requirement for Earth is to take on a physical body at birth. We must also drink from the cup of amnesia and forget our planet of origin.'

Joanna nodded. She had heard this before.

'At the time of Atlantis visitors came to Earth quite freely from various planets, either in their spirit bodies or in space ships. The need for amnesia had not then been established.' He threw his head back and gazed lovingly at the night sky as though remembering the halcyon days when heaven and Earth were one. 'The people of pure Atlantis in the early times had enormous spiritual powers and could communicate with telepathy and crystal power. Later their technology and computer skills were beyond belief. They could communicate with their friends from other planets with computer links.'

'Really! That's incredible!' Marcus found this awesome.

'Indeed. Me! I can't use a computer now!'

They smiled. It was hard to think of this simple man knowing anything about computers.

'You mentioned Sirius,' prompted Marcus.

'Ah, Sirius! Another training establishment!' he replied unexpectedly. 'The beings from Sirius are cerebral people. They are instigators. In Sirius they are trained in advanced technology, medical science, holistic healing, computer studies, science of all kinds. That is what they bring to Earth. You get my drift?' He eyed them with a question mark.

'You mean people like Bill Gates would come from Sirius?' Marcus asked, his mind focused on the mention of computer studies.

'Absolutely right.'

'You mean you've heard of him?'

The shaman grinned, exposing his gums. 'I have my feet in both worlds. The computer revolution and in fact most of the benefits to the planet are Atlantean and the people who instigated them came from Sirius. Brunel, who brought construction skills, was one of the first in the latest wave of Atlanteans trained in Sirius. They bring in practical knowledge.'

'But he lived years ago.'

The black man chuckled. 'Human time and the time of spirit are different.' He went on, 'Sirians who are now incarnated on Earth are aiming to expand the mind and raise the intelligence of everyone. Their higher purpose is to teach and alert us to what is really going on round the planet. They are helping people to notice and acknowledge what is happening. Many of those from Sirius are incarnating in capitalistic countries; their divine mission is to turn the minds of people away from capitalism, which does not serve the light. Many rebels come from Sirius; some are acting out old karma and have forgotten the spiritual laws. By the way, Osama bin Laden was on Earth at the end of Atlantis, one who helped cause its destruction.'

'Really!'

'I thought it was the technology gone mad that caused the downfall of Atlantis,' queried Joanna.

'Not the technology itself but turning it into a God.'

'That makes sense.'

'So all those who caused the downfall of Atlantis came from Sirius, did they?' asked Marcus.

'No, but many of them did. They used their great knowledge for greed and control. During the last centuries of Atlantis they were given chance after chance to change and work for good but they ignored all warnings and selected destruction. After Atlantis those people did not ascend but returned to Sirius to be . . .' He paused and the corners of his mouth twitched as if he were trying not to smile. He picked up a stick and whacked a leg of the chair. 'I'd like to say to be knocked about a bit. Re- educated to put it politely. Now they are getting a second chance. But, I must emphasise, some from Sirius served the divine and tried to stop the horrors of the last days of Atlantis. They are also reincarnating now. Sometimes they come into the same family to create a balance.'

'That must be difficult,' murmured Joanna.

'Indeed.' He inclined his head.

'So the good and the bad are back now as the planet is trying to ascend?'

'Yes. That's why the battle between dark and light has intensified.'

'And did Sturov come from Sirius?'

'He has trained in Sirius and elsewhere but his soul has gathered evil during a long descent. He is a descendant of the dark Annunaki warriors of Nebiru, and their servant, of course.'

'Nebiru?'

'It's a technologically advanced third-dimensional planet, sometimes called Anu. The beings live on lower astral energy and minerals, which Earth had in plenty, so this planet was and still is a prime target for them. Their technical advancement enabled them to help build many of the great monuments on this planet.' He shook his head slightly. 'But the Annunaki included control structures in the architecture of the buildings, the inverse of sacred geometry. They were also able to generate lower vibrational electromagnetic frequencies, which bound human minds to limiting beliefs. The warmongers and corrupt leaders on Earth are their servants.'

Marcus was listening intently. 'Are those lower vibrational frequencies now sent out through television and computers?'

'I believe so, yes.'

'And is that why the leaders on Earth don't get together to feed the starving or do something about the ozone layer?' demanded Joanna. 'Because the influential ones are servants of the Annunuki?'

'Indeed.'

'And Sturov is their chief representative on Earth?'

The shaman nodded.

'No wonder he foments fear and chaos. The dark energy feeds the dark aliens,' said Marcus.

As if on cue a distant animal screamed in agony. Joanna felt a sudden rush of sweat to her palms and the back of her neck tingled. She was determined to raise the tone. 'And light-workers have the power to bring freedom, love and peace to Earth. Let's talk about that!' she exclaimed.

'Have you heard of the Dogon tribe?' Bede spoke suddenly and they jumped, for they had almost forgotten he was still there. 'It's a totally fascinating story. They are a primitive tribe not far from here and they seem to know all about Sirius.'

'How?' demanded Marcus.

'I don't know,' admitted Bede. 'But I bet he does?'

He nodded to the sangoma who stood up quietly and said, 'It is indeed connected to what we are talking about and important for the healing of the world, especially Africa. But I must leave you now.'

'When will we see you again?' Joanna's voice sounded faintly querulous. She heard it herself and stopped, consciously continuing in a changed tone. 'What I mean is, please will you give us the information.'

He eyed her seriously, then smiled. 'Indeed yes. The Dogons. I will tell you about the Dogons of Sirius. There is a lot to explain.' He shook his head. 'I will come tomorrow. But remember those who caused the fall of Atlantis aren't just incarnating into human bodies.' He pulled his cape firmly around his shoulders and moved away, seeming to melt into the darkness and disappear, leaving them to their thoughts and the starlit African night.

They looked at each other. 'What did he mean by that?' Joanna asked aloud into the empty darkness of the night.

Their conversation with the sangoma had put all thoughts of the elephants out of their minds but next morning they found the intelligent beasts had left them a gift. A mountainous, steaming turd had been dropped strategically outside the door of their cabin as if to say, 'That's what happens when you watch someone chasing us with a stick.'

'Those naughty elephants!' exclaimed Aunt Monica when she saw it. She was not so pleased when she saw that they had casually pushed over one of the trees inside the compound so that its roots lay gasping for sustenance, like octopus tentacles out of their element.

Bede arrived late for breakfast. He was unshaven and furious. 'Those damn elephants have pulled out the water pipe to my bungalow! I'll have to go to town when we get back from safari for some more pipe to repair it!'

Joanna could not totally suppress a little grin of satisfaction.

Chapter 12

Already the limitless sky was washed a monochrome blue as though painted by a giant paintbrush, fading where the fierce white-hot sun lit it. A family of zebra marched along a track in single file, almost invisible behind leafless branches. Bede, who was driving the safari vehicle, pointed out a large bird, sporting a beak like a big banana, which graced a solitary tree. 'That's a yellow-billed hornbill. They mate for life and in the mating season the female stays inside the nest for two months. She loses all her feathers and then lays her eggs on them. The male covers the entrance to the nest with mud. When the chicks are hatched he makes a hole and feeds his family through the hole. Then when the feathers grow she can leave with the chicks.'

'Ah!' responded Joanna. 'That's lovely!'

Marcus grinned and before he could comment, a flight of tiny iridescent blue birds with red bills rose like a cloud of butterflies in front of their vehicle, and distracted him.

An African tracker, called Drake, was sitting on a lookout seat over the bonnet. His incredibly sharp eyes missed nothing and he alerted Bede with a movement of his hand to the big game and small animals, which blended into the bush. Drake pointed a finger and Bede stopped, then jumped down and ran back a few paces to pick up what looked like a stone but transpired to be a two-inch baby tortoise, which he said was about a week old. Suddenly he laughed and held it out as a stream of urine precipitated from the tiny creature. The tortoise put out its ugly wrinkled little head and looked at them with a knowing expression in its bright button eyes. They watched it for a while, then Bede returned it to the roadside.

'There!' Bede pointed and their vision adjusted to an immobile herd of springbok, seemingly etched into the landscape. Then in one movement, their black and white tails waving, they turned, leaping away with curious stiff-legged bounces and vanished into the grey petrified scrub.

Joanna and Marcus were longing to see a lion. 'That's what I really want to see,' Joanna told Bede three times just to make sure he got the message. And the trackers did their best. Again and again they got out of the vehicle and examined tracks but they were always too old. They came upon three big male buffalo, placid-looking but dangerously short-tempered, who snorted and tossed their heads in unmistakeable warning. Several times they crossed over the wide, dry, sandy river bed, which was full of tracks, including the slithery trail of a python, which Drake assured them would be six feet long. Two handsome male kudu with magnificent spiral horns walked through a clearing for their benefit and several giraffes appeared to stand by the road to say hello, but lions eluded them.

When they stopped for a coffee break by a large muddy

water hole, Marcus, Joanna and Bede sat on a log over-looking the water while Drake wandered round the lake. All was silent for a time except for the high-pitched whine of the cicadas and the intermittent drilling of a wood-pecker in some hidden tree.

'You were going to tell us about the Dogon tribe?' Marcus reminded Bede.

'Oh yes. It's quite an extraordinary story.' Bede picked up a stick and doodled with it in the mud as he spoke. 'The Dogons are a primitive African tribe, who live in Mali and appear to have advanced astrophysical knowledge.'

'My goodness!' Marcus looked stunned.

'They believe they came from Sirius, the star, and all their dances and ceremonies represent the movements and characteristics of Sirius.'

'What do you mean?'

'Well, their ancient dances involve revolving in certain directions in a precise way, with a prescribed number of steps, which they said was to mirror the movement of Sirius, and it turned out to be exactly right.'

'No!' Marcus exclaimed.

'Oh yes. And they said that a small star, which they called a heavy star, revolves round Sirius every fifty years and maintained that it orbited elliptically round the big star.'

'That's very exact!' exclaimed Joanna.

Bede nodded. 'It is, isn't it? They also said it takes a year for the heavy little star to rotate on its axis. Naturally scientists scoffed, saying that there was no second star near Sirius. There is nothing visible to the naked eye. It was only in 1970 that a photo was obtained of Sirius B, the tiny star. It's a white dwarf and this star, the smallest thing in the sky, is also the heaviest, consisting of a metal called sagala, which is so heavy that humans can't lift even a tiny piece. The Dogons proved to be right about the timing and everything else.'

'What an amazing thing! How did the Dogons know all this?'

'I don't know but the ancient Egyptians also spoke of a civilisation coming from Sirius. Apparently it's depicted in their hieroglyphs.'

Joanna glanced at Marcus. 'We ought to let Mum and Tony know. They'd be fascinated by this and could go to see the hieroglyphs while they're in Egypt.'

'We'll try and ring them again.'

Bede clearly wanted to continue. 'The Dogons had other advanced knowledge. Their dances also described the circulation of the blood round the body. The Chinese apparently knew about it in the second century BC but it wasn't understood in the West. And when William Harvey published his book on it in the early 1600s people thought he was insane.'

'Unbelievable!'

'There's more. The Dogons knew the Earth goes round the sun long before we in the West were putting people to death for saying so!'

'Wow!' It was Joanna's turn to exclaim. 'Anything else?'

'I'm sure there's lots more. Some things are rubbish though. The tribe claims that the gods who founded their civilisation were amphibious creatures with fish tails. Apparently they too are depicted in the ancient Egyptian hieroglyphs.' He laughed rather derisorily and Joanna found her hackles rising.

It seemed terrible as well as premature to deride a tribe for their understandings when other, seemingly ridiculous, aspects had been scientifically verified. She breathed in the hot fragrant air and sipped her cold drink, feeling bemused and excited by what Bede had told them. She looked up at the artificially blue sky and thought, Tonight we'll be able to see Sirius. Perhaps the lion shaman will come and tell us more. Maybe he'll tell us how the Dogons have this knowledge. She looked at Marcus and knew from the expression in his grey eyes that his thoughts were identical.

Chapter 13

That evening's safari was even more impressive. By now the eternal miles of desiccated bush, interspersed by the occasional tree fully clothed in emerald leaves, were no longer a novelty to Marcus and Joanna. But the feel of the wind in their hair and the anticipation of the unexpected could never lose their magic. They were ready to be charmed by a big grey Egyptian goose with a vivid white stripe, which took off into the pink early evening sky like a fat-bodied jet. A pair of fish eagles on top of a dead tree flapped off laconically at the approach of the safari vehicle, the smaller male behind his female. They watched a cringing hyena skulking along a parallel path. And then they came across the lions.

There were three lionesses, who looked at them with a bored expression, and six cubs, with smiling mouths and soft round ears, who peeped out from behind their mothers, without fear but with a good deal of curiosity. None of them was white.

'Can you talk to them?' Marcus whispered to Joanna. She swallowed and projected thoughts of love to the lions, then made herself receptive. They sat there for a long time watching but nothing came to her. No response. No form of communication. One of the lionesses yawned, a cavernous contemptuous yawn, then closed her eyes. At last it was time to move on. Just as Bede was putting the vehicle into reverse, Joanna received full into her third eye: 'Soon. The white cub will be born soon.'

Her eyes shone and she clutched Marcus's hand. He looked at her. 'What?' he whispered and she told him what she had been given. It was his turn to look amazed and delighted.

'We must let Helen know. Something is about to happen!'

His girlfriend needed no second bidding. As soon as they returned to the safari lodge she hurried to their room to indulge in a long conversation with her mother. Her mood of exhilaration changed to shock as she learnt of the explosion at the Sphinx and the danger that her parent had been in. 'At least you're safe now in the Great White Lodge,' she responded, as much to soothe herself as Helen.

Why did parents always expect their children to phone them? she thought to herself, conveniently forgetting the times her mother phoned her. She added as an admonition, 'Promise you'll phone immediately if you have any news about anything!'

'I will,' responded Helen meekly.

After supper they sat on the bench overlooking the water hole. It was if anything darker than the night before and the stars seemed even brighter. There was a sense of anticipation in the air. They silently prayed that the lion sangoma would come, trying to send him an invitation on the air waves.

But when someone slipped up to them, they were disappointed to find it was Bede. He did not seem to notice their disappointment, however, and quietly pointed out a cluster of gazelles creeping down to the water to drink.

With ironic timing, just as they had decided to retire to bed, the lion shaman materialised. None of them saw or heard him coming. He simply arrived.

Immediately their tiredness evaporated and Joanna told him excitedly about the lions they had seen and also the communication she had received from them.

The African merely nodded as if he were well aware that the white lion cub would be born soon. 'There is great danger and we must stay very alert,' he said. 'We will talk about it later. Tonight I wish to talk to you about the cosmos, for the white lion is an important part of the web of light. It is intimately connected with All.' His head swivelled in a wide arc as he looked at the heavens above. 'Our world is linked to the vast universe out there. We must not forget that. Do you think the white lion is a big cat just born on Earth? No, no. It enters from out there.' He waved his arm to indicate the heavens.

'Is it from Sirius?' Joanna ventured.

'No! No! Later I will explain where he comes from and why. First we are talking of Sirius.' He paused with a faint frown on his face. 'The Dogons!' he announced. 'I will start with the Dogons.'

Marcus looked at Bede, who as usual had been sitting silent, invisible and almost forgotten by them.

'I told them about the Dogons this morning,' Bede spoke up.

The old man nodded. 'What did you tell them?'

And the young man gave him a potted version of their conversation. 'But could you explain how the Dogons know all this about Sirius?'

'Right,' said the wise man, with a faint hint of amusement in his voice. 'What do you know of the fish people?'

They shook their heads and he could see the whites of their eyes shimmer in the light of a flare.

'It's a myth.' Bede shrugged.

The shaman ignored his comment and started to talk in a sing-song voice. They all listened intently. 'In Atlantean times there was a clan of wise and evolved priests, led by Nommo, a mighty being or god from Sirius. The word Nommo means Pure One or Christed One. At the fall of Atlantis, this tribe was saved and went to Egypt, then eventually moved south, deeper into Africa. They always kept their connection with Sirius. Remember, the Dogons are enlightened beings, who have a special mission on Earth and like most ancient cultures their faith is based on the universal myth.'

'The universal myth?' queried Marcus.

The shaman nodded. 'They understand that Nommo is the pure light and that man descended after temptation by their equivalent of Lucifer. In order to atone for human impurity the Nommo was crucified on a tree, acting as a sacrifice for us and to purify and cleanse the Earth. He gave his body to help humanity. Then he rose again. The Dogons believe that he will come again and a special star will appear in the sky to show us.'

'It's the same story as Christianity!' exclaimed Joanna.

'And the same story as many cultures and religions,' added Bede. 'They all have the same basic ingredients.'

'If only everyone in the world knew we all have the same fundamental myth,' Marcus was saying, 'surely that would expand people's minds and stop certain religions thinking they were the only one.'

Joanna was puzzled by the quirkiness of Bede's knowledge and asked him how he knew all these things.

'Part of the deal when I came to Africa was that I continue my studies through the Open University,' he replied. 'I chose myth and religion, mainly to upset my parents, especially my father who hated anything you couldn't see, touch or prove.' His eyes hardened and a cold feeling hit Joanna in the solar plexus. 'But Aunt Monica backed me to the hilt.' His voice softened as he mentioned his aunt as if there were an intangible bond between them.

I guess it was through Monica that he returned to his roots, she thought, for she had noticed their closeness before. They must have known each other in previous lives and had a soul contract that she would bring him back to his homeland as he grew older. Her thoughts were about to wander into the complexities and wonders of soul choices when she stopped herself, suddenly realising that the shaman was watching them in silence.

'So what is the Dogons' special mission?' she asked him.

'Ah!' he said. 'Their divine work is to keep the connection to Sirius open, active and growing. As I mentioned yesterday Sirius is a training college for medical and holistic science, advanced technology, astronomy and astrology.'

'What do you mean by medical and holistic science?' Marcus asked for clarification.

'The Sirians don't just expand the knowledge and use of drugs. They work with medical science in the broadest sense, which includes holistic medicine, herbal healing, acupuncture, homeopathy, sound vibrations – all things that heal the physical, emotional, mental and spiritual body. Then they beam out this information, a bit like a lighthouse, so that appropriate souls can access it.'

'Give us an example,' Marcus requested.

'In the last century they brought in medical information from Sirius and beamed it out. Pasteur picked it up and used it to push forward the boundaries of human science.'

'I see. So is that why scientists in Russia or China or America make exactly the same breakthroughs at the same time?'

'Indeed. Receptive people pick up the broadcasts, quite unconsciously, of course.'

'Right. I've heard that before but it explains it more clearly.'

The shaman nodded. 'So the life purpose of the Dogons is to keep the portal to Sirius open for science and technology to reach Earth so that seed thoughts of new ideas can be passed through it without distortion,' the shaman reiterated. 'Another example is the way they bring through astrological knowledge not just about Sirius but the cosmos. This information carries the vibration of the

Christ consciousness, their Nommo. In this way they spread pure light.'

Marcus sat forward as if he were about to ask a question, then thought better of it and sat back, deep in thought. No one said anything for a while. It seemed a lot to digest.

Joanna was convinced that the star was shining more brightly. She was sure it flashed but decided that was her imagination.

At last the shaman stirred and started to speak. 'In the glorious early days of Atlantis, it was the task of the wise initiates to keep the portals to the cosmos open and often there were visitations from more evolved planets. In this way they had access to cosmic knowledge and wisdom and were linked into the vast web of light. You know the names of some of the high priests and high priestesses of Atlantis I am sure. Ptah, Osiris, Isis and Horus, even Thoth himself. They became mythical gods in Egypt but they were real people in Atlantis.'

'They really lived in Atlantis!' Marcus repeated, sounding amazed.

'Oh yes. As the Pure Ones of Atlantis they were in constant communication with the divine. When the dark priesthood took over the continent and cast it into a downward spiral of terror and abuse, the Pure Ones were forewarned that the flood was about to take place. They sent twelve groups of Wise Ones to different parts of the planet that had been prepared for them. Each group held part of the ancient esoteric wisdom of Atlantis. None had it all. But there are mighty beings incarnated in an

unusual form who hold all twelve strands of the knowledge in keeping for us. They will hand it over when we
humans are ready.' A sudden movement from Bede, who
had tilted his head to hear better, made him hesitate.
'Enough of that. It is not the time,' he muttered.

Joanna was willing him to continue. 'They sent twelve
groups to different parts of the world?' she prompted.

He considered for a long minute and they thought he
might get up and vanish as he had done before. At last he
settled back and repeated, 'Yes, twelve soul groups.'

'Could you tell us where they went?'

He murmured to himself, 'Is it important for them to
know where they went?' and then answered his own
question. 'Not yet. Too much too soon. Later.'

Without replying he continued on his former tack.
'Since the fall of Atlantis the initiates in these soul groups
have endeavoured to keep the portals to the galaxies
open, like the Dogons. At the present time these are the
men and women who lead enlightened cultures or
esoteric branches of religions throughout the world.' He
looked at Marcus. 'You understand this for you received
the Scroll of Atlantis and you were sent to Machu Picchu
to learn how the Inca initiates kept the divine portal there
open.'

Marcus thought about his extraordinary meeting with
the Inca shaman in Peru, and nodded. He certainly had
been given awesome esoteric information about
Machu Picchu. He felt stunned even now when he
remembered it.

Joanna suddenly remembered the comment made by

Bede earlier in the day. He'd said that the Dogon tribe claimed that the gods who founded their civilisation were amphibious creatures with fish tails. Now she asked the sangoma about it. His answer surprised them.

'Indeed. Dogons are fish people. Recall what the fish represents.'

'It's the symbol of Christianity, isn't it?' Joanna put in.

'The Christ. The Nommo. The energy of unconditional cosmic love. The Dogon legend said that the Nommo would return and when he did it would be called the Day of the Fish. Think.' He looked at them with his deep black eyes.

Marcus said, 'The symbol for Christianity was a fish and now we await the second coming of the Christ. Is that what they refer to? I thought—'

The shaman stopped him. 'All you said was right, so far. The Christ consciousness is an energy carried by beings who are sufficiently pure. Remember that in your quest to heal the web of light.'

'Buddha's symbol was a fish and so was Vishnu's,' interjected Bede.

Marcus nodded and looked at the shaman, inviting him to continue but the wise man merely said in a soft voice, 'Now, Marcus and Joanna, you must go and swim with the dolphins. That is the next step in your quest.'

With that he rose and walked away without a backward glance. The night soon swallowed him up and Marcus, Joanna and Bede were left staring into the dark.

Chapter 14

Placed in a healing cocoon by Edward and Zoranda, Helen slept a deep dreamless sleep that night and woke feeling she had been in the arms of the angels. She knew she was safe at the Great White Lodge. All the fear of the previous day had evaporated and she was gracefully anticipating the new one. She glanced at Tony and saw that his eyes were open and he was watching her, as if gauging her emotional state. She smiled a happy lazy smile and he responded by opening his arms, inviting her in.

They could hear the joyous early morning twitter of birds greeting the day, the distant bark of a house dog and the soft swish of sandals as people went about their business in the house. All was well.

'The cloud has lifted,' murmured Helen as she kissed her husband good morning. 'I feel we can start again today.'

And it felt like a new beginning when they drank tea with Zoranda on the generous patio, shaded with ferns and palms and cool green vines. The big, bald man scanned Helen's energy fields with his all-seeing blue eyes and smiled. 'You feel better this morning.' It was a statement not a question. 'I'm glad. We have brought you here for your own protection, of course, but also for another reason.'

She tensed in anticipation. Here it comes! she thought. What do they want of me?

He continued softly, 'It is time now for people everywhere to know things that were previously hidden. The masses are ready to understand some of the esoteric information that has been kept secret for aeons and handed down through initiation on pain of death.'

Helen thought, What's this got to do with me? She said aloud, 'Oh?', managing to make it sound somewhere between a squeak of anticipation, an exclamation and a question.

Zoranda's words had thrown her equilibrium and he was, of course, aware of it. Kindness exuded from him as he said softly, 'There is nothing to fear, Helen. You are no longer in danger.' He looked at her steadily. 'Unless you choose to place yourself in such a position.'

'Oh no! No more. I'm finished with adventure. I'm ready for a quiet life,' she affirmed, touching her husband's arm as if to make sure he had heard her. 'What do you want me to do?'

Zoranda responded with a faint smile of knowing compassion. He understood that Helen consciously wanted peace and safety. At another level she craved change and excitement, unconsciously attracting drama and danger. Now was not the time to confront her with the deep unconscious messages broadcast by her soul.

'We want you to write a book containing special information, in a form that will be accepted and understood by people everywhere, possibly as a novel.'

'What?' she gasped as if unable to believe her ears. 'But why me?'

'First, because we trust you to keep the purity of the information. There are many who would distort it for effect or through ego. Second, because you have written esoteric books in past lives, many past lives. And you have tried to write a book in this one, though you have never mentioned it.'

Helen went red. What he said was true, of course. How did he know? He seemed to be aware of everything. For a moment she felt as naked as a new-born baby, as she wondered what else he read in her aura. She always had this sense with him, and if he were not so eternally loving and serene it would be very uncomfortable. Her thoughts darted down corridors of doubt. A book was a major responsibility. Was she worthy? What if she couldn't do it? Then she took a deep breath and remembered what an honour this was. Her spirit guides and angels would surely help her. So would Tony. So would Zoranda. Of course she could do it!

Zoranda had watched the colours round her change from the grey of confusion and self-doubt to a wonderful swirl of gold, violet and sparkling blue, denoting angelic connection, true service and communication.

'Good!' he said. 'You're ready.'

Helen laughed aloud, suddenly fired with enthusiasm. 'You read me so well. Not only will I do it, it'll be the best book I can possibly write.'

'Thank you.' Zoranda nodded in acknowledgement.

'Good for you, Helen,' said her husband proudly and she smiled at him, her brown eyes warm with gratitude for his steadfast support.

'What do you want me to write about?' She turned to the wise man, her cheeks flushed and her chin tilted slightly forward, like a child trying to hide its excitement and ready to handle anything.

Zoranda rubbed his fingers together as if contemplating where to start. 'I think you know that those who caused the destruction of Atlantis, through trying to substitute technology and materialism for the power of spirituality, have reincarnated on Earth. So too have those whose purity and light maintained the heights of that age. The battle between dark and light is being played out once again throughout the world and in many dimensions.'

Helen nodded solemnly.

'To put it in a nutshell, it is important for the world to understand the impact this is having now, from terrorism to New Age philosophy to the Bermuda Triangle. Because we have reached the same point of choice on Earth now, we want you to tell people about the glory of Atlantis, then how and why it fell. Include what happened to the groups that survived the flood.'

'There were twelve groups, weren't there?' interrupted Helen.

Zoranda nodded. 'Indeed. I'll give you all the information you need about them, as well as their interstellar connections. It is time to reveal the riddle of the Sphinx, the pyramids and the dolphins.'

Helen startled, exclaimed, 'The dolphins! What have they got to do with it?'

But Zoranda gently and patiently waved her question away. 'I'll explain later.' He continued with his faint enigmatic smile, 'Finally and most important of all, we want you to write about the white lion cub to be born, for it is of awesome moment, representing, as it will, the return of the Christ consciousness. In order to do this you will have to understand a little of the true story of Jesus and the cosmic Christ.'

'Is that all!' responded Helen, sarcastic in shock and excitement.

'What's the point of it?' Tony wanted to know. His interest piqued, he had been listening intently, his eyes slightly narrowed in concentration, unaware that the filtered sunlight was creating a halo round his silver-grey hair.

'Partly because it's time for people to wake up and grow up but mostly because we must now strengthen the web of light round the planet so that the glory of the golden days can return. This book is one of the tools we wish to use.' He added almost as an afterthought, 'We particularly need to facilitate the healing of Africa. You know there is a ley line which runs from the Sphinx to South Africa, don't you?'

Helen had not known that. Nor did Tony.

'It runs along the seam of gold, placed by the divine on Earth and which has now been plundered. Gold, as I'm sure you know, represents enlightenment, and when it was wrenched from the planet the web of light was torn along the length of Africa, with cataclysmic results for that continent and the world. In order to have peace on Earth, we must replace the physical gold with spiritual awareness and light.'

'Oh!'

'Your book, Helen, will help to do that. It will spread the message of wisdom and unconditional love, which the white lion is to bring to Earth, as well as much esoteric knowledge.'

Helen felt adrenaline fizzing through her body. Surely they could see her heart glowing with delight?

Chapter 15

'In order to talk to you of the Christ consciousness, which will illuminate the web of light, I must explain a little of the true story of Jesus the Christ.' It was late morning and Zoranda, in his customary cloud of tranquillity, was about to impart information to Helen for the book she was to write.

Helen keenly felt the responsibility of the task she had been allotted. Pride, fear, a sense of unworthiness and determination to do her best ricocheted round her brain. Determination was the dominant feeling. She gripped her Biro tightly, without realising that she was so tense, and nodded.

A slight breeze puffed round them from time to time, making the heat bearable, and a lizard, almost hidden by the dappled sunlight, lay on its stomach with its feet in the air as it tried to keep cool.

Zoranda began, 'Over the millennia many avatars and those named Sons of God have been sent to Earth and almost every culture has a similar myth about their birth and life. The saviour's birth is always anticipated by the Magi of the time. It is heralded by a bright star or comet. The child has a lowly birth, often in a stable, to a virgin on 25th December. He is attended by three Wise

Men. His teachings are disputed and he is killed, usually crucified, then resurrected.'

Even Helen, who had a very rudimentary knowledge of religion, knew this was the story of Christianity.

'You're saying it's not just a Christian story?' she checked.

'Indeed not! It is a cosmic mystery. According to old Essene and Rosicrucian records, when Krishna was born a great star in heaven proclaimed the fact and the Magi brought him sandalwood and perfumes. At the Buddha's birth a bright, moving star proclaimed his divinity and Wise Men visited to bring him gifts. Initiates observed a bright star, which enabled them to find the birthplace of Confucius. It was the same with Mithras, the Persian saviour, Socrates, Aesculapius, Bacchus, Romulus and others. Remember the Magi of all cultures underwent a very high degree of initiation and were learned in the sacred art of astrology. They were the Wise Ones of the mystery temples and the chief instructors of esoteric knowledge.'

'That's amazing. I had no idea.' Helen was lost in thought for a moment. Then she asked, 'Was it really a virgin birth? I've always wondered about that.'

'Indeed it was.' Zoranda was smiling gently, his blue eyes appraising her with a hint of humour.

Helen frowned, trying to keep an open mind. 'It seems incomprehensible,' she commented.

Zoranda rebuked her gently. 'It only seems impossible to the Western mind, for we are so steeped in logic that we have lost the mystic truth and power of divine law.'

Helen flushed. 'Please explain.'

'Joseph and Mary were both Essenes, the religious sect into which Jesus was born. The members of the sect spent several hours each day in mystical practices and the development of spiritual power. This is what made possible the miracles and healings they performed. They were taught the Great White Brotherhood teachings and in turn passed them on.' He paused. 'I think it would help if you had an understanding who Mary really was.'

She waited in keen anticipation while the big man moved slightly to let cool air blow under his perspiring legs, which were sticking to his chair, and put his finger-tips together as he often did if he wanted to emphasise something.

'The Essene brotherhood had a great secret temple at Heliopolis in Egypt where the highest ceremonies were held. It was known as the Temple of Helios or some called it the Temple of the Sun. The young daughters of the highest members served here as vestal virgins. They were educated by the organisation and were spiritually trained to a high degree of cosmic awareness, so that their essence was pure.

'Joachim was the high priest in the Holy Temple of Helios and when his wife, Anna, gave birth to a girl they agreed she should become a dove in the holy temple. That means her life would be dedicated to service there until she became a woman at twelve or thirteen. Then they could make a choice about her future.

'When the baby, Mary, was six months old they took her to the temple where her past lives were revealed by the Magi. One of her previous incarnations was as Isis, the High Priestess of Atlantis, who gave birth to Horus, the sun god, who represents the solar logos. He was the bringer of enlightenment to Earth for that time. Those who were his followers were custodians of the wisdom of the Sphinx and in Egypt he was known as a Lion King.

'Before that, in Lemuria, she was known as Ma-Ra, which means "the goddess who is the mother of the sun". She was the first initiate of that civilisation. Later she developed the Lemurian Mystery School and was the first Lemurian to ascend from Earth. So you can see, Mary was not a lowly maiden. She was a mighty soul.'

Helen gave a little gasp of surprise. Zoranda smiled and continued.

'Even as a small child Mary was spiritually aware and miracles happened around her. As a symbolic way of keeping her pure, her feet were not allowed to touch the earth and she always walked on a white holy cloth. So you understand, she was prepared before she was born and throughout her life to be the mother of Jesus, who was to carry the Christ light.'

Helen nodded. 'I still don't understand the concept of a virgin birth.'

Zoranda sighed very slightly. 'In order to understand spiritual conception, you have to let go of the analytical mind. You must comprehend the higher mystical and spiritual laws as taught by the ancient Masters. To become a Christ of the time is so sublime, so utterly beyond the comprehension of human mind . . .' He stopped as if overcome by the impossibility of expressing so ineffable a concept and added simply, 'Mystics everywhere know that only one who was divinely conceived could become a Christ of his time. The vibration of God was implanted into Mary.'

Helen had a sudden and complete revelation of the meaning of divine conception. It was as if a light had entered her mind and swept away all previous beliefs. The awesomeness of this cosmic mystery overwhelmed her for a moment as a million tingles shivered and splintered through her body. She could not speak.

In a little while Zoranda continued, 'In every age and time avatars had divine conceptions. Krishna, Buddha, Lao-Tsze of China and Horus, as I've already mentioned. Then there was Ra of Egypt, Zoroaster of Persia, Quetzalcoatl of Mexico and there are more. Plato's father was said to have been told in a spiritual dream to keep his wife pure until after the divine conception and birth of a holy child. So was Pythagoras's father. In times and places when the consciousness was higher and the divine mysteries accepted, it would have been considered inconceivable for a holy being to have been born from a physical mating.'

'I think I understand.'

Zoranda said, 'I want to explain where Jesus was born. It certainly was not in a stable.'

'Oh!' exclaimed Helen. More of the received story was about to be changed, she could tell. 'Where was He born, then?'

'I'll tell you what happened. In AD 325 at the Council

of Nice, many important traditions of the Christians were discussed and decided. There were so many variations in the story about Jesus's birthplace that a man called Eusebius brought the matter to the council for a definitive decision.

'Many ancient records refer to the birth in a cave. Rosicrucian and Essene records from that time state He was born in an Essene grotto on the highway near Bethlehem. The Essenes built grottoes, containing ten to twenty rooms, which were warm and dry and, most important of all, safe from attack by Bedouins. They were comfortably equipped for that time. Oil lamps hung from the ceiling so there was plenty of light. They were always close to a well so that there was fresh water. Floors were smoothed stones and the grottoes were furnished for sleeping, eating, rest, recreation and the care of the sick.

'The grotto where Jesus was born was a hospice. We would call it a hospital now. And it was quite common for Essene women to go to one for birth. However, at this council held by the Church fathers, they voted that He was born in a manger. This fitted the story they wished to perpetrate about His life.'

'But I don't understand. Why?' asked Helen, perplexed.

'Remember the Church fathers wanted control of the masses. The myth they decided on keeps people in perpetual poverty-consciousness. And the more unworthy people feel, the more they will look to the Church for leadership.'

'I suppose it's like parents who put their children down constantly,' reflected Helen. 'If the kids have no self-confidence they'll never stand up for themselves against their parents.'

'Sadly that is why the story was decided on. It has been a theme in many religions and has nothing to do with the original message of love and the true magnificence of the soul brought to Earth by the avatars.'

Helen felt enraged about the gullibility and suffering of so many people. She thought bitterly about the slaughter of witches, the damage done by zealots and wars in the name of so-called religions. Her hands clenched tight and she frowned.

Zoranda saw her expression and gently put the situation into perspective. 'Remember too that the Christian myth and that of most religions has helped people and given them a sense of comfort. It is also true that many were not able to accept the cosmic mystery of Jesus's life. I don't believe I am qualified to judge the Church fathers who made the original decision. They were subject to the conditions of the time.'

Helen sighed. 'I suppose so but it has always made my blood boil to hear of missionaries who take their restricted understandings into happy cultures and cause immeasurable damage to the spirits of the people. And the way the Church has kept women down.' Her face was redder than the heat would suggest.

Zoranda spread out his big hands in a gesture of peace and comfort. 'You know there are no victims, only volunteers, on Earth.' She nodded slowly and he added gently, 'Eventually balance returns. In times when women had the upper hand they emasculated men. In subtle ways many still do but from a position of perceived power-lessness. And now is a time to put the record straight and bring untruths into the light of knowing, so that we can all move forward in our true power. The time will come when all recognise that men and women are equal but different.'

Helen nodded. 'I know. The Codes of Power told us that.' She referred to esoteric information revealed during the initiation she and Marcus and Joanna had under-taken in Australia. She flushed, feeling embarrassed that she should need to be reminded of this but there, she told herself, she was human.

Zoranda was speaking again. 'Astrological records show that there was a bright comet in the sky at or about the time of Jesus's birth. Of course, the movement of the stars was observed for many months prior to the advent of the Holy One and the Wise Ones knew of the imminent arrival. The Magi who were selected by the Mystery Schools to present greetings to Jesus had set out several weeks beforehand and were waiting at Bethlehem for the delivery. Mary had arrived three days before and was lying in at the hospice.'

Helen's forehead wrinkled as she asked a question she thought might be considered foolish. 'Is it true one of the Wise Men was the Master St Germain in another incar-nation?'

'Quite true. He is in charge of human evolutionary development and his symbol is the winged lion. And the other two were Dwjhal Kuhl and Lord Kuthumi, who also had incarnations as St Francis and Pythagoras.'

Helen nodded. She liked things to fall into place in her mind. Then she asked with a touch of irony, 'And the shepherds minded their flocks in the snow at Christmas?'

That drew a belly laugh from the big man. 'Of course not. There's never been snow in Bethlehem in December or lambs for that matter but,' he added with a flash of humour, 'it makes pretty Christmas cards.

'No. Jesus was born in the late spring but it was not until the fifth century, after years of dispute, that His official birthday was decreed by the Holy fathers as 25th December. That date was already celebrated as a religious festival in the ancient civilisations of India, China, Egypt, Mexico and others. Isis, Osiris, Horus were all said to be born on this date as were Bacchus, Adonis, Hercules and many of the great Masters. The Christian fathers fell into line.'

'Same old story!'

'Yes, but there was a reason for it. The 25th December is a time of mystic significance. That is chiefly why the date was chosen as Jesus's birthday. Each year a cosmic change occurs at midnight on 24th December, bringing in a rush of new divine energy. The Wise Ones throughout history have understood that special energy is more readily available to humanity on that day. So by making it a celebration day the Church fathers were ensuring that the masses could have the possibility of drawing in this higher cosmic energy, including the Christ consciousness.'

'Oh. Wow. I had no idea.' Helen felt awed.

'The Church has distorted the form, which has

disguised the glory of the truth,' Zoranda said very softly. 'Now the great flame of truth must be revealed again to everyone.'

Then he sat back for a moment, surveying the beauty of the garden before he announced, almost casually, 'In two weeks' time an extra-bright comet is forecast across Africa. It is heralding the rebirth of the Christ consciousness. A creature of pure innocence is to be born, a white lion cub, who can carry the Christ light!' As he looked deep into her soul, his eyes glowed violet. 'I shall have the privilege to be there soon after its birth.'

Helen felt soft tingles flow through her entire body.

Chapter 16

In Egypt it is almost mandatory to pause in the bustle of life to watch the glorious sunset. Helen and Tony did not even have to set aside the time, for they were relaxing on the western verandah of the Great White Lodge, enjoying a cool drink.

'I love it when we can just be,' murmured Helen dreamily. 'The birds sound like an orchestra.'

'You sound like a hippy,' Tony responded flippantly and Helen was pleased to see how much more playful and at ease he had become.

The great ball of orange light was dropping rapidly behind the horizon when Zoranda joined them, a peaceful smile on his lips as he watched the ritual wonder of life. Even when it had completely disappeared they all sat in silent appreciation for some time.

'I know it's a platitude but I have to say it,' Helen commented at last. 'For thousands of years people have watched the sun rise and set and it's awesome. It's the one thing people have always had in common; it's no wonder they worshipped it in the olden times.'

'It's a symbol of the continuity of life,' agreed Tony. 'I can understand why they used to be terrified of eclipses.'

Zoranda smiled. He wondered whether to talk about

the true significance and power of the great Central Sun but decided this was not the time, so he said, 'In the days of Atlantis they had good reason to be afraid.'

'Why? I thought they had such advanced knowledge.' Helen sat erect, acutely interested again.

'Sorry. Not now. It's a fascinating subject but I'll go into it later. This evening I want to tell you a little more of the life of Jesus.'

'I thought it had all been written in the Bible,' put in Tony.

'There is very little in the Bible about His childhood and education, though it is well documented in the ancient holy archives,' Zoranda responded. 'But it was not to be revealed until humanity was ready to understand the mystic significance of His training for the role of the Christ.'

Helen and Tony were now looking intently at the wise man. Helen noticed how grey his eyebrows had become. They seemed to stand out because of his shaved head.

Zoranda continued, 'He was called Jeshua Ben Joseph as a child. This reflects His past incarnations as Jeshua and Joseph of Egypt. Of course He also lived as Adam and Elijah and had other truly extraordinary lifetimes. As I'm sure you know He was a highly evolved being, who had already mastered every lesson He had undertaken on Earth.'

'Really!' exclaimed Helen, leaning forward to catch his every word.

Zoranda nodded and went on, 'Naturally the preparation of the Messiah was not left to chance. He was educated, trained and prepared to be an attuned instrument for the Christ light.'

Helen and Tony both nodded slowly, thinking that made sense.

'His birth was expected and His education was well planned by the Essene Brotherhood and the Great White Brotherhood. After the three Magi visited the Holy Baby, they went on to Mount Carmel to report that the sacred birth had taken place. Here they left instructions for the care and instruction of the Divine Incarnation before they journeyed on to Egypt to report to the high priests of the Brotherhood.'

'What sort of child was He?' Helen wanted to know.

'Even when He was a child people saw the light around Him. Remember the Essenes had such pure auras that many people who could not normally see auras were aware of theirs, but Jeshua Ben Joseph was luminous even in His childhood. People were often astonished to see a pure light emanate from Him.'

'Wow!' exclaimed Helen.

'How was He educated?' asked Tony, who liked facts.

'When He was six his father took Him to Mount Carmel, which housed the Great Mystery School for the Great White Brotherhood and was a deeply sacred place. Here many of the most ancient manuscripts were translated and illuminated on parchment and sent to the various archives of the brotherhood throughout the world.

'At the Mystery School He was registered as Joseph. He learned Aramaic, Hebrew and the Greek languages, astrology, astronomy and the natural laws of the universe. An important part of His education was to study the major religions but He also studied the sacred mysteries and was taught to practise mind control. During His training He also underwent the most stringent initiations.

'When He was thirteen He left Mount Carmel and the Magi took Him to His home for a week of reunion and celebration, before they set off with Him on extensive travels to experience the world.'

'Where did He go?' Helen asked eagerly.

'First they travelled to Jagannath, now known as Puri, on the east coast of India. This was chosen as it was a centre of pure Buddhism and they stayed there a year, so that He could study Buddhism.'

'Who do you mean by they?'

'He was always accompanied by one of the Magi. His entire education was very carefully planned.

'After that they went to the Ganges, to Benares, where He studied ethics, natural law and languages and was also taught the Hindu principles of healing. Then He returned to the monastery of Jagannath, where He remained for two more years, studying documents sent from Tibet by Mengtse, considered the greatest of all Buddhist sages, and other subjects of course. He also went out among the common people and taught the lower castes. It was while He was here He heard that His father, Joseph, had died, which was a bitter blow.'

'Did he go home?'

Zoranda shook his head. 'No. He travelled on to

Persia, where the Magi provided many teachers for Him. It was quite incredible that at the end of each day He taught the teachers. After His years of studying healing He became very aware of the mind-body connection and realised that often the mental attitude of the patient blocked their healing. That's why He is later quoted as saying, "Go and sin no more." '

'Oh, I see!' exclaimed Helen. 'Did He mean, "Go and change your thought patterns which have created the problem?" '

Zoranda smiled. 'That's a more accurate translation of what He said.'

'That makes sense.' Tony and Helen glanced at each other and nodded.

'Quite an education!' commented Tony.

'Yes,' the big, wise man responded. 'It was considered important for an avatar to go to the source of each of the ancient religions to study their authentic documents and intimately understand their rituals and practices. And there's more, much more. For instance, while He was in Persia, He practised Entering the Silence to obtain divine instruction. He taught the importance of deep meditation for spiritual growth.'

'Can you just imagine meditating with Him!' exclaimed Helen. 'His energy would take you into the Silence.'

Zoranda nodded absently as if contemplating the possibility. Then he continued, 'After a year in Persia, Joseph, who was not yet known as Jesus, travelled to the Euphrates. Here He met the greatest sages of Assyria and again talked to the people. Then He moved on to

Babylon, then to Greece, under the personal tuition of Apollonius, and on to Alexandria. Finally He travelled to the Supreme Temple at Heliopolis where He started his preparatory initiations for entrance into the Higher Grades of the Great White Brotherhood. So you see He had a long and arduous training.'

'I had no idea,' said Helen. 'It makes me feel humble. I thought He was born with all his gifts.'

'He was but He developed them so that He would be ready to be a pure instrument for the cosmic Christ,' Zoranda told her.

She nodded slowly, remembering we all have gifts but we have to polish them up and tune them like a musical instrument.

'When did He become Jesus?' queried Tony. 'I always presumed He had been christened by that name.'

'No. He attained the name and finally became known as Jesus the Christ at the greatest secret ceremony there has ever been within the Great Pyramid.'

'Really!' exclaimed Helen, hoping he would say more.

But Tony asked with a look of concentration on his face, 'And where does John the Baptist come in? Surely he baptised Jesus?'

'Yes he did. That was Jesus's public acceptance of the Christ consciousness,' Zoranda replied. 'Let me tell you how baptism came to be of such importance as symbolic purification. I think it's relevant for you to understand.'

He glanced at them and they nodded.

'Have you heard of the great avatar, known as El Morya?'

Helen nodded. Tony shook his head.

'In one of his early incarnations El Morya learned through cosmic illumination that water does not just clean physically. It is a cosmic energy, which offers divine purification and spiritual regeneration as well. Most people nowadays think a splash of water is a symbol but it is much more. John the Baptist recognised this. He went to a sacred place on the banks of the Jordan and told those who would listen that, if they let go of the past, they could be cleansed, purified and spiritually regenerated by baptism so that they could move on to a spiritual path and see the Messiah.' He paused thoughtfully. 'At that time Pontius Pilate was persecuting the Jews. There was much unrest and talk of holy war. It is at such times that many people are open and receptive to a different way.'

'A bit like now,' commented Helen.

'Yes, a bit like now.

'Jesus heard of John's work and decided He should set an example among the people. He walked to the river and waited in the huge crowds for His turn to be immersed in the holy water. John the Baptist recognised Him as the Messiah and Jesus indicated that He wished to be immersed. As He rose from the water a magnificent, blinding light came down and surrounded Him. Then, as everyone watched, a white, luminous dove alighted on His shoulder and the cosmic Christ energy entered Him. This brilliant luminous light remained with Jesus, the Christ, until it was surrendered on the cross.'

The silence between them was like the void. No one spoke for a long time.

Chapter 17

'I've always wanted to swim with the dolphins,' Joanna burbled happily for the umpteenth time. 'They say they can heal all sorts of illnesses and lift depression. They're amazing creatures. I can't wait. It'll be fabulous.'

In her heart of hearts she was sure she would be able to communicate with them. She knew they held incredible wisdom.

Joanna and Marcus never doubted the shaman's guidance, so they did not question why they were to swim with the dolphins. They only asked where and how. As always when someone is clear about their next step, the universe opened doors for them.

Bede had been sitting quietly with them in the darkness. He spoke suddenly, startling them. 'I know of a dolphin camp over the border of Mozambique, where they take you out in boats to swim with them.'

'What's it like?' demanded Marcus.

'It's a gorgeous place,' he told them, his face glowing with enthusiasm. 'You sleep in bamboo huts right on the beach. And what a beach! White sand stretching for ever and the bluest sea. The dolphins are there all the time. You'll love it.'

'Sounds perfect,' breathed Joanna.

Bede added cautiously, as if suddenly remembering a downside. 'It's a bit basic. The facilities are in a central block, but the place itself is magic.'

'You've sold it to us,' responded Marcus. 'Let's find out how we get there in the morning.'

And they slept that night on a rainbow of anticipation, in their dreams already floating in the silky blue waters of the ocean.

Next morning before they left for their early morning safari Monica put a bit of a damper on their hopes. 'You'll need a visa to get into Mozambique. That could take some time.'

Marcus frowned impatiently. 'Let's find out. Have you got a contact number?'

'Leave it to me.' Monica smiled soothingly. As owner of a safari lodge she was very used to impatient clients who wanted the moon today or even yesterday. The bush was infused so deep in her very being that she could not understand anyone wanting to leave it, let alone for the restless, unfathomable ocean, but she could see from their faces that they were raring to move on.

'You go out on your safari now. Bede's going to take you to look for the rhino this morning and I'll sort out what I can while you're away.'

They heard a cracking sound with which they had become very familiar. 'Oh, those naughty elephants,' Monica scolded, shaking her head in frustration and making Joanna smile.

Carrying her cup of coffee, Joanna made her way to the

reception area and crossed it. Then she stepped out in front of the lodge. She could hear the elephant though it was some distance away. I've got to try to communicate with it, she thought, holding her hands round the cup for warmth and reassurance.

She imagined a soft pink light going from her heart to the elephant. Then she sent it telepathic thoughts of love. She fancied it flapped its ears towards her, so she beamed white light from her third eye to it and sent a loud clear thought: I'm sorry about the other evening. She was certain it would be aware that she had watched it being chased away so ignominiously, and wanted to put the record straight.

The elephant turned and faced her, so she knew it had received the message, though it did not stop munching. Then she felt a soft buzzing in her forehead and sensed it was all right. It had heard, acknowledged and accepted the apology on behalf of them all.

She flushed with pleasure and her heart felt as if it had expanded as she quickly finished her coffee.

Half an hour later they were out in the bush, traversing the eternal grey petrified scrub, and exhilarated by the chill wind, the extra-vivid pink and purple sunrise and the promise of rhino. Bede pointed to a pair of huge marabou storks, their legs hanging down, which floated above them, circling. They travelled in silence, watching for signs of life of which there were precious few that morning. A red protea, a hardy desert flower, provided an isolated splash of colour in a desolate landscape.

Then as the pink morning sky transformed into vivid blue and they replaced sweaters with sun cream and sunglasses, Bede decided not to waste more time procrastinating. He accelerated like a man with a mission towards the haunts of the white rhino. They glimpsed deer flitting between the trees and once a startled steenbuck leaped across the road and darted into the scrub.

At last they were in open terrain where monstrous buffalo with flat shiny noses and menacing horns raised their heads and peered at them with angry eyes.

'They're dangerous creatures,' Bede reminded them. 'Unpredictable and nasty-minded.'

Joanna silently sent them clouds of love and peace, telling them they were safe. Indeed the black beasts watched intently as they passed and soon returned to their grazing. Joanna sat back again and relaxed.

'Now watch out for rhino,' Bede told them as he drove on to a higher plateau. 'They'll be around here looking for some shade to shelter from the sun.'

Within five minutes he had spotted two of the enormous dinosaur-like creatures plodding along, one in front of the other, grazing as they walked. They were so much bigger than either Marcus or Joanna had imagined that they stared in surprise at the great beasts with their strange horns and small pricked-up ears.

'Very poor vision but incredible sense of hearing and smell,' Bede murmured quietly and they needed no prompting to be quiet.

'What huge mouths they've got,' whispered Joanna,

sounding like the grandmother from *Little Red Riding Hood* as she clicked busily with her camera.

The two armoured tanks ignored them and lumbered past on their short chunky legs, heading, as Bede had predicted, for a shady tree. There they turned very slowly in circles for ten minutes, like a dog when it gets into its basket. Then they lowered their heads as an indication to each other that they were about to lie down, and sank down, facing outwards in opposite directions to protect each other.

Marcus and Joanna watched enthralled and felt a performance had been staged for their benefit.

Bede made his way back more slowly for lunch. The sun was blazing white gold. It sizzled as if to evaporate the moisture from every living thing and Joanna was glad she had brought her sarong to cover her shoulders.

They paused at a water hole to watch two pairs of eyes peeping above the water, which was the most they saw of hippos. At the next muddy pool Bede pointed out ripples, which marked the scaly back of a lurking croco-dile. On the bare branch of a tree three eagles cuddled together, one a brown juvenile and two black adults. Silhouetted against the bright blue backdrop, the birds eyed the whole scene with impassive disdain.

When they arrived back at the safari lodge in time for their late breakfast, Monica had good news for them. 'I've booked you into the Dolphin Beach camp. A friend of mine is on the lunchtime plane today to Johannesburg. He can take your passports and get your visas for

Mozambique. I've booked you on tomorrow's plane to Jo'burg and he'll meet you there with all your documents! Then you can catch the afternoon plane to Richard's Bay and take a taxi to the border at Mozambique. You'll have to walk through the customs and someone from the Dolphin Beach camp will meet you.'

Marcus and Joanna stared at Monica in surprise and delight. 'You've organised all that while we were out!' exclaimed Joanna.

'You're amazing, Monica,' added Marcus and gave her a huge bear hug.

'To be honest it was a miracle. You know Africa. It normally takes for ever to get things done but it all just fell into place.'

Marcus and Joanna glanced at each other. So the hand of divine providence was playing a part. What would the dolphins reveal to them?

They hoped that the lion shaman would materialise that evening. Bede joined them after dinner on the seats overlooking the water hole, and this time he did not sit in silence but chatted about the animals and life in Africa. He was more relaxed than they had seen him and, though they were disappointed not to see the lion shaman, it was a pleasant evening. They would have time for a safari before they left next day for the airport and perhaps they would see the lions again.

They did. This time there was a male and three females. They had made a kill in the night and the females were lolling on their backs careless of danger, paws in the air and full protruding stomachs as tight as drums. The male sat up watching them impassively. Their hearts leaped when Bede said that there was a pregnant lioness in the pride. 'She's got a week or so to go yet,' he told them.

Was there any possibility it was the mother of the white cub? Did she carry any white genes? When they plied him with questions Bede was non-committal but he did not rule out the possibility. Marcus and Joanna looked at each other.

'Ask them,' whispered Marcus, nodding in the direction of the prostrate trio.

Joanna took a deep breath and opened her heart, sending out soft pink unconditional love to the lioness. 'Are you the mother of a white lion cub?' she beamed out on a ray of white light to the beast. There was no flicker of response. Disappointed, Joanna glanced at Marcus and shook her head.

Just then she was hit in the forehead by a shaft of light coming direct from the huge male lion. It seemed to say, 'Come back soon. Important. We will need you.' She jerked slightly under the force of the energy.

'Yes,' she returned with all her might. 'Yes. We'll come back soon.'

Confused, she repeated what had transpired to Marcus.

'Are you sure?' He stared into her eyes seeking reassurance.

'Positive.' She felt unreal and wanted to change the subject. 'Do you think we ought to go to the dolphins if the cub is to be born soon and the lions need us?'

'The shaman said so and I think it's right to go. We must follow the signs. The fact that we were both so enthusiastic about the idea is a signal in itself.'

'Perhaps we should arrange to come back next week. Then we'll be here to help the lions if necessary.'

'What could they possibly need from us?' Marcus demanded.

'I don't know. I can only tell you what the lion said.'

Monica said she would be delighted to put them up when they returned from Mozambique and they set off to catch their flight to Johannesburg feeling that the universe was well and truly on their side.

What they did not know was that Sturov had booked into the most expensive hotel in Johannesburg. That day he was meeting some very influential people, planting seeds in their minds that it was time to have a cull of lion cubs in the Timbavati and backing it up with cash incentives.

After that he would be moving to the Black Rhino Lodge, a place of darkness, not so very far from where they were staying.

Chapter 18

A cheerful, bronzed young man with blond curly hair, who introduced himself as Hugo, met Marcus and Joanna at the bleak and dusty Mozambique border and loaded their luggage into a four-wheel-drive truck. 'Welcome!' He smiled, drawing them into his capable aura and they felt immediately comfortable. 'I'll be taking you out on the dolphin swims. Have you swum with them before?'

They shook their heads. 'We're really looking forward to it,' Joanna told him, her brown eyes shining like highly polished stones.

'You'll love it. How well do you swim?'

'Strongly. Both of us,' replied Marcus.

'Great. That's even better.' Hugo grinned broadly at them. He was experienced enough to know he would not have to nanny these two and he relaxed, pleased.

They could see for themselves that the infrastructure in Mozambique had almost collapsed as a result of years of civil war. Even the four-wheel drive had difficulty negotiating the track from the border to the resort, for the compacted sand that was all that was left of the road had reverted to soft deep sand. In the great undulating dunes they watched a driver taking a run at the downhill slope in order to give his car the impetus to climb the other side. Another man tipped out his passengers, who trudged up the hill carrying heavy boxes, while the vehicle made it empty.

As happens all over the world, a relay of small barefoot children raced along beside the truck. When one fell back, the next took over, calling, 'Sweets! Sweets!' or more commonly, 'Money!'

Joanna was disturbed by the look of desperation in their young eyes. They were not laughing at the game as children did in some countries. Here they seemed sad and she wondered if their families had been torn apart by the civil war. This thought clouded her enjoyment of the beautiful countryside and anticipation of the week ahead.

But all such sober contemplation disappeared when they reached the camp and wandered through the palm trees on to the endless miles of white sand, which fringed the ocean. When Joanna half closed her eyes the water looked like a turquoise dress, spangled with silver sequins and edged with pure white lace. Further along the shore the sea was rougher and waves pounded a vast expanse of flat rock, where locals fished. A couple strolled barefoot along the edge of the waves with a brown mongrel shadowing their steps. Later they learned that the local dogs walked with the tourists, seemingly wanting nothing but the pleasure of their company.

Hugo warned them not to leave the beach. 'The area behind it is peppered with landmines,' he said, nodding towards the innocent-looking dunes, which rose steeply behind them.

They stared, silently mesmerised by the area where danger lurked unseen, the result of human insanity.

Almost immediately Hugo turned back to the ocean and pointed. 'Look, dolphins.' And there a pod of perhaps ten dolphins arced together in graceful and perfect synchronicity as they crossed the sun-drenched bay.

Joanna and Marcus broke into smiles. 'They're beautiful!' exclaimed Joanna.

'What is it about dolphins that makes people so happy?' Marcus asked.

'Oh, they're really special,' Hugo told him. 'People always light up when they see them. I used to swim with them every day, recording their activity, but now I drive the boat and Sue and Anna go into the water with them and keep the records. I know them all and they certainly know me. They're highly intelligent, you know.'

Marcus inclined his head. 'I know.'

'Wait till you hear their sonar,' Hugo carried on. 'That's the way they communicate with each other and it's how they know where the fish are from a long way away.'

'Do you think they can heal people?' Joanna queried.

'I've no doubt of it. In my first season here I took a child out who'd been given months to live. His mother told me he made a turn for the better after going into the ocean with them and he's still going strong five years later. We're always getting grateful letters from people.'

'What else can dolphins do?' pressed Marcus.

Hugo shrugged. 'I don't know. They're clearly very clever and I suspect can do things we've no idea of. But basically they're fish with incredibly evolved sonar and they love playing, especially with humans. I think they're here to show us there's more to life than material things and worry.' He laughed and glanced at his watch. 'Look, I'll leave you now to chill out. Come down to the shop when you're ready and you can hire masks and snorkels. Tomorrow morning I'll take you out in the boat and you can get close to them then.'

'Thanks, Hugo! See you later.'

For a moment they watched him stride down the beach and when they turned again to the ocean to look for the dolphins, they had vanished.

That evening Joanna and Marcus perched on a log, which had evidently been lying on the beach for years, and looked out to sea. Everything was bathed in the silver light of the full moon. The sea swelled and rippled like a giant magic carpet in front of them, while behind them occasional lanterns formed pricks of light among the silhouetted reed huts and palm trees. It was a silent night.

Joanna had the same feeling of anticipation in her solar plexus as she did before she tried to communicate with the lions. She gazed at the luminous ocean and focused on the dolphins, telepathically calling them.

It was ten minutes before Marcus noticed a solitary fin. He inclined his head and, when Joanna followed the movement, she immediately saw the dolphin swimming

147

towards them. She felt a clutch of excitement. Had it come in response to her call?

She sent out a message that they would be going out in the boat tomorrow. 'We greet you in peace and goodwill. Please swim with us and share your secrets.'

She had no idea if her message had been received, for the dolphin seemed to be on a quest of its own, but Marcus assured her that it must have picked up the clear intent she was sending out. 'I hope so,' she murmured. No sooner had she spoken than the dolphin leaped out of the water three times in a splashing cascade, then disappeared. She and Marcus looked at each other and nodded, their faces once more wreathed in smiles. What would happen tomorrow?

But the wind had come up in the night and the seas were huge next morning. They trudged along the soft white sand towards the boat, each privately thinking it was too rough and cold to swim but buoyed with excitement. A diverse cluster of holidaymakers, swinging masks and snorkels, and weighed down with towels, sweaters, sun cream, bottled water and all the paraphernalia of a trip in the tropics, were milling round the huge rubber dinghy. At last Hugo and two girls in wet suits turned up and gave them instructions and an endless safety brief.

Five minutes later they were clutching the side of the boat, their feet firmly anchored in straps, as the turbulent sea flung the dinghy all over the place. Then they saw the macho side of Hugo emerge. Standing at the helm he roared round in semicircles and negotiated huge waves with audacity and skill. Joanna suspected he was adrenalised by the screams of his passengers as the white waters threatened to submerge them. But they passed safely through the crashing waves near the shore and reached the heavily undulating ocean. Here the blond driver appeared to concentrate on racing across the bay. We'd be galloping if this were land, Joanna decided, holding on for all she was worth. At the same time she was trying to emulate Sue and Anna, who had relaxed into the movement of the boat. The girls pointed to something neither Joanna nor Marcus could see, and Hugo changed direction. Within moments they were in the middle of a huge pod of dolphins. Most were swimming just under the surface of the water.

Suddenly it was all worth while. Everyone was animated, exclaiming and watching the dolphins, hoping they wouldn't swim away too fast in search of fish. Because of the swell Hugo only let four of them enter the water together. By the time Joanna slid into the cold, rough element most of the dolphins had passed, but one swam under her then dived down deep and three others swept past. She could hear their sonar clicking and tried to click back with her tongue, sending telepathic messages of peace, but all seemed to ignore her. She looked up and saw Hugo indicating several dolphins to her right and headed that way. These swam right under her and she had a feeling that there was some cognition on their part. But it could have been her imagination, she conceded.

She wished it was warmer and calmer. She longed to be more receptive to their information but Hugo was calling her back to the dinghy and she felt frustrated and disappointed. Marcus had returned to the boat before her and reached down a strong arm to heave her over the side. He eyed her with a question mark but she shrugged and sat quietly for the rest of the trip, trying to link with the dolphins who passed by. Perhaps she could make a connection tomorrow, she consoled herself.

But that night she had a dream. Some dreams are messages from the soul, others pigeonhole your day-to-day life and others, always vivid, are spirit communications. This dream was an interspecies link, she knew.

She was swimming in the sea, in warm, calm blue waters, with a beautiful silver dolphin. It said, 'We were trying to talk to you this morning but the conditions were not right. Our pod carries knowledge from Atlantis and we want to pass it on. We are waiting for people who are ready to receive it.'

She reached out a hand as if to touch the gracious creature but it glided from her reach.

'I want to make amends,' it sighed. 'I want to put things right.'

She frowned, not comprehending. 'What can you tell me?' she urged.

'Look into my eye.' She gazed into his incredible Egyptian-looking eye. There she saw a jumbled scene of futuristic houses, half-human, half-animal slaves, people

flying, humming rocks and a gory bullfight. Then everything disappeared into swirling sea and blackness.

'I don't understand.'

'The end,' it said. 'Find another way.'

At that moment Marcus moved in his sleep and Joanna
woke feeling nauseous. She stared into the dark, still
seeing the pictures in her mind. The dream had disturbed
her profoundly. She touched Marcus. 'Are you awake?'

He grunted in denial, but she persisted. She had to talk
to him. When he was sufficiently roused, he switched on
the light and gave her his full attention but his frown of
puzzlement deepened as she related the dream.

'I don't get it. I thought dolphins carried the wisdom of
Atlantis.'

'So did I, but he said knowledge. And it was horrible.
I can still see people with hawk heads and a bull with a
human head.'

'Calm down.' Marcus took her hand gently, for he
could see she was very agitated. 'I think the dolphin
showed you the end of Atlantis. We know that it fell
because they abused power with slavery, genetic modifi-
cation, cloning humans and animals. And bloodlust, of
course. But why show you that in your dream?'

'It doesn't make sense. Surely they also had masses of
information about vibrational healing, computers and
amazing technology? Why not show me that?'

'I don't know,' replied Marcus. 'They used crystal
power too, didn't they?'

'Yes. That's what I mean. Why show me the dark side?
Why would a dolphin pass on horrible things rather than

the spiritual light of Atlantis? I don't understand it. I need to find out more.'

'I think you're right. Perhaps the dolphins carry layers of information we don't know about yet and at least they've made a kind of communication. Let's stay open to anything they want to impart.'

'Okay. It was just a shock. Why did he want to make amends? What did he do? And why is he a dolphin now?'

'I don't know,' Marcus replied. 'But we're in the right place to find out.'

And he was right. Next day the picture expanded considerably.

Chapter 19

Overnight the wind calmed and they hoped the sea would follow suit. But when they rose the waves were still high and Hugo declared it was too rough. Marcus and Joanna did not let the disappointment spoil their day, which they spent exploring the rockpools and examining the local crafts. The following morning they rose early, keen with anticipation, but Hugo still looked dubious about the prospect of going out at all. Sue and Anna, the girls who swam every day and kept the dolphin records, were watching him closely, awaiting his verdict. At last he nodded. 'Okay. We'll go,' he proclaimed.

Sue and Anna gave a cheer and organised everyone to push the boat into the sea. Joanna was not sure how she felt after her disturbing dream but Marcus was full of enthusiasm. His intuition told him that the dolphins held a key to the enlightenment of the planet and he wanted to find it.

This time the boat ride seemed easier, possibly because they had already braved it once. Joanna slipped into a meditative mood and tried to detach herself from expectations. That was probably why a dolphin swam round her as soon as she entered the water. It did not want to play or come too near but she sensed it scanning her energy fields and she stilled her mind. A telepathic communication started to flow in, like a stream of energy. 'We store in our consciousness the vast knowledge of Atlantis, ready to restore it to humanity when they are ready.' Then a picture came into Joanna's mind, showing a graph, marked from one to ten. 'On a scale of one to ten, dolphins hold the full range of understanding for this planet. They are at ten,' came the flow into her head. 'At present humans only have the consciousness to access up to three. People must raise their frequency to understand what we hold. We keep the key to the future of the world.'

'What sort of knowledge do you hold?' Joanna beamed the thought. She had forgotten she was cold and was lying on the surface of the heaving ocean, turning in circles as the dolphin swam round her.

'Regeneration, healing, crystal power, superior technology, the keys to the portals to other galaxies and more. Little by little we are opening people up again to their psychic and spiritual powers.'

Joanna was silent. Awed. Suddenly she remembered dolphins were reputed to be able to heal depression.

The dolphin picked up her thought immediately. 'We scan the person's energy fields so we know all about them. If someone is depressed we reconnect him to his soul and sometimes to his planet of origin.'

Joanna decided to consider that later. She found herself thinking of a distant cousin who had two autistic children. She knew they had swum with dolphins in America but there had been no improvement.

The dolphin responded. 'We can read the akashic

records, for we can connect to the Hall of Records within the Sphinx,' it clicked at her. 'The autistic brother and sister came from Sirius and represent the forces of good and evil. One served Atlantis and one helped to destroy it. The rivalry was and is so great between them that if they were whole and perfect the good sister could search out the wisdom of Atlantis to protect it but the bad brother would be on her tail to destroy it. As autistic they can't interact with the world so they don't have the freedom to pursue the information from Atlantis.'

'Then why did they choose to come to Earth as autistic?'

'Their souls wanted to be born.'

'So you could not help them?'

'We cannot interfere with a soul choice.'

A tangled skein of questions milled in Joanna's head but before she had time to focus on a specific one, the dolphin had drawn out one of the threads and was responding.

'Regeneration is about connecting the soul, the spirit and the brain into alignment with the nervous system. A man swam with us who had a withered hand. We connected with his soul and made the necessary realignments so his hand started to improve. But his mental scepticism blocked any further healing. He had enough faith to come to us but not enough faith to heal. We could do no more for him.'

Joanna could understand that. She wanted to know about the power of Atlantis but the dolphin pulsed something urgent into her mind.

'I was one of those who misused the power of Atlantis. I chose to reincarnate in a dolphin body so that I could not risk abusing it again in this lifetime. I am working through my karma in ways you could not conceive. Seek out an angel dolphin. They hold the treasures of the universe.'

'Angel dolphin! Where. . . ?'

But it had vanished. She looked up and saw that everyone on the boat was waving to her to come back in.

That afternoon she and Marcus walked miles along the beach, accompanied by a different friendly brown mongrel. They talked over all that the dolphin had imparted, and contemplated the prospect of angel dolphins.

'We need more information from the Scroll,' commented Marcus, not even noticing the sand crabs scuttling from his path. 'There's been nothing for ages.'

'You're right,' agreed Joanna. 'This has been the longest period without a transcript since we brought it back from India.' The Scroll was being translated by a professor in London, an academic not used to the pressures of inquisitive youth but with a profound fascination for his task.

'In fairness we often get several translations close together and then a gap.'

'I suppose you're right. What made you think of it?'

'I've got a feeling that the energy of Atlantis is returning and somehow the dolphins are instrumental in it.'

'What about the birth of the white lion cub?'

'That's to do with the return of the Christ conscious-ness. That's coming back to Earth now too. They must be linked.'

'It's an amazing time to be incarnated,' commented Joanna. 'We're being given incredible information which makes me realise how little I know about the universe.'

'I know. I feel totally ignorant too,' agreed Marcus. 'I wish I understood more.'

'So what's our role in all this?' Joanna wondered aloud, absently picking up a pearly pink shell and running her fingers over it.

Marcus sounded very serious. 'Well, we know we're to help protect the white lion cub when it is born and I sense that you are to receive a message or maybe several messages from it.' He frowned thoughtfully. 'I still feel it's in danger?'

'Then why aren't we there? Why are we here playing with dolphins?' Joanna's voice was suddenly shrill with anxiety.

Marcus spoke slowly to calm her fear. 'We were sent here for a purpose. Perhaps it was to find the angel dolphins.'

'We still don't know who they are! Or even if they're here,' Joanna butted in.

'That's true. They could be here or anywhere in the world but at least we know of them. I'm sure they hold information which will help the light, and you know as well as I do, Joanna, if we need to find them the forces of the universe will guide us in their direction.'

Her shoulders dropped an inch as she relaxed. 'You're

right. I know you're right.' She took his hand and squeezed it. 'But I think we ought to go back to the Timbavati tomorrow. And I want to phone Mum and tell her what happened today.'

'I didn't bring the mobile with me. No point as there's no signal on the beach. We'll walk up the road when we get back and try to find one. Then we can catch up with any news from your mum and Tony. And I think you're right. We'll go back tomorrow.' As he spoke a little white feather floated down to land at his feet. He laughed as he picked it up. 'The angels are confirming that's right,' he said.

They had both learned to trust the signs and omens of the universe, which come as synchronicities and co-incidences. They always watched for the appearance of a white feather when an angel of light was reminding them of its presence or guiding them that a decision they had taken was right. They noticed other angel symbols too, like rainbows bringing hope.

Joanna remembered a time when she asked the angels if she should apply for a particular job. Within seconds someone wearing an angel T-shirt passed her and she took it as a favourable sign. She got the job. Helen was always reminding her that it was important to watch the signals.

'Ask for what you want, listen or watch for guidance, then take action,' she used to say. Joanna smiled as she thought of her mother and hoped she and Tony were enjoying themselves in Egypt.

*   *   *

It was not really surprising that there was a rather faint message from Helen on Marcus's mobile when they got back to their reed hut. 'Contact us when you can. We've got another translation from the Scroll. It's unbelievable.' There was no disguising the excitement in her mother's voice and they both felt thrilled and curious as they sprinted up the track leading from the camp to the village, hoping to find a better signal. They could not wait to share their news and hear what the Scroll had to reveal now.

Chapter 20

Helen was impatient to tell Tony, Edward and Zoranda of her conversation with Joanna. She had to wait until after supper as Edward had gone out for the afternoon and Tony had accompanied him.

Helen smiled as she remembered the two of them leaving together. Edward thought he was doing Tony a favour, believing that the older man was bored while his wife was engaged in writing. Tony considered he was helping Edward by keeping him company on a longish trip. But it works, she thought. They respect each other even though they are so different. The two men had become friends and Tony treated Edward in an avuncular way, rather as he did Marcus.

Edward was thin and aesthetic. His thoughts and his conversation were all aimed at his spiritual journey. He was intent on learning and was quite intense about information presented to him. No wonder he had taken so hard the disaster of his mission to collect the papers from the Tibetan monk. And he seemed to take personally his failure to protect Helen when she went to the Sphinx to meet the Crocodile and the Shark, even though she had arrived so early for the rendezvous that he was not even there. At first she had not realised that he believed the danger she had been in had been his fault. But when she did become aware, she tried to allay his doubts and was pleased at the way he relaxed with her. He was almost the warm, light person Marcus had described when they first met at Kumeka House.

It's strange, she mused. Edward is always the one to smooth other people's lives but he's not so accepting about his own. She contemplated her own life and decided that she could often help others with their problems while she agonised over her own. Perhaps he was presenting a mirror she needed to look at.

When at last she gathered the three men together, they all sat on the western verandah, just as they had done on the night Zoranda told them about Jesus the Christ. This time it was later and the moon was hovering above them, a luminous ball of light rendering all silhouettes black and the paths and lawns silver pearl. They could hear the fountain tinkling in the distance. An owl hooted in the shadows and the night seemed enchanted.

She felt as excited as a child with a glorious secret as she related Joanna's dream and the messages the dolphins had given her. Tony was listening with a doubtful expression, which irritated her and brought her down to Earth. Edward looked as excited as she felt.

Zoranda, on the other hand, nodded sagely and did not appear in the least surprised. When she paused for breath his comment was enigmatic. 'The web of light is being restored and there are many beings and creatures who are linked into it. At this time ancient wisdom is being revealed so that Atlantis can rise again.'

'Atlantis can rise again?' questioned Helen. 'What does that really mean?'

'It's figurative. It means that the pure energy of Atlantis will return.'

'I see,' she responded thoughtfully, then, remembering her mission, added, 'Is it important for the book?' Her heart skipped suddenly with excitement as she realised it must be.

Zoranda smiled at her. 'Very important. An essential ingredient I would say.'

Helen sighed happily, giving him her full attention.

'Can you tell us more about Atlantis than the Scroll has already imparted?' Tony spoke with caution.

'A little. In translations to date the Scroll has mostly given us information about the latter days of Atlantis, by which time the people had closed down their right brains and therefore their spiritual and psychic links. That was after the pure energy of the early days became sullied.'

'Let's start at the beginning,' said Tony. 'Where and when was Atlantis?'

Zoranda was amused by Tony's down-to-earth, logical approach but he answered him carefully. 'It was a huge continent with a glorious climate and rich soil, which lay between Europe and America. The civilisation spanned from 52,000 BC to 10,000 BC, a long time!'

'It's beyond comprehension,' agreed Tony, impressed despite himself.

'It was destroyed twice in that time. There is some evidence to suggest that around 50,000 BC they used atom bombs to try to kill the wild animals, which were overrunning the world. That destroyed the equilibrium on Earth and the North Pole shifted, with the result that land was lost and Atlantis became five islands. Then in 28,000 BC there was another collapse, but the final destruction came with the flood around 10,000 BC.

'Each time Atlantis was about to be destroyed, the people were given an opportunity to reform. In fact before the end times, they were offered chance after chance to change but they persisted in their evil ways.'

Helen was startled. It was unlike Zoranda to use such a strong word and she could see he had intended to shock them as he had sat forward slightly, watching them intently, his eyes violet in the moonlight. Now he relaxed again.

'When was the golden period?' Helen asked.

'The pure times started in 20,000 BC. The golden days of Atlantis were the nearest there has ever been to heaven on Earth in a physical body.'

'I thought the early times in Lemuria, before Atlantis, were heavenly?' queried Edward.

'That's true but the people were in etheric bodies and not fully physicalised. However, when Lemuria was finally to be terminated, the continent of Atlantis was prepared.' Zoranda paused and pursed his lips. 'These things take hundreds and probably thousands of years, you know.'

Helen nodded and noticed that Tony had sat back, slightly withdrawn from the conversation, whereas Edward was sitting forward drinking in every word.

Zoranda continued, 'The first thing created by the deity in charge of the experiment of Atlantis was the Cathedral of the Sacred Heights, the crown of Atlantis. It is sometimes spoken of as the Temple of Poseidon. Anyway, the cathedral was sited in the heart of high mountains, surrounded by seven peaks, representing the seven pillars of the universe. It was a great House of Initiation, for those who sought divine illumination. Only the purest of the pure could gain access.

'In order to enter the cathedral you had to be able to levitate, which meant having control over your frequencies. Even in those times only the most dedicated had this ability.

'The cathedral was awesome, constructed in pure white material, which shimmered in the sunlight.' Zoranda hesitated fractionally, then glanced at Helen to gauge her reaction as he continued. 'The eastern entrance was guarded by an enormous statue of a Sphinx.'

She responded as he predicted. 'A Sphinx!' she exclaimed, startled.

The big man chuckled. 'Indeed the Sphinx is a symbol of purity. It was the representation of the deity of Atlantis.'

'Really! Is the Sphinx here a copy of the one from the Cathedral of the Sacred Heights?'

'Just a second. People are always asking about the Sphinx and when it was constructed. Listen! The Sphinx is and always has been and always will be. It has always existed. The Sphinx is the God of Atlantis as people perceive God today within the tight religious framework of the Church. Its role is to be the source of power on Earth. It is actually a deity, represented by a statue.'

'Does it still have power?'

'No. It has lost its power. It was placed on the Giza plateau because that was the optimum place on Earth at that time for its energy. It is the guardian of the planet and was able to put a force field round the planet to protect it. But it only has two per cent of its power left.'

'Why? What happened?'

'Humankind drained its power. The Sphinx represents purity. As people became greedy and self-centred, they diminished its ability to guard the planet. As we increase in spirituality so the Sphinx's ability will increase.'

'What was it saving Earth from?' asked Tony, sitting up suddenly. 'You make it sound like *Star Wars*!'

Zoranda spoke softly and very seriously. 'In a way it is. There are aliens who have not entered Earth by the spiritual process of incarnation, who desire our minerals as their own planets are scarce of them. Some even crave our emotional and sexual experiences and suck this energy from us, for it feeds their lower frequency. They try to gain access through breaks in Earth's auric field. There are many of these beings of less than good intent towards us out there! The Sphinx watched over Earth and placed an aura as a buffer around us so they could not harm us.'

'You mean just like a person's aura?' asked Helen.

'Exactly the same,' agreed Zoranda. 'As you know, if a person is weak and unhealthy their aura, which is an electromagnetic field, will be thin and may be full of holes, which lets in viruses, germs, entities or other people's negative thoughts, and these can harm the person mentally, emotionally or even physically. If someone is strong, healthy and positive their strong aura acts like a shield, which repels everything so that they are totally safe from harm. Furthermore the light of a powerful aura will dissolve any darkness that comes near it. The light will even reach out to embrace negative energy in the room and transmute it. It's just one reason why a positive attitude keeps people healthy.'

'It makes sense,' agreed Tony.

'And that is the Sphinx's role for the planet,' Zoranda confirmed.

'Were mosquitoes astral entities, which pierced Earth's energy field?' asked Edward. 'Is that how they came to the planet?'

'Many people think so,' replied Zoranda. 'Certain viruses have certainly come in from space because Earth's aura let them in.'

'What more can we do to help the planet?' murmured Helen.

'You already are doing your best, Helen. And everyone can play their part. Every time someone focuses on peace instead of war, on love instead of dislike, on serenity instead of anxiety, it increases the power of the Sphinx again.'

'Will you answer me something that has long puzzled me?' asked Tony. 'Is the Sphinx a lion, as we are told in tourist literature, or a dog, which I have also read?'

'Neither,' replied Zoranda. 'It is a generic animal which

represents purity. It is universal. It is a deity beyond our current level of understanding.'

Helen was quiet for a moment, contemplating what Zoranda had told them. Then she remembered he had been telling them about the Sphinx in the Cathedral of the Sacred Heights in Atlantis and prompted him to tell them more.

'Just one last thing for now,' Zoranda responded patiently. 'The Sphinx was placed at the eastern entrance in such a position as to be visible to the populace in the valleys below. On holy days when the people gathered on the tableland below the cathedral, a huge door would open under the paws of the statue. The initiates, who were highly trained priests, would pour cosmic light down on to the people. It helped to raise the spiritual level of everyone.'

'Like mass spiritual healing,' murmured Edward. 'It must have kept everyone's frequency high.'

'Exactly.'

'How do you know all this?' Tony's chin was sticking out slightly in a gesture Helen recognised. His interest was piqued but he did not want to be taken for a ride.

'That's a good question,' agreed Zoranda equably. 'Some of the information comes from ancient records like the Scroll, but none written as early as that. A certain amount comes from archaeological information and carbon-dated items, which have proved to be from that era. Yet more understanding comes from the myths, which are remarkably similar throughout the world. The Atlanteans had enormous capacity for memory, beyond anything we can conceive of now. In our society, once we developed symbols and writing, we used our memories very little, and that part of the brain has consequently gone into disuse. In early Atlantis all knowledge and information was handed down verbally. And in later Atlantis, even after they could write, groups of wise women were trained to memorise the sacred knowledge and the ancient stories. The twelve soul groups that left Atlantis at the fall took these stories and passed them down the generations until they were considered to be myths.'

'I can see that,' Tony said and Helen was surprised at his easy acceptance of this concept.

'There is also channelling,' continued Zoranda, smiling faintly as he observed Tony's eyes become hooded. 'There have always been a few gifted psychics who can access the akashic records, the records of all that has ever happened. Nowadays there are more people of high frequency and good intent being prepared, who are channelling consistent information.'

'I still distrust channelled information. How do you know if it's right?'

'You have a point,' admitted Zoranda. 'Currently there are many people who are channelling without a proper spiritual foundation and who are not necessarily accessing the purest information. Anyone who has become psychic through drug use may be entering the astral planes rather than the spiritual planes and will be presenting tainted information. There is false information filtering round in some circles, which tends to cause confusion, a tool used very effectively by the dark forces. So your contention is quite valid. However' – Zoranda lifted his head and looked Tony full in the face, penetrating his soul with his clear blue eyes – 'you and most others are perfectly able to feel the resonance of truth and use discernment about what you accept. Discernment is one of the lessons of our time.'

Tony cleared his throat. 'I accept that. Remember I am left-brain trained.'

During this conversation Helen was racking her brains to remember what she had heard about the Sphinx. 'Doesn't it contain the Hall of Records?' she asked Zoranda.

He smiled. 'Indeed. There is much more to tell you but not tonight.'

'You still haven't explained why it was specially important for Atlanteans to know when there would be an eclipse,' Helen urged him.

But he rose with a smile, said, 'When the time is right. Thank you for the pleasure of your company,' and left the verandah with a soft, 'Goodnight.'

Chapter 21

The following morning Helen enjoyed the most fabulous meditation. She entered the sacred and eternal garden of her third eye and there a gate to a higher world opened. Here everything was brightly coloured and bathed in light. For the first time she heard the music of the spheres, the magical notes of the heavenly bodies in motion and felt a sense of pure bliss.

Afterwards she sat quietly looking at the physical garden of the Great White Lodge with its small well-watered emerald lawn and tubs filled with vibrant blue, gold and red flowers and felt perfect contentment. She wanted to stay in this space for ever. Suddenly she had a blinding revelation that this was the feeling she had enjoyed when she had been incarnate in early Atlantis.

Later in the morning a translation from the Scroll was faxed through to her and when she read it, she knew the universe was validating her intuition, for it was about the golden days of Atlantis. Zoranda himself brought it to her and watched her face as she read it.

'You're glowing,' he told her quietly when she looked up.

She smiled, for she could sense it herself. 'I'll get Tony. I'd like to share it with him.'

She made a move to get up but Zoranda put out his hand gently. 'No. You sit there and absorb it. I'll fetch him.' She sank down gratefully and as he walked away he asked if he might bring Edward in too.

'Of course.'

Zoranda, Edward and Tony glided into the room moments later. They had hurried but contrived to make their movements look leisurely, for no one really moved quickly in the Great White Lodge.

They pulled up chairs around her and clearly expected her to read the translation aloud to them. Tony was surprised to see how his wife's eyes were sparkling and her skin seemed translucent. Even her hair was glinting golden in a stray shaft of sunshine. He smiled at her encouragingly and decided he must learn to open up. If reading whatever it was could make Helen so radiant, perhaps he should be more receptive too. Perhaps I've been a bit too logical and scientific, he thought, and found himself attending to what she was to read without the constant judgement that went on in his head.

'It seems to be a continuation of the translation we received yesterday,' Helen said at last, smiling. 'But it is quite extraordinary. It's about life in the golden times of Atlantis.'

'In the pure times?' Edward wanted confirmation.

She nodded and again the sunlight played with her hair. Then she held the script closer and started to read.

' "In the time of Atlantis when the pure white angels

walked among all life forms, people had such high vibrations that they could see and communicate with these wondrous beings of light at all times. There was no veil between the worlds. The people considered that to be psychic was a natural condition. Everyone was clairvoyant and telepathic. All was open." ' Helen glanced up at the men. 'Now this is the important piece.' She paused to read it again before speaking and the three men waited patiently.

' "The power of Atlantis was its purity. The frequency on the planet was so high that everyone could draw from a pool of pure energy and manifest with the power of their minds. They created buildings and all their needs by imaging for the highest good. They were highly creative and nothing existed except as pure energy." ' Helen lowered the sheet of paper as if deep in memory.

Edward remarked, 'So they were living fully in the fifth dimension.'

'You mean a high frequency?' asked Tony.

'Very high. We've been told that at the fifth-dimensional frequency people can manifest without taking action. The power of the mind is enough. Whereas at the lower dimensions in which we live now, we must visualise our wants and then take action in order to bring things into our lives. I think at the third dimension it's fifty per cent thought and fifty per cent action.'

Zoranda said, 'Even now there are certain yogis who have the power to draw material things from the unmanifest world into the manifest one at will.'

They nodded. It was something they had all heard of

and regarded with scepticism or at least imagined was way beyond their capabilities.

He added, 'Those who live such pure lives that they are fully in the higher dimensions rarely use the power. They know the material is an illusion which can distract us from the spiritual purpose of our lives.'

'But the Atlanteans used it properly. They kept their minds very clear and light,' commented Helen quietly and started to read again. ' "People imaged from this pool of energy for the highest good. They were creative, artistic people. Whatever they shaped the energy into had grandeur and style. This is how they manifest their crystalline structures, their round buildings, their magnificent temples. Everyone could tap into some part of this pool of energy.

' "In the early days certain people by birth or training had the right and the power to use this energy in its entirety and they did so with wisdom and integrity." '

'What happened to change things?' Tony enquired.

Helen scanned the page. 'Your question is answered here, Tony. It says, "Eventually greedy people realised that this energy could be shaped and used personally. Then ordinary people learned to access it without integrity. However the ability to maintain the high frequency of purity in their lives and manifest for the highest good is one of the great secrets of Atlantis." '

'Back to greed and darkness,' sighed Edward. 'Even when we have all we want, it seems hard for humanity to maintain a pure frequency.'

'So how did they remain in the fifth dimension for so

long in the golden years?' asked Zoranda in his quiet voice.

Helen searched the page again. 'Ah, here it says, "They lived a relaxed, contemplative life, spending much time outside in nature. Their needs were simple and acquired by manifestation or co-operation with the plants. They had lots of time for leisure and spent it in art and creativity. They loved to walk in beauty and communicate with the birds, animals and elementals." ' She added with emphasis, thinking of herself and most of the people she knew, ' "It was only when personal ambition came in that they became busy and lost their psychic powers." '

'It says it all, doesn't it,' commented Tony. 'Our lives nowadays are geared to work.'

'And ambition.'

' "They also used the power of their minds to control their bodies. They could control their temperature, make the blood flow to certain parts or withdraw it for anaesthesia. There will always be Atlanteans on Earth who hold this power for everyone." '

'I guess the yogis in the Himalayas who can sit in freezing snow and dry wet sheets by raising their body temperature are descendants of Atlantis. Do you think they hold the key to that power for all of us?' asked Edward.

Zoranda nodded quietly.

'I wish I could do it,' added Helen. 'It must be about constant mindfulness and focus.' She glanced at Zoranda, who was sitting quietly listening. He had trained for years in mind control at Kumeka House and she knew that he had extraordinary powers that he rarely demonstrated. She realised that he radiated an aura of magnetic power and had no need to tell people, for they could feel it. Yet again she made a resolution to be more centred and focused. She glanced back at the sheet of paper.

' "They could use their mind, usually with sound, to alter the rate of vibration of physical objects. To dig a well a stone would be made so heavy it sunk to the required level into the earth. The atomic structure of stones was changed. They were lightened, moved and relocated by thought control and placed accurately where they were wanted. This was often done with the assistance of beings from other planets and always under the direction and guidance of the angels." '

'That's just what you did when you moved the lintel at Stonehenge back into place,' exclaimed Helen, looking at Zoranda, who smiled his assent. That had been a night Helen would never forget. She and Joanna and Marcus had meditated at Mount Shasta in California, which is a very sacred place. They had projected their thoughts and certain symbols contained in the Scroll along the ley line to Stonehenge in an effort to restore the mighty interdimensional portal for the light. At the same time Zoranda and the men from Kumeka House had focused sound and the power of their minds on to one of the lintels to levitate it back into position. By harnessing the power of the full moon their initial task had been accomplished.

'Those who have reached a certain level of cosmic illumination will be aware that many of the ancient

sacred buildings of the world were built in this way.'
Zoranda was speaking. 'You saw it, Helen, when we
were at Machu Picchu and Cuzco.'

'Yes. It's amazing. Row upon row of huge cut stones
and not the space to put a razor blade between them,'
Helen replied. 'Didn't the Scroll say that the angels
oversaw the building of Machu Picchu?'

'Yes, the building of all the great and sacred structures
was overseen by high beings from other planets or by the
angels.'

Tony was sitting forward slightly, indicating that he
wanted to contribute to the conversation. 'I understand
that ancient stone tablets found in Sumeria state that
sound can lift stone.'

'Really?'

'Isn't Sumeria one of the places where the descendants
of Atlantis fled to?' asked Edward.

Zoranda nodded a quiet affirmative.

'So all the information from early Atlantis is beginning
to come back. Perhaps we are to gather it together.'

'All those who incarnated in early Atlantis are reincarnating with their spiritual and psychic gifts. So are those
who caused its destruction with their technical minds and
desire for personal gain,' Zoranda reminded them. 'We
must play our part in tipping the balance so that pure
Atlantis can rise again.'

'And we will,' declared Helen fiercely.

Tony reached over and squeezed her hand. 'I'm with
you. Now read the rest of the Scroll.'

Chapter 22

Edward fetched them each a glass of cold clear water. Helen wasn't aware of how dehydrated she had become until she felt the refreshing water in her mouth. 'I didn't realise how hot it is in here even with the fan on so it must be boiling out there.'

'It is,' Edward replied. 'Just think of the poor people working outside all day in the heat.'

'Not a pleasant thought,' said Tony, who felt the heat on account of his somewhat expanded waistline.

'Can I read the rest of it now?' said Helen, looking at the translation of the Scroll, the paper already beginning to look limp in her damp hands. She carried on without waiting for a response. 'Apparently in early Atlantis the people worked in harmony with the elementals and cycles of the moon, tides and so on.' As an aside to Tony she murmured with a faint smile, 'Elementals are fairies, elves and the creatures of folk tales, only, of course, they really exist in an etheric state which is invisible to most people.' She expected Tony's face to shut down but he reminded himself that there was more in this world than meets the eye and responded with a nod. Surprised and pleased, Helen continued to read.

' "The Atlanteans communicated with those elementals who are in charge of the growth of plants and responded lovingly to their needs. As well as caring for their physical requirements, the people sang to the plants and played music. As a result plants, fruit and vegetables were large, nutritious and easy to grow. They were also filled with a vibration of harmony, which matched that of the people, so they were easy to digest." '

'You know,' said Helen, laying the script on the table. 'There have been so many experiments done nowadays showing that plants respond to different kinds of music and to people talking to them, yet we still prefer to drench them in chemicals and try to modify them genetically.'

'Isn't that the point,' said Tony. 'Just as Zoranda said, the early Atlanteans bringing the higher way have reincarnated and so have the technologically advanced late Atlanteans. All is drawn to our attention now so that we have another chance to get it right.'

'What you read from the Scroll is just what they do at Findhorn!' exclaimed Edward. 'Have you been there, Helen?'

'Yes, I have and you're right. Findhorn is a magical reminder of early Atlantis.' She turned to Tony. 'Have you heard of it?'

He shook his head.

'Well, years ago three people, Eileen Caddy, her husband Peter and a friend of theirs, Dorothy Maclean, who communicates with elementals, lived in a caravan in this remote, windswept part of Scotland called Findhorn. The soil was arid and thin but Eileen meditated each night for guidance and they scrupulously followed the messages she received. They also communicated with the devas of the plants and animals, and honoured their needs, with the result that they grew enormous vegetables, which attracted widespread attention. When I say enormous, they were incredible. Now people from all over the world live there and it's a huge community.'

'One difference though,' said Edward. 'In Atlantis the soil was rich and fertile and the weather perfect, so they probably grew even bigger crops then.'

'True. Because of the simplicity of their diet and of their needs, and their close connection with the vegetable kingdom it meant that very little time was spent in growing food,' Zoranda commented, 'and that offered them more space for their spiritual contemplations.'

They nodded and Tony murmured thoughtfully in a voice of regret, 'I'm always too busy.'

Helen had picked up the script again. 'It says here that the early Atlanteans were vegetarians. They believed that eating meat would close down their psychic abilities. Listen, I'll read it. "The pure Atlanteans would never touch flesh, for they knew it would diminish their psychic abilities and make their minds coarse. Indeed this proved true as will be explained."

'Then it goes back to the elementals. Ah, listen, this is interesting. "If they wished to light a fire, they would communicate with the salamanders, the fire elementals, and ask for their co-operation. Before they entered the water to swim, they would ask for the protection of the water elementals." '

Edward put in, 'Once, when I was in Africa, there was a fire out of control and they thought it was going to reach the houses. Some friends and I went as near as we could and connected with the salamanders. We honoured them and asked them to withdraw as it was not appropriate to burn the houses. The fire was out within hours and it never touched the properties. The papers called it a lucky break but we were convinced that the salamanders had responded to our request.'

'I'm sure they did,' agreed Tony, to everyone's astonishment.

'Hey, you're not supposed to say things like that. It's my role,' exclaimed Helen and found herself laughing with surprise and delight.

Tony's eyes twinkled. 'Is there more, Helen?' He wanted to add that a fairy was tickling his nose but he thought that was going too far. Besides, he was fascinated with the revelations of the Scroll. In some ways it was similar to the information about early Lemuria, which he had found difficult to comprehend. To be honest he had considered it completely off the wall. I must be opening up despite myself, he thought wryly.

Helen shook the sheets of paper slightly to indicate she was ready to continue and the men fell silent. ' "The early Atlanteans also communicated with birds and animals. They befriended all animals. No one wanted to harm anything, so the animals had nothing to fear." '

'I suppose what we call horse whispering was normal and natural in the everyday lives of the people,' said

Edward. 'It must have been wonderful. I suppose everyone was like St Francis of Assisi.'

'He incarnated to remind people of the Atlantean times when people and animals lived together in harmony,' said Zoranda quietly. 'He came to show people that it is possible to live in such a way.'

'Didn't you say he was an incarnation of the Master Kuthumi, who was one of the Wise Men?' asked Helen with a slight frown of concentration.

Zoranda nodded agreement, adding, 'And Pythagoras.'

'I remember.' Helen nodded and continued to read down the page. 'Ah, it's coming up. I think you'll be interested in this bit.'

'It's all fascinating,' replied Edward, a lock of hair falling over his face making him look more like a teenager than a man in his mid twenties.

Helen smiled at him. She felt very warm to him and wondered if she had been his mother or aunt in another life, or perhaps it was just that they were on a very similar wavelength. She read aloud, ' "The abilities of clairvoyance and telepathy were encouraged and nurtured in everyone. Even untrained people could communicate with each other telepathically over long distances. This was the chief means of communication.

' "The development of all spiritual and psychic gifts was so highly prized that reading, writing and use of symbols were not considered appropriate as they can diminish psychic powers.

' "Children were taught by priests in the temples. They

would be taken into deep relaxation by music and the priest would telepathically impart cosmic information. Sometimes pure white beams of light were played on the child's mind so that certain information could be accepted more easily. At this time the frequency was so high that the only aim or intention was to acquire divine knowledge and wisdom. Children were also taught to remember stories, which they chanted round the stone circles at ceremonies to raise the energy." '

Again Helen put the page on the table. 'I don't understand it,' she commented, with fire in her voice. 'We know that pressure and anxiety make it difficult for a child at school, or anyone for that matter, to absorb information, but we herd them into large noisy classrooms; we constantly tell them they have to do well or pass exams in order to be worth while, stressing the poor little things out. We force boring information into them with archaic, left-brain teaching methods. We take away the power and authority of the teachers and then we expect them to do well. Yet again and again studies show that children learn better when they are relaxed and listening to baroque music.'

No one spoke for a moment, then Zoranda said softly, 'And what are you going to do about it, Helen?'

She flushed. 'I'm going to write about it in the book. Clearly we can't teach children telepathically. They've lost the ability to receive but we can simply and cheaply help them by applying some of the methods used in Atlantis.'

'Good for you, Helen,' said Tony and she felt well supported. 'Is there a bit more information on that page?'

'Yes, just a bit about the priests. It says, "The priests were developed in many psychic and spiritual areas and were highly gifted healers." '

'And it just ends like that?' asked Edward, appalled. 'There's so much more I wanted to know, about their healing methods and religion.'

'And their technology and use of crystals.'

Helen smiled at Zoranda, a question mark in her eyes. She knew he had read the translation before he handed it to her.

'Shall I tell them or not?'

He chuckled. 'I never thought of you as a tease, Helen. Go on, tell them.'

'Right!' By now she was grinning broadly. 'At the end of the page is a list of headings of information which will be sent shortly.'

'So you were holding out on us!' Tony laughed. 'Read the list.'

And Edward's eyes sparkled. 'Yes, Helen. Read it.'

'Okay,' she responded. 'There's Healing, Marriage, Dress, Crystal Power, The Great Crystal of Atlantis. I really want to know about that. And Transport, Portals, Galactic Connections. Then another heading Later Atlantis but there aren't any subheadings there. Perhaps they haven't got so far in the translation.'

'Wow!' exclaimed Edward. 'I can't wait.'

'Nor can I,' agreed Helen. She looked at Tony. 'Right now I think we'd better tell Joanna and Marcus. They'll be on their way back to the Timbavati now. I wonder what's been happening to them?'

Chapter 23

Marcus considered every journey as an opportunity to meet new people. Invariably he chatted to someone who had something interesting to impart. Several times such a seemingly chance encounter had slightly changed the direction of his life, but even he did not expect quite such an interesting flight from Richard's Bay to Johannesburg.

The flight was full so that he and Joanna had to sit apart, not that it bothered either of them. Joanna wanted to be silent and contemplate the dolphin messages. Marcus was in chatty mood.

Next to him was seated a thin, elderly, slightly dour-looking man, with the greyish tinge of those who worry and overwork. Pity, Marcus thought, disappointed for a moment. Nevertheless this is the person the universe has seated me next to, so perhaps he has some information for me. It was a game he and Joanna often played and this time, as so often before, this attitude was to reap dividends.

He asked the stranger in his direct, friendly way why he was on the flight. The man responded to Marcus's openness. He introduced himself as John and was soon telling Marcus about his business. He confided that he loved Mozambique. 'I used to spend holidays there when

I was a child. It's so beautiful and the people are absolutely delightful. For years I've wanted to take business in there to help them and since the civil war I've gone there several times to talk to the officials.' He sighed, then shrugged. 'That's an uphill struggle.'

Marcus nodded encouragingly. He had already discovered that John was managing director of a refrigeration business, and that he had a keen philanthropic bent. He and his brother had built up the company over the years but now it had hit hard times, and he did not feel his nephew, who was lined up to take over, was making wise decisions. 'At least, his decisions are commercially sound, I'm sure, but they'll hurt a lot of people who have been loyal to us.' Marcus invited John to share some human stories and the young man caught a glimpse of how deeply the older man felt for the African people. No wonder he looked unwell, as if he were carrying responsibility for the lives of many who were less fortunate than he was. John explained, 'My wife and I have all we will ever need financially so I would like to be able to give something back.' He stopped with an embarrassed half laugh. 'I don't know why I'm telling you all this.'

Marcus knew why. He was interested and listened whereas, he surmised, most people probably wanted something out of the old man or were trying to force their opinions on to him. So he told John a little about his work helping ailing companies, and shared some of his experiences in return.

As the plane was landing John said, 'I don't feel we met by chance. You seem heaven-sent.'

Marcus smiled. 'I'm not sure about that but it's been very interesting and the flight has gone really quickly. Thank you.'

Fleetingly John was far away, in his own youth perhaps, when he too had had a vision and the fire to fuel it. Then he asked hesitatingly, 'I know that you and your girlfriend are only in Johannesburg for one night but I would esteem it an honour if you would both have dinner with my wife and me tonight.'

Marcus replied with a smile, 'I'll check with Joanna but I'm sure we'll both be delighted.'

The elderly man could tell he meant it. It gratified his soul. For an instant his tired and faded hazel eyes searched the young man's warm, shining grey ones. Then he added, 'There's something I'd like to discuss with you. I have a proposition for you.'

Suddenly Marcus remembered what Helen had said to Joanna. 'I've a feeling you and Marcus are meant to be in South Africa a bit longer.'

'Well, if that's right, let's just ask the angels to arrange it,' Joanna had replied lightly.

'Okay.' Her mother laughed. 'I know how rapidly things work for you, so if I'm right something'll happen soon.'

Instantly Marcus knew that John would offer him a job in South Africa and he knew without a shadow of doubt that he must accept it.

But the wheel of fate turned not just once but twice. John sent a car to fetch them at their hotel and they were driven to his gracious and beautiful home in Sandton, a suburb of Johannesburg.

His wife Marcia proved to be slim, grey-haired, elegantly dressed and delightful. She must have been in her late sixties but she had more vitality and life force than many women half her age and within seconds had introduced herself, given them drinks and made them laugh, so that they felt at home.

John took Marcus off to show him some boy's toys, while the women sat in the lounge. Despite its palatial size, Marcia had managed to make a corner cosy with luxurious, soft white sofas, glossy green plants and colourful paintings. Joanna's mouth fell open in surprise as she saw the pictures, for they were all of fairies. She glanced at the older woman, who was smiling at her, and immediately knew that she was with a kindred spirit.

'I saw a fairy once, here in that flowerbed,' Marcia told her, when they had relaxed back on the comfortable sofas looking out over the landscaped garden.

'I've always wanted to see one,' responded Joanna eagerly. 'What was it like?'

'It was about eighteen inches tall and like a ball of yellowy orange light. It was hovering over the roses and was exactly the same colour as they were. I watched it for perhaps ten to fifteen minutes fluttering from flower to flower. Sometimes it rested on one. Sometimes it hovered over another. I looked away several times and each time I looked back it was always there, until the phone rang and I had to answer it. Then I couldn't see it any more.'

'What a wonderful experience!' exclaimed Joanna,

staring at the roses and wishing she could be so fortunate.

Even before dinner Marcia had told Joanna of a holiday when she had swum with dolphins in Hawaii. 'It was magic,' she remembered. 'Hundreds of dolphins around us. We swam out from the shore and floated on the surface watching them. And whales in the distance. We even saw the turtles.' Her eyes were shining with a light, which Joanna recognised. When she saw it she called it an angel light.

On impulse she said, 'What kinds of dolphins were there?'

'Oh, spinners and bottlenose. I can't really remember the others.'

'Was there an angel dolphin?'

'An angel dolphin?' Marcia was searching her memory. Her forehead puckered in concentration. 'I don't know. There's something. . .' Her face cleared. 'I know. We were on a dolphin boat trip and Big Bella, who ran it, was behind me. She said to one of the helpers, "Look there! Angel dolphins – that's lucky!" I tried to see where she was pointing but there was just a turmoil of white water where they had jumped and dived. Now you mention it, she spoke very quietly as if it were really special and she didn't want everyone to hear.'

'And that was it?' said Joanna.

'As far as I can remember. Strange, I've never heard of angel dolphins before. Oh yes, her helper said, "They're so blue!" '

Angel dolphins! thought Joanna, her eyes shining. Now she knew one place where they could find them, but Hawaii was an awfully long way away.

At that moment the maid, Esmerelda, came in to tell Marcia that dinner was ready and the men returned from examining John's gadgets. Joanna could tell they had been discussing something important and had not just been looking at toys. From time to time she glanced at Marcus's face and knew he was pleased. John too seemed to be more relaxed and some of the tension had left his face. She was impatient to know what it was but had to force herself to concentrate on the food and the conversation.

After dinner John and Marcia strategically withdrew for a few minutes, leaving Marcus to tell Joanna what had been mooted. 'John's offered me a job with his company, mostly based in Cape Town but travelling here to Johannesburg and other places. He wants me to find a way for it to be humanitarian and profitable. Not that that's easy but it'll be interesting. Money's crap as you would expect with the rand the way it is but we'll be able to keep an eye on the white lion cub when it's born and do what we can to help.'

Joanna was surprised to sense a note of pleading in his voice. He really wants to do this. Is it the job or the white lion? she wondered. Probably both, she decided. Well, she wanted to please him and it was time she had a break from her job. Marcus was watching her closely as she made her mental deliberations.

Then in her usual practical way she responded with a barrage of questions. 'Can he get you a work permit? What about housing? When does he want you to start?' Then, almost as an afterthought, 'Can he get me a job too?'

As she spoke he threw his head back and laughed. 'Come on, give me a hug. I love you, Joanna. You're a woman in a million.'

She laughed too as his arms enveloped her. 'Get off, you great bear. Answer my questions.'

'Okay. Yes, he'll sort out the work permit. Start as soon as possible, probably after Christmas as you'll have to give notice at your job. He's sure he could get you work and a permit too. They've got a house in Cape Town, which they use when they stay there. We can live there at least until something else is sorted.'

'I see you've thought of everything?'

'It will be a bit of a rush,' Marcus admitted. 'We'd have to let the flat in London.'

'Oh, I can sort that out. We can put the stuff in Mum and Tony's house. There's plenty of room.' It was fortunate, she thought, that her mother had moved in with Tony when they got married. Her mother's old house was much too small to store their things in as she had discovered when she worked abroad before she met Marcus. It had forced her to have a major clear-out of her life and possessions and that had to be good. Possibly throwing and giving away what she no longer needed was necessary in order to let Marcus in. However, it was amazing how quickly clutter re-accumulated. It was time for her to move on from her job too, though she would miss the people at work. It would be a great opportunity to see South Africa properly and Monica had said they were always welcome at the safari lodge. She jumped suddenly, stopping the flow of her mind chatter as a thought intruded above all others.

'Marcus. We can't go back to England until we know the white lion cub has been safely born.'

'I know. I have explained a little to John and he understands. Don't worry. We'll be there! Maybe we can spend Christmas in the Timbavati.'

'As a matter of fact, I don't think so. We're going to have to get a bank loan. I've discovered where some angel dolphins are. I think we should go to Hawaii for Christmas!'

Marcus stared at her. 'Life with you will never be dull, Joanna!' he responded.

Chapter 24

There was a feeling of thunder in the air and black clouds were rolling across the sky when Joanna and Marcus returned to the Timbavati. Bede glanced at the grey pall and told them the weather could break at any time. It was appallingly hot and even the birds were silent.

'Rain would be more than welcome,' he commented. 'Everything's gasping for it.'

If possible the trees looked even more desiccated and tinder dry than they had a week ago and the huge white thorns on the acacia seemed to stick out like dehydrated weapons of torture.

But the rain did not come.

Monica was delighted to see them again and even her husband, Peter, greeted them with a friendly smile. Since Joanna had learned he was very ill, she had understood that his quietness was not lack of friendliness but rather that he was in pain. Monica took Marcus to look at the latest damage inflicted by the elephants and for a while Joanna sat with Peter in companionable silence and did not try to engage him in conversation. He seemed to appreciate it and she wished that someone had told her before that he was so ill. But every family handles illness and dying differently, she thought. So, who am I to judge.

Thank God I've never had to deal with the sickness of anyone I love.

They were in the same room as before and were pleased to see the familiar wooden bed with its mosquito net. Joanna looked out of the window and exclaimed, 'Quick, Marcus. Look. Warthogs.'

He rushed up in time to see the mother and babies, their tails in the air, trotting away from the water hole and disappearing into the bush.

'They're so sweet! Oh, I'm so glad we're back.' She took a deep breath. 'I just hope the white lion is born soon. I don't know why, but I feel anxious when I think about it.'

'Me too! Though we don't even know for sure that a white cub is going to be born.'

'I know it. We have to have faith. It is time now for a demonstration of the cosmic Christ into the world. I sense we'll be called on to do something to help it.'

'You're probably right. Though what I've no idea.'

By now they were walking across to the shimmering blue pool for a dip, both thinking about the possibilities ahead. Monica came rushing out of the office, calling them, her face alight with smiles.

'Guess what? Edward has just phoned. He's coming next week bringing two friends with him. I do hope you can stay that long. It'll be quite a party.'

Joanna and Marcus glanced at each other. 'Edward's coming!' repeated Joanna. 'But he's in Egypt!'

'Yes. He's flying down with a couple of friends but

they're only staying two nights.' She looked perplexed. 'It's a long way to come for such a short time.'

'Maybe they're going on somewhere else.'

'No! He said they were staying two nights and then flying back to Egypt.'

'Which day is he coming?'

'Thursday.'

Something struck Marcus. 'Did he say what his friends were called?'

'One was something odd. Z something. Ended in "anda".'

'Zoranda!' exclaimed Joanna and Marcus together, wide-eyed with astonishment and delight.

'Yes, that's it. Do you know him?'

'Oh yes!' they replied together. Zoranda here! Edward and Zoranda here! They must be coming for the birth of the white cub. Only a few days to wait! They looked at each other and grinned.

'Who is the other man?' asked Joanna impulsively.

Monica did not know. 'He seemed to be someone important. Edward asked for the best room for him. Lucky we aren't full, which is strange because we usually are at this time of year. I was just saying to Peter it's worrying how there have been lots of cancellations.'

Joanna and Marcus were in no doubt as to the reason. The universe had made space first for them and then for Edward and Zoranda. But who was the other man? Wild guesses were flying round in their heads, like birds in a cage.

At last when they were alone Joanna dared to voice her thought to Marcus. 'I know it's impossible but do you think it could be the Master?'

'Could be! The birth of the cub is a cosmic event,' he replied. 'And I imagine that's why they are coming.'

And they both knew this was right.

From that moment they asked every question they could think of about the lions. In the mornings and evenings they went out on safari with Bede and the other guests, always hoping to see the king of the beasts. But they did not see the pregnant lioness again.

'She's got to be somewhere,' said Joanna to Marcus in despair. 'Even the trackers haven't seen her.'

'If she's carrying the sacred white cub, she'll need to be careful,' replied Marcus to reassure her. But he too was becoming anxious, not knowing that the cub was safe until its cosmic birth had taken place. 'Don't worry. Edward and Zoranda will soon be here. They have powerful energy which will protect it.'

And with that Joanna had to be content. They meditated each day, sending love, light and protection to the white cub.

Then, when they'd almost given up hope of seeing him again, the lion shaman reappeared.

They were sitting outside after dinner as had become their custom, silently watching the activity at the water hole, when a shadow flitted from nowhere and sat in the empty chair. They saw his dazzling white teeth shining in the light of the flare when he smiled and found themselves beaming with joy.

'At last,' shrieked Joanna. 'It's you! We thought you'd never come back.'

'Oh, hello!' Marcus said, more moderately. 'It's good to see you.'

The sangoma laughed with pleasure at their surprise and delight. 'I come. There is work to do.'

At once they were alert and ready. 'Where is Bede? Is he not with you tonight?'

'He's taken the truck down to the village to see a girl we think. Aunt Monica is not pleased! But Bede said he'd only be a few minutes.'

'Then he hasn't gone to see a girl,' said the shaman with a wink. 'A girl needs longer time. But we need transport.'

'Why? Where are we going?' asked Marcus.

'To a sacred quartz mountain. We must place a symbol on the hill,' the sangoma replied.

'A symbol? What for?' Joanna was intrigued.

'What symbol?' echoed Marcus.

At that moment they heard the roar of the truck and within minutes Bede had joined them. He seemed slightly ill at ease and Joanna wondered if he felt unwelcome so she did her best to make him feel comfortable by inviting him to sit down and join them.

Marcus made a teasing comment about the hazards of getting involved with a woman but it fell on stony ground and they all knew the shaman was right. He had not been to see a girl. But why lie? Later Joanna realised that Bede had never said anything about a woman. Others had assumed it and he had let it ride. So where had he been? she wondered, but his face was inscrutable.

Bede eagerly agreed to drive them to their destination and seemed relieved that the attention was no longer on him. It was cold despite the cloud cover and Joanna could tell that the shaman hoped the wind would stir and move the blanket that covered the stars. He kept glancing upwards but he said very little.

After a half-hour drive Bede pulled the vehicle to a stop.

'Five minutes' walk from here,' said the lion shaman. Each of them had a hefty-sized torch and Joanna for one was very grateful. She was also comforted by the fact that Bede held a rifle as they walked single file through the bush. The sangoma read her mind and said quietly, 'There is nothing to fear. The animals are our friends. Only fear can call in attack.'

'I know,' she whispered back. But it did not stop her from feeling very nervous and walking close to Marcus.

Very soon they reached a clearing, which seemed to be littered with lumps of quartz. The shaman directed them to place the crystals in a huge cross with a double circle round it. Then a smaller circle was created in the centre with five equal-sized stones in each segment. They hardly noticed that the cloud had all but vanished as they worked, leaving only a few wisps over the Milky Way. When it was finished the four of them looked at the huge symbol in awe. The crystals were gleaming and glittering in the light.

'I feel it can be seen from the heavens,' said Joanna at last.

'Indeed,' agreed the shaman. 'That is the intention.'

'Why five crystals in each segment?' asked Marcus. 'Is there a special significance in five?'

'All numbers are sacred. Each number is connected to a great cosmic energy, which influences all of life. By the time it has filtered to Earth the power of the number is but a pallid reflection of its cosmic significance, but nevertheless important.

'Five represents the lion. It is the cosmic number of Orion from which all cats come. The lion is the ruler, the bringer of justice, might and majesty so we have placed it here to call to Orion that we are ready for the great being we await to enter our planet.'

'I thought the white lion was going to carry the Christ consciousness for humanity, like a second coming?' said Marcus, awed and puzzled at the same time.

'It is. Let me explain. In the cosmic plan every star, planet, asteroid, galaxy has a significance and a part to play. Orion is a training centre for all spiritual people. Not in the physical you understand?'

They all nodded.

'In the inner planes,' he continued. 'It is the mightiest spiritual university available in this universe. All the great spiritual people who incarnate come via Orion. At very least they will have done a course of training there.'

'Oh!' said Joanna.

'Spiritual leaders like Gandhi and all the Dalai Llamas have come from Orion.'

Once more Marcus and Joanna were struck by the breadth of his knowledge.

'The cat people are the Wise Ones,' he added. 'Orion is about spirituality not intelligence.' Then he chuckled and looked at Joanna. 'Yes, Orion was the last place you and your boyfriend were educated before you arrived for this incarnation, and your mother too.'

Joanna flushed with pleasure. 'What about the indigo and crystal children? Are they from Orion?'

The sangoma nodded. 'These children are bringing in enlightenment. They are from Orion.'

'Are they also from elsewhere?'

'No, but Wise Ones from elsewhere come to Orion to teach them. These children have knowledge of other places but no experience of them. They are the cat people.'

'I see,' said Joanna, 'and one more question. Does the white lion cub come from Orion?'

The sangoma was pensive. 'The white lion represents Christ. The Christ energy is from everywhere and has it all. Orion is the channel He will use to arrive because it is a spiritual place.'

'I see.'

'And now we will make prayers and chants to invite the Christ energy,' said the shaman and started to walk round the outside of the circle. They fell in line behind him.

Chapter 25

There was an air of peace and stillness at the Great White Lodge. Several of the brothers had been meditating in the beautiful room set aside for that purpose and all could sense and feel the angelic presences in the room.

'And now,' said Zoranda to Edward, quietly shutting the door as the brothers left, 'we must discuss the visit Helen is to make to the pyramids.'

'You want Helen to visit the pyramids?' Edward repeated, surprised. 'I thought. . .' He stopped.

'You thought?'

Edward had been trained to use his inner sight and then to keep silent about what he perceived unless he could directly help someone. After all, what was in someone's aura was a very personal matter. He knew Zoranda had clearer vision than he had, though the wise elder rarely revealed what he saw. Now that he was being invited by the older man to share what he had seen, he resumed. 'Well, I had the impression that Helen is afraid of the power of darkness. This is from many lifetimes ago but it has left a scar in her aura, which renders her vulnerable. She draws in situations; look at the bomb attack. Look at what happened to her in Australia. As long as she has that mark in her aura it will continue to happen. I thought it might be dangerous for her to go to the pyramids.' He paused and added, 'Yet I know she has been consistently used as an instrument for the force of light.'

'Go on.' Zoranda's light eyes appraised the young man and he was pleased with what he saw.

Edward took a deep breath. 'I believe her unconscious fear is her Achilles' heel. Consciously she believes she can protect herself and nothing can touch her. At a deeper level, the scar itches when there is evil around and she unconsciously remembers some distant event.'

The older man nodded occasionally as Edward spoke. 'Good. Your assessment is true.'

Edward said, with a puzzled expression, 'There's one thing I don't understand. I'm told that when you were all at Machu Picchu protecting the portal from the dark forces of Sturov, Helen's light was as steady as a rock.'

'Indeed. Her mother instincts came to the fore and looking after Joanna, who was injured, left no room for fear. Second, some of the purest light-workers in the world had assembled there and she was in their aura of protection.'

'I understand. So she is untouchable while she is in the protection of the Great White Lodge but if she goes to the pyramids and the Sphinx, she may be vulnerable again? Is that right?'

'Yes. That's true. As you know moths flutter round the light and her light is very bright. When she leaves this house, they may be able to harm her unless we can exorcise the ancient fear.'

'But Tony will not be touched?'

'No. Tony's quite safe. He's not particularly interested in this spiritual path, so his light is clear but it's not shining like Helen's. He's no threat to the dark, so the darkness is not interested in him.'

Edward pondered. 'Dare we let her go to the Sphinx and the pyramids?'

'She must feel the energy for herself before we impart that which must be revealed in the book she is writing.'

'I see.'

'So, Edward, what do you suggest?'

'We must talk to her and offer to help her heal the scar!'

'Excellent. And it is urgent. I have information for you about a journey we are about to undertake.'

Edward wanted to ask what it was but Zoranda said mildly, 'Perhaps you could fetch Helen now. We must talk with her as you so rightly say, and I will be preparing for this in the blue healing room.'

When Edward brought Helen to the healing room a few minutes later, Zoranda was sitting quietly in a chair. He smiled at Helen, motioned for her to sit down and indicated to Edward that he was to explain.

Edward decided to be direct. 'We want you to visit the Sphinx and the pyramids again but before you go we feel you need a little healing.'

She was surprised. 'I thought I'd had enough healing to transmute the energy from the explosion. It doesn't bother me any more, you know.'

'Good. That's really good. But we feel there is something deeper, from another life which is calling danger to you.'

Even as he spoke he had a vision of a black coven in another dimension, which had a cord into Helen, right into the place where he had seen her scar. Suddenly he felt slightly sick and knew he was picking up the link. She might have fallen from the path of grace in a distant life and belonged to the coven but he thought it more likely that the line had attached to her when she was trying to release one of its members. It was a deeper and stronger cord than he expected, and even within the sacred space of the lodge it was not a task he relished. He breathed deeply and centred himself, aware that Zoranda was watching him closely.

Helen gave her grateful permission for him to do what-ever needed to be done and sank back in her chair, closed her eyes and surrendered into deep relaxation. As she did so a feeling of great strength and confidence came over Edward. It was a sense of solid, unshakeable power. He was a high priest who could command the forces of light.

Under his direction Helen went deep into a trance so that she could re-experience the original event. 'Now tell me what's happening,' he commanded softly when he knew she had regressed sufficiently.

'I'm wearing a long white dress with a sapphire at my third eye,' she murmured. 'I'm in charge of a Temple of Light, a priestess. It's Atlantis.' She shivered suddenly. 'Corrupt Atlantis. Terrible things are happening. I try to keep my temple pure and inspire the people who believe in the light but the clouds of darkness are gaining power.' She paused and Edward let her remain silent for a moment as he sensed her distress.

She continued, 'There's a coven of dark priestesses, who have pillaged the sacred stones of a powerful circle and built a sacrificial altar on the ley line not far from our temple. They are directing black energy to us. They are telling people that they can see demons and spirits, who want to harm them. Oh no! They are saying that they have influence with these beings and can intercede to prevent horrible things happening. They infer their children will die of plague and their crops will fail unless they give them money and blood. So many bad things are happening that the people believe them.' Tears were pouring down Helen's cheeks. 'I can see the shadows round the evil priestesses but the people are frightened and bewitched. They are forsaking the light.'

Suddenly her voice rang out loud and clear as she made up her mind. 'I must help them. I will go into the coven myself and radiate such pure light that they must see the truth.' She described how she did a ceremony of purification round herself and set off towards the meeting place of the coven, little realising that her own power had been sucked dry by the constant battle against the enemy. She thought her light would protect her but her aura was seriously depleted.

It was full moon, which would energise her mission, but she noted with some trepidation that heavy grey clouds had rolled over the sky and the light was obliterated.

When she entered the coven the Dark Ones gathered

round her and taunted her. 'You cannot harm me. I am of the light,' she declared loudly but a snake of fear, somewhere inside her, rendered her vulnerable. Instantly the darkest witch among them, her fingernails like talons, leaped forward and struck through Helen's broken aura, piercing her physical body across the chest.

At that very moment the clouds rolled back and the moonlight shone full on the evil woman's face. The Dark Ones fell back, and Helen, the pure priestess in that life, fled. She ran, hearing their comments, knowing all was lost.

Her cut was not severe but her spirit was wounded and she died a week later, feeling she had failed the light.

Edward led her in a ceremony to enable her to forgive herself and the perpetrator, who, they could see, had been in a hell of her own making ever since. She had lived life-time after lifetime of dark misery, returning to the coven in the inner planes between lives. A well of compassion rose in Helen, allowing Edward to cut away the foul bondage and transmute the magnetic pull of the scar. So powerful was his energy that the remaining evil ones of the coven, still active in the inner planes, did not even attempt to intervene. Finally Helen sent love and light to the coven. At last it streamed into their dark world in a way it could not in Atlantis.

Full circle, Edward thought as he brought Helen to consciousness again. He told her that she was totally safe from now on and was no longer calling in darkness or danger.

She smiled a beatific smile and thanked him warmly.

'I've never been able to get a handle on what caused all the trouble. I knew there was something but not what it was.'

'That's because it was so deep. And the dark is cleverly manipulative. It can hide its tracks.'

She nodded. 'I'm so grateful.'

Zoranda spoke. 'Thank you, Edward. You did a magnificent job. The tentacle has been completely removed. As long as you do not let it re-enter through your fear, you will be safe, Helen.'

She nodded. 'I'm never going to let it in again,' she declared fervently.

I hope you're right, thought Edward. I really hope you are right. He knew it was too easy to succumb to old thought patterns and fears.

'Come,' said Zoranda, rising from his chair. 'It is time for breakfast. Helen, please would you fetch Tony, for I want to talk to you both. Edward, please wait a moment. I have something to tell you.'

Helen left to find her husband and Zoranda gave Edward news that he had not expected in his wildest dreams. He felt honoured and elated but most of all surprised.

Over a simple breakfast of fruit and juices, Zoranda told Helen and Tony that he would be flying to the Timbavati for a few days with the Master and Edward. He said it so softly that the information floated in like a petal on the tide and it was a moment or two before it registered.

Tony understood immediately and looked at Helen, waiting for a response.

Edward too was watching Helen. She hesitated in the act of moving a piece of pineapple to her mouth, then continued with her task almost as if she had heard but it was too much to take in. She ate the fruit with careful concentration and, when her jaw stopped moving, looked up at Zoranda.

'You're going to the Timbavati!' she repeated. Then her eyes lit up as full realisation filtered in. 'You're going to see it? Has it been born?' They all knew she meant the white lion cub. 'Why? Why the three of you?' Suddenly she was full of questions. 'When are you going? Will you see Joanna and Marcus? What else do you know?' And all the time she wanted to say, 'Can I come too?' but she didn't.

Zoranda could read her mind easily enough but he did not engage with her desire. Instead he said, 'We are honoured to be chosen to represent our order. According to the calculations of our astrologers and the Wise Ones of our brotherhood, the glorious birth will take place on Friday, a week today. A specially bright comet will be seen in the skies over Africa on that day. We will leave here on Thursday and stay with Edward's aunt and uncle for two days.'

Why Edward? thought Helen. He was only a kid after all and not of the same stature as the Master and Zoranda, even though he had done that deep exorcism on her. Perhaps it was because he had relatives on the spot and knew the area. But she knew that could not be the reason. She turned her head to look at him and realised that something within the young man had changed. He seemed to have grown physically in the last half an hour and she could see a glow of light around him. As he smiled at her his eyes were bigger and more luminous than she had ever seen them.

She became aware that they were all looking at her.

Zoranda spoke again and Helen wondered if she detected a hint of reproof. 'Edward has been chosen because of his pure heart and the quality of the light he carries. He has earned this over lifetimes. He may be young in years but he carries the wisdom of ages. He was chosen on merit to accompany the Master and myself to greet the white lion cub, who is the hope of the world. We take no gift other than the purity of our hearts and our offers of service.'

Helen bowed her head. She could not disguise a tiny wisp of envy.

Tony said, 'So you will see Joanna and Marcus. They should be there right now and will probably stay for a while.' He did not yet know about their new plans to remain and work in South Africa. A thought struck him. 'Didn't you say that Sturov also knows where and when the cub will be born?'

'Ah.' Zoranda spoke gravely into the sudden shocked silence. 'That is true. We all have work to do to strengthen the light.'

Helen noticed he said to strengthen the light rather than to prevent the work of evil.

The big man nodded to Edward who rose silently and

fetched a map of Africa from a drawer in one of the beautifully carved chests that graced the room. He placed it on the table in front of his mentor.

'See,' said Zoranda, pointing to a thick line, which had been drawn in gold from the Giza plateau along the Nile and straight down through Africa.

'As I think you know the Giza plateau is a perfect star map, which mirrors the heavens. In other words the pyramids were constructed to replicate the three belt stars of Orion and are in alignment with them. This line of gold, which is drawn on this map, follows the Nile to its source on Earth, while above it streams the Milky Way. It continues through the Great Zimbabwe.'

'What's the Great Zimbabwe?' interrupted Tony.

'Ah! Good question!' responded Zoranda. 'It's known as the sacred site of the lion and used to be an important trading place and centre for smelting gold. Historians say it was built between AD 900 and 1500.'

'But?' breathed Helen and the big man smiled at her.

'But it is a site of great legend and mystery, a sacred place of lion spirits. Indeed totem lions have been found here. It was originally built by a lost civilisation who created the most stable empire on the continent on the seam of physical gold, which runs through Africa.'

'The gold of enlightenment that holds the Earth together,' murmured Helen.

Zoranda nodded and continued. 'The gold line then goes straight through the Timbavati, where the white lions are seen and down to Durban.'

They all looked at the map and Edward pointed out

that the Sphinx, the source of the Nile, the Great Zimbabwe and the Timbavati were all on the same longitudinal line, 31 degrees 14 minutes east.

Tony drew in breath and scrutinised the map more carefully, while Zoranda mindfully picked five crystals from a bowl. He held the stones in his big hands and blessed them. Then he placed a black obsidian at the top of the map on the Giza plateau. Below it he put a yellow citrine on the source of the Nile, further down a red garnet on the Great Zimbabwe, a green malachite on the Timbavati and finally a blue lapis over Durban.

He stepped back and they all looked at the map with its line of gold through Africa and strategically placed crystals. 'The greatest thing you and other people can do now to bring in the Christ consciousness and heal Africa is to visualise the gold line of enlightenment drawing Africa together and picture the crystals lighting up the points they are placed on.'

He spoke with such conviction and authority that they all felt the power of what they were being asked to do.

'And now,' said Zoranda briskly, 'there is a great deal to prepare. Helen, we wish you and Tony to visit the Sphinx and the pyramids tomorrow, for there is much to explain.'

Helen could not disguise her delight but Edward was praying that the healing would hold. He felt Helen needed a couple of days at least for the energy to integrate at a mental and emotional level before she was totally safe.

Zoranda watched his thought forms. Oh, Edward, let go of your attachment to results, he thought, or your fear could cause the link to reactivate. But he said nothing. The young man had to learn by experience.

Chapter 26

It was late afternoon when Tony put his head round the door of the room where Helen, surrounded by books and pieces of paper, was staring at the computer screen.

'Guess what?'

She looked up and smiled. 'I couldn't begin to guess. Every day here is full of surprises.'

Tony waved a piece of paper. 'Another translation from the Scroll.'

'Already!' Helen's face lit up. 'Have you read it? What does it say?' She saved her file, then sprang up from the chair. 'Is there more about early Atlantis?' She was grabbing for the piece of paper like a child while Tony laughed and held it out of her reach.

'Come on, let's look at it on the verandah. It's cooler there and you need a break from that computer. What a way to spend a honeymoon!' He shook his head, though she could see his eyes were laughing.

'I know,' she replied, automatically feeling guilty. 'I'm so sorry. It must be terrible for you.'

'You're not sorry at all!' he exclaimed, still chuckling. 'You're loving it. Go on, admit it.'

'Well, it is fascinating. I have to admit I am enjoying it.'

'Told you.'

'But it's very important. It could make a difference—'

He stopped her by putting his finger over her mouth. 'And I'm enjoying having the time to read and relax. So it suits both of us and you are right. I know your book is important. We've got years and years together to do other things. Come on, Helen. Let's get Edward and Zoranda if he's available and see what the Scroll has to say.'

And, taking her by the hand, he led her out to the verandah. A glow of love and gratitude filled her heart. She was so fortunate to have this man by her side.

Edward and Zoranda were already waiting for them on the verandah. 'The office told us about the new translation from the Scroll and we guessed you'd come out here to read it. May we hear what it says too?' said Edward, while Zoranda smiled his quiet all-knowing smile.

'Right,' said Tony. 'Possession is all important. I've got it and I'll read it!' Helen was tempted to say something but wisdom prevailed and she indulged him. He put on his glasses and cleared his throat. 'It starts with the powers of the priests in early Atlantis,' he announced, starting to read. ' "The priests were extensively trained in many psychic and spiritual areas. They were highly gifted healers. They could levitate, teleport, bilocate." ' He looked at them over his glasses. 'I'm afraid I don't understand. Obviously I know what levitation is but what is to teleport and bilocate?'

'Bilocation is where someone can be seen in two places at once,' Edward told him. 'A person can leave their physical body in one place and can be seen in the etheric body somewhere else by psychics. That's relatively common and people often don't realise that they have done it. The other way of bilocating takes real training and power. You project yourself out of your physical body so strongly that others can see you and talk to you.'

'I think I get it. And teleporting, what is that?'

'It's the ability to move objects from one place to another, usually by dematerialising it and then re-forming it somewhere else.'

'I see.' Tony cleared his throat and Helen knew that meant he was finding this difficult to comprehend. 'You'd better take over, Helen.' He put the paper into her eager hands.

'I'll start again,' she said. ' "The priests were extensively trained in many psychic and spiritual areas. They were highly gifted healers. They could levitate, teleport, bi-locate and communicate with other galaxies." '

'What?' Tony really couldn't contain himself. 'Communicate with other galaxies!' he repeated and even as he spoke, he realised that his mindset was about to be expanded again. Helen felt a little stab of irritation so she ignored him and continued.

'It starts with healing.'

She read. ' "Health was considered to be the normal condition. Any deviation from perfect health was under-stood to result from an imbalance in the spiritual, mental and emotional state. Therefore healing was seen as a holistic realignment. The divine has placed on this planet everything we need for our human journey in the form of medicinal plants. Throughout its history Atlanteans had a thorough knowledge of the symbiotic relationship between plants and humans. Trained healers were expert herbalists and used the essence of plants to heal the auric field." '

'That sounds like homeopathy,' commented Edward.

'Yes,' agreed Helen. ' "They also used sound, colour, crystals and laser light to clear the aura and the physical structure of the body. Bones, for instance, were set and mended with sound healing. Healing chambers were made of various crystals, which were programmed to purify and heal different states. Healers channelled divine energy through the crystals.

' "Certain healer priests were trained in psychic surgery. Those who held this secret gift at the fall of Atlantis took it to South America, where it was practised by those who kept the knowledge." '

'And still is,' interposed Zoranda. 'Atlantean healer priests are reincarnating with these gifts now in other parts of the world.'

Helen nodded and commented, 'I had psychic surgery once. It was unbelievable. I don't know exactly what happened but the pain I'd had for ages disappeared completely. Anyway, to continue: "Sick people were often placed in sleep chambers where their dreams were analysed and the correct healing offered.

' "Later they used computers to scan the body, which told them if the blockage was physical, emotional or spiritual. It would for instance say that the cause of the dis-ease was karmic and healing could be affected by purification and crystal therapy." '

'There are bio-resonance machines now, which can scan the body and give all that information,' put in Edward, but no one responded.

'I hope the Scroll says something about their use of computers,' commented Tony, feeling he was on safe ground there.

Helen smiled at him. 'The next section is about marriage. Just listen to this. "When a couple wanted to marry, the priest would examine their auras to see if they were compatible. If they were, the marriage was sanctioned. If not they were not allowed to marry."'

'That sounds like common sense,' said Tony, nodding, 'but rather dictatorial.'

'This continued in the Essene tradition after Atlantis,' Zoranda commented.

'And in some Native American tribes, I think,' added Edward.

'There's a snippet about dress now. "In early Atlantis, dress was very simple. The people wore sandals and a tunic, which was often purple. Priests wore pale green, pale blue or white robes depending on their level.

' "The only adornment might be a crystal attuned to enable them to achieve higher consciousness. Later, as the consciousness degenerated, people wore heavy adornments and many jewels."'

'It's that link between sophistication, complication and lower vibrations again,' mused Tony.

Helen considered this. 'I guess spirit is simple and ego is complex,' she responded, and continued, 'Now there's a line that has been printed in bold. I guess on the original script it must have been made to stand out in some way. "Men and women are different but equal."'

'I think we discussed this earlier. That truth is honoured and understood in the esoteric branches of all spiritual cultures,' agreed Zoranda. 'It is only when purity is tainted that the masculine seeks to undermine the feminine. In truth man and woman have always been equal.'

'So are you saying any culture or religion that claims women are inferior to men is tainted?' asked Tony.

'Absolutely,' he responded quietly.

Helen was reading ahead. 'This part is about criminals and how they treated them. It's totally fascinating. It says, "Prisons were unnecessary. The Atlanteans used humane methods to realign a miscreant to the glory of his soul, so that he never re-offended. A convicted person was examined for the source of the problem within himself. First he was hypnotised by magnetism. While his spirit was out of his body, he was diagnosed by a trained intuitive, who marked the man's head and neck to indicate where the physical manifestation of disorder was located.

' "Healers and magnetic technicians beamed energy into these specific points. The aim was to atrophy the blood vessels serving relevant parts of the brain or to flood the cells with blood as necessary.

' "While this was taking place a trained priest communicated telepathically with the criminal's spirit, raising the consciousness of the guilty party to a higher moral plane."' Helen put the paper down. 'What about that!' she exclaimed. 'Isn't that amazing!'

Edward said thoughtfully, 'I'm sure we have the skills to do that now.'

'There are too many off their paths – and it would be considered interfering with civil liberty,' commented Zoranda mildly.

'Surely not if it's done with consent and if the criminal was shown his higher pathway and given help to stay there. Those who were treated would have such a sense of satisfaction, contentment and enthusiasm that the concept would spread,' argued Helen.

'Maybe. But the number of healers who could do the work are minimal. They'd be flooded by the sheer volume of criminals,' Edward responded.

'Well, not necessarily,' Tony came in unexpectedly. 'So many people are weak and simply follow the ringleaders. If the consciousness of each leader was raised, they would bring their acolytes into the light. But you're right. I don't think it would work yet. Go on, Helen, what's next?'

She had as usual been scanning ahead while listening to the discussion. 'Aha! There's a bit about portals here. Listen. "Portals. The purity of the initiates kept the portals from this planet to the universe open and protected. This allowed initiates and other highly trained people to communicate inter-galactically. It also enabled free travel between our planet and others. The wisdom of the universe was therefore available to Atlantis."'

'Is that all it says?'

'I'm afraid so. Maybe there'll be more in the next translation.'

'I hope so,' said Edward. 'I'm sure they could fly and I'd love to know how they did that.'

Helen's eyes shone as she looked at him. 'I could always fly in my dreams as a child and I'm certain that was an ancient memory from early Atlantis. I hope the Scroll tells us more.'

Zoranda's eyes were sparkling. He knew so much more than he ever revealed.

Chapter 27

They did not have to wait long for more information. Less than an hour later a second fax arrived, which should have come with the first one. Helen was settling down to listen to Zoranda, who was giving her esoteric information about the pyramids for her book, when Edward interrupted them. 'More from the Scroll,' he announced.

Zoranda, in his quiet voice, suggested that Edward fetch Tony, who was in the pool. By the time the latter arrived Helen and Zoranda had read the information, so Tony settled quickly into a chair and his wife handed him the typescript to read aloud.

'The first heading is Religion. "In the earliest phase of Atlantis before the polar shift, the Sons of Belial, those who were materialistic and sought sensual pleasure, were in conflict with the Children of the Law of One, whose lives were dedicated to spiritual knowledge and who focused on oneness. However the force of black magic was so terrible that the experiment was terminated and Atlantis sank.

' "With eternal hope in the heart and mind of the divine, Atlantis was reinstated. Alas the outcome was the same and the experiment was terminated for the second time.

' "When it rose for the third time, high beings of light had prepared the Cathedral of the Sacred Heights to overlight Atlantis. This was the purest time in the history of the planet. At the height of its purity the people honoured the oneness of all things. There was no separation between humans, animals, plants or trees." '

'That's what the Scroll said about early Lemurians too.'

'Yes. I think that automatically happens when the frequency is higher and the veil between the worlds is thinner,' agreed Edward.

' "They always had a belief in the continuation of the soul and reincarnation. They prepared the body for its onward journey and subsequent return to Earth.

' "In the pure times they worshipped outdoors in nature, which kept the energy clear. Trees, flowers, birds, animals, water, stones and all of the nature kingdom were considered to be part of the oneness.

' "When conditions were right they danced, chanted and told stories at ceremonies around sacred stone circles. The circles were carefully placed with their centres over underground water, so that the energy of prayer and ritual was spread by the water throughout the Earth. Stones were individually chosen and brought from long distances. Many were slightly concave to act as sound chambers for healing and the enhancement of spiritual light. They act as amplifiers and produce spirals of energy.

' "The Atlanteans were aware of the power of the sun, with its mighty solar deity, and honoured it, so stones were often angled towards the Great Central Sun or a particular planet to connect with its radiations. The priests understood the particular qualities of the friendly planets. That which was beamed down to Earth was magnetised by the rituals and ceremonies at the stone circles and enhanced the power of the light. The special energy waves at these stones will persist throughout the life of planet Earth.

' "Special ceremonies were held at full moon as well as on mid-summer's day, to take advantage of extra power flooding the planet at those times." '

'Hm,' said Tony.

Helen could tell he had in his mind pictures of witches dancing by moonlight, so she added some scientific information. 'Hey, scientific tests have shown that ultrasonic sound waves from sacred stone circles are more powerful at sunrise. And at the sites that haven't been disturbed the static magnetic field is shown to be stronger than at broken ones. Also tests reveal that more than usual amounts of electromagnetic energy circulate in and around them.'

Tony's eyes lit up and he nodded. He liked scientific results. However, he did not comment. He put his head down and continued.

' "Before the fall of Atlantis the dark priesthood took control and used their knowledge and energy for personal power and control. Then religion was once more dominated by black magic and sacrifice as at the end of Lemuria. The pure priests and priestesses, who kept and honoured the sacred wisdom, stood alone and isolated, until they were killed and the light of Atlantis expired." ' He frowned and said dryly, 'Very dramatic.'

'I guess those of us who worked for the light at the end of Atlantis still hold the memory in our consciousness,' protested Helen. A picture of a priestess resolutely making invocations to the light, while the dark priests desecrated her temple and finally killed her, came into her mind. This was followed by quakes and a great tidal wave of water. She shivered and shook herself as if to exorcise the vision. Then she focused her attention on Tony and the Scroll again.

Helen knew he had reached the part about levitation and flying, so she watched him closely. Edward, who was trying to read over Tony's shoulder, exclaimed, 'Levitation. Read what it says aloud, will you, Tony?'

'All right.' Tony obliged. ' "Those priests who had a high enough consciousness mastered gravity with mind control. They could create a rotating energy field round themselves and travel within it." '

'Unbelievable, isn't it?' commented Helen. 'Perhaps that's why spirals represent the energy of Atlantis.'

' "The people could use energy from sound waves to lift themselves short distances in the air," ' continued her husband, ignoring the interruption.

'Wait for it,' said Helen excitedly.

Tony went on, ' "Metal discs that you could sit on were tuned to an individual's voice. When charged by being hit like a gong and with the sound of the voice and mental concentration it would lift people. Even children could do this." '

'So they could fly. Like a magic carpet,' said Edward.

'I suppose that's where the magic carpet myth came from.'

'I read somewhere about a Caribbean folk story. In the olden days when people wanted to climb a hill, they hit a plate, sang the appropriate song for where they wished to go and immediately flew through the air to that place,' Helen told them. 'It's fascinating how the old tales and myths are based on actual happenings which are lost in the mists of time.' She was thinking of some of the Aborigine myths that she had learned from Uncle George in Cooktown. 'I wonder if the songs were two-line rhymes, like our magic spells. Perhaps the rhythm and rhyme help to activate the power.'

'You mean like, "Make him wriggle, make him squirm. And turn him into a lowly worm,"' chanted Edward unexpectedly, with an impish schoolboy grin.

Helen laughed. 'I was thinking more of "In the glory of Thy will, Take me to the highest hill, And there enhance my healing skill, To cure and help all who are ill."'

Edward laughed back. 'Much better,' he responded.

Tony said to his wife, 'I don't know how you do it off the top of your head.'

'Words flow like a constant stream through my head.' Helen laughed. 'I just wish they were more erudite. Read on, Tony. The next bit is quite incredible.'

'The next heading is "Ley lines",' he obliged. '"Molten iron within the Earth generates a current that produces a magnetic field. The mighty Thoth, who was incarnate for some time in Atlantis, channelled this force into straight lines to create an energy grid around the planet. This grid linked the portals, through which connection to the divine was made. They formed a spiritual communication network and the origin of the web of light.'

'Hey, that's what the earlier section of the Scroll told us,' commented Tony, pausing. 'That the ley lines linked all the sacred sites and portals.'

'It says more now,' said Helen, pointing to the paper to urge him to continue. He took the hint.

' "However it was also a force that could be used as a roadway. People could tune into the energy of the ley lines to travel along more easily in the air. They were sacred lines, and the magnetic force was more powerful at full moon. Witches and other healers with sacred esoteric knowledge would fly these lines. They would gather at full moon because it was quicker to travel then." '

'Isn't that amazing!' burst out Helen. 'It's so terrible that the energy lines have been corrupted and broken.'

'There are many people sending pure energy down the lines to purify them and re-energise them now.'

'Yes, I know. It must have been amazing at full moon to see all the people flying on the lines.' She giggled suddenly. 'No wonder in the dark ages when they tried to kill off the psychics and healers they depicted them as black witches on broomsticks moving across a full moon. It was enough to terrify anyone. I don't know why I'm laughing. I'm sure I was burned at the stake.'

Zoranda slipped in quietly, 'Now you know why it was important for Atlanteans to be able to forecast eclipses. They harnessed the power of the sun and the moon to fly.

When it was eclipsed, everything and everyone fell to Earth.'

They stared at him. 'What a horrible thought!' exclaimed Helen.

Tony had been pondering the revelations. Now he said unexpectedly, 'I understand that the intensity of the magnetic field round the planet is decreasing rapidly.'

'It is,' agreed Zoranda. 'Humanity must raise its frequency again in order to re-energise the force field that protects Earth. It is imperative we help the white lion to survive so that it can bring in the Christ consciousness, for that will raise the light of people more quickly than anything else.'

They looked at each other and each made a vow to do their best.

Chapter 28

The trackers were tense. Bede was talking continuously into his eternally crackling radio. A trio of lionesses had been spotted entering the Timbavati and all the safari vehicles were watching out for them, for it was believed one was the pregnant lioness nearing her time. Everyone had heard that a white lion cub might be born and rumour had it that this cub would have magical powers. Another tale spreading faster than soft margarine on a hot day was that a star or comet would explode above the Timbavati when it was born, causing a terrible fire. Yet another that this lion, when it grew up, would cause the destruction of Africa.

It was Monica who first told Joanna these rumours. She was laughing as she spoke and shrugged. 'That's Africa for you. You wonder where these things start, don't you!'

Yes, thought Joanna, going white. You do! Her mind was churning over the repercussions of such rumours. Maybe locals would try to kill the cub. Perhaps they would curse it or force it out of the Timbavati. Where was Marcus? She must talk to him. She raced off to find him and blurted out everything she had heard.

He looked gloomy and very worried. He said, 'Thank goodness Zoranda will be here soon. At least while he's in the Timbavati the lions will be safe. He and the Master have the power to protect anything in their auras, and they can project their auras quite a distance.'

'You mean, a bit like sending out a finger of energy from themselves to surround the cub?'

He nodded and she hoped fervently that he was right.

And so they kept their ears open for information. Bede had become very quiet. He often slipped off for an hour or two and was shifty when his Aunt Monica asked him where he had been. 'Off to see a friend,' he muttered, sounding like a sullen teenager when she spoke to him in a perfectly civilised way. She, too, looked more upset than seemed reasonable. Something about the way Bede responded and even more about the way his aunt watched him with big anxious eyes concerned Marcus greatly.

On the morning safari Bede seemed to be very withdrawn. He pointed out fewer animals. Perhaps I'm imagining things, Marcus persuaded himself. Probably it's because the rain still hasn't started and it's so hot. He decided that the weather was getting to him, for the drives seemed longer in the furnace-like heat. That morning they had crossed several times, or so it seemed to him, a wide dry sandy river-bed, full of tracks and dead branches, rewarded only by a glimpse of a snake and a troop of chattering monkeys.

The track undulated and wriggled ahead, winding through the beige-yellow soil, and round the piebald trunk of a merula tree. They stopped to allow a giraffe to amble across in front of them but nothing seemed exciting. Of course, it was because they were all wondering about the birth of the white lion cub and the rumours around it. They all desperately hoped to see lions but none showed themselves that day. Nor did any other trackers report seeing them.

Monica approached Marcus that afternoon. She looked pale and her eyes were puffy as if she hadn't slept.

'Can I have a word, Marcus?' Her voice held a pleading quality, which worried him. He wondered if her husband, Peter, was sicker than they thought.

'Yes, of course.'

She drew him by the elbow towards the water hole where they could not be overheard. 'Marcus, I'm really worried about Bede. Something's the matter with him. Has he said anything to you?'

'No. Nothing. I'm not really on that sort of terms with him.'

She looked at him directly and he noticed that her soft blue eyes looked faded and fearful. 'Please will you do something for me?'

'If I can,' he responded cautiously. That was unlike Marcus, who was usually willing to do anything for anyone.

'I want you to find out where he's going and why. Follow him if necessary.'

'No!' Marcus was aghast. 'I can't possibly do that.'

He saw Monica's face crumple as if she were near tears. What on earth was this all about? She was Bede's aunt, for goodness sake, not his keeper. Hastily he added,

'Look, I'll talk to him and try to find out if anything's wrong.'

'Oh, would you, Marcus? Thank you. Thank you. I must go.' Her shoulders hunched, she hurried back to the office without a backward glance.

Marcus noticed, with concern, that she looked thinner and more fragile than when he had first met her a few short weeks ago. He hoped there was not some horrible can of worms waiting to be opened. He decided he would have a word with Bede and then back off. That would fulfil his promise to Monica. Only it did not work out like that.

Half an hour later Marcus noticed Bede disappearing behind one of the bungalows. Ah, he thought. I'll do it now. Get it over. He made no particular attempt to be quiet but, as he turned the corner, Bede had his back to him and was leaning against the building, talking into his mobile. Evidently he had not heard Marcus approaching. What Marcus heard made his heart freeze.

'The white cub. Sure! How much?'

Marcus leaped back out of sight, his heart pumping. How much! What did Bede mean? He listened hard.

'Of course. At your service, sir.' Bede's voice was low, sounding obsequious. 'Tonight? Okay.' Another pause as the youth listened. Then he shrugged. 'Your place. I'll be there.'

Marcus did not listen any longer. He sprinted back to the room and told Joanna what he had heard.

She was equally horrified. 'Bede! I don't believe it.'

'You just better, Joanna. I heard him.'

'Who was he talking to?'

Marcus shook his head. 'I've no idea but I am going to find out.'

'Marcus, be careful. What can you do?'

'Let me think. Monica wanted me to follow him but that's ridiculous. Another vehicle on the road would be too obvious.'

They sat talking and thinking for some time. Then Marcus stood up. 'I'm going to see if Monica can track down the lion shaman. He might be able to help.'

'How?' Joanna began but he was already out of the door and striding across the baked earth to find Bede's aunt.

The sangoma turned up an hour later. He had not received a message but simply responded to a feeling that he was needed and they marvelled at the man's intuition. As Marcus told him everything he observed the lines on the black face deepen with concern.

'You say he has been disappearing from time to time?'

Marcus nodded.

'Come!' The shaman jumped up and led the way to the safari vehicle, parked in front of the lodge. He examined the wheels carefully. 'See?' He pointed to mud in the treads. 'There's only one place that comes from. Not in the Timbavati. Rich man place. Private.'

Marcus was silent as the wise man considered the situation. 'Soon Bede will take you on safari to find lions, right?'

'Yes, we'll be leaving in half an hour.'

'You can drive, yes?'

'Yes.'

'Ask the boss if you can borrow a vehicle. After dinner make sure Joanna talks to Bede and keeps him occupied. I'll meet you by the car.'

'And then what?'

'Leave it to me. Lot to do. Must go.'

And he trotted away along the path towards the servants' huts.

Joanna and Marcus scarcely enjoyed the safari despite the most spectacular pink, orange and violet sunset and the fact that every night animal seemed determined to show itself. Rare wild dogs, with their soft round ears, trotted across their path, hyenas slunk along the track, the eyes of civet cats gleamed in the searchlight. They glimpsed a leopard, which would normally have filled them with joy but tonight almost seemed an irrelevance. They even came across a pride of lions with their cubs, but not *the* pregnant lioness.

Bede too was preoccupied, though two elderly sisters, who were staying at the lodge and were in their vehicle, plied him with questions and expressed enough ecstasy for all of them.

After supper Joanna did her best to engage Bede in conversation, while Marcus disappeared. She asked him the names of all the stars, and the two grey-haired women, with their insatiable desire for knowledge, made her task easier.

* * *

The lion sangoma was waiting in the pitch dark when Marcus left the lodge. Even though he was expecting him, Marcus still jumped when he materialised. They climbed silently into the four-wheel drive, hoping no one would see them. The engine sounded loud and rough when he switched it on and the headlights so bright that someone must surely come out to see what was going on. Act normal, he said to himself. You have Monica's permission to drive this vehicle. You can say you are taking the shaman somewhere. But he felt like a conspirator, his hands were sweating and he knew he would be a poor liar if Bede came out now and asked him what he was doing.

They followed the main road to the entrance of the safari park. The sangoma knew all the men on duty at the gates and they readily agreed that Marcus could park for a while in the shadows. There was little traffic to disturb them.

'Now tell me what the plan is,' whispered Marcus, even though there was no need to be quiet.

'Bede will pass in about an hour, I think,' replied the shaman. 'He will be driving to a private safari lodge called the Black Rhino Lodge. Very luxury. Private. Invitation only. Powerful men stay there. Meetings. Bad energy. Bad decisions. Someone there is trying to stop the white cub bringing in the higher consciousness. And more. I think much more.' He stroked the side of his nose in a universal gesture of knowing. 'We will go there and find out.'

'What do you mean, we'll go there? That's impossible. It'll be guarded.'

'Sure. Dogs. Trained guard dogs. I know it.'

'Stop!' exclaimed Marcus, putting his hand over his ears as if to stop the words penetrating. 'This is madness. First, Bede will see the lights and know we are following. Second, how do we get into the grounds? Third, how do we pass the guard dogs? And then how do we find out what's going on?'

'Leave it to me,' replied the sangoma airily. He made a gesture suggesting that the higher forces were on their side. Marcus would have preferred something more concrete. 'We wait until he passes. You can see lights for a long way in the dark but when he goes off the road to the Black Rhino, he must go down the hill and our lights will be hidden by the ridge. We wait. Then turn lights off and coast slowly to the house.'

Marcus was opening his mouth to protest, when the sangoma grabbed his arm. 'This is him. Sooner than I expected.'

'How do you know?'

'Sound of engine and anyway I know.'

Marcus could see his companion's white teeth flash like snowdrops in the headlights of the passing car.

They waited until Bede's lights were far in the distance. 'Go!'

Marcus drove out of the shadows and set off down the road like any other late traveller about his business. Just as the sangoma had indicated the lights ahead swept to the left and wound down the hillside. The lights were out of sight by the time they reached the junction.

'Now,' ordered the shaman, 'lights off. Go slow.'

Marcus needed no telling. The track ahead was a whisper of white in the moonlight and he had to concentrate hard as they negotiated holes and ruts. 'If they are that rich you'd think they'd make up the road better,' he muttered. But his chest was tight and he was wondering what on earth had possessed him to come out on this mission to face dogs, dangerous men and possibly guns.

Huge gates faced them at the end of the path, a barrier that was almost certainly alarmed, so they would have to announce their presence over an intercom to gain entry. 'To the right,' whispered the shaman.

Marcus veered off the road. The scrub had been cleared round the edge of the high wire fence, which surrounded the property. He turned the vehicle to face the road and stopped under a large leafless tree.

The shaman eyed the fence and his eyes glinted white in the moonlight. 'Electrified!' He laughed softly and Marcus could have sworn he thought this was a game. Perhaps this was the childish sense of humour he had heard Africans possess.

But he had no time to find out. On the other side of the barrier a pack of German shepherds raced, barking, towards their car. Thank God for the fence! thought Marcus, his heart thumping.

A door of the house opened and a man stood silhouetted in the light. He yelled at the dogs to be quiet but they ignored him and, if anything, increased the volume. With an oath the man started to shamble towards the gate, shining a torch in their direction.

The shaman slipped out of the car and over to the

electrified wire mesh. He made strange whining sounds and the dogs stopped barking. He appeared to be talking to them, not in the way Joanna did but really communicating. Their ears were cocked as they listened and their tails wagged. Weird, thought Marcus.

The man with the flashlight, presumably a guard, was getting nearer. The shaman moved quickly along the fence towards the gate, calling the animals to follow on their side, until the guard picked him up in his light and shouted. The shaman spoke softly for some time until the guard stood, still and silent as a petrified rock, seemingly hypnotised. Then the powerful sangoma hurried to the gates with the willing pack of dogs trotting beside him on the other side of the fence.

'Come.' The magic man beckoned to a doubtful Marcus, who reluctantly edged himself out of the four-wheel drive and followed. In a trance the guard opened and closed the gate, like an automaton. Marcus could see that his eyes were glazed and staring as the shaman ordered him to sit on the ground and the dogs, at a command from the shaman, encircled him and lay down. When the African medicine man spoke again the lead dog's ears twitched and Marcus knew the guard would not move. He looked as if he had gone to sleep sitting up.

'Come,' the sangoma urged Marcus. 'Quickly.'

'What did you do?'

'Told the dogs to surround the guard till we get back.'
That was not what Marcus meant by the question.

He confessed later that his legs were wobbling and his stomach felt like jelly as they crept towards the lair of sharks, with a pack of wild hounds lying on the ground between them and their exit. But he did it. The shaman directed him with movements of his hands and soon they were behind a bush in front of an open window, streaming with light.

Marcus dared to raise his head and peep into an enormous room. Eight men and one woman, of mixed nationalities but all hatchet-faced, sat on sofas deep in negotiation.

Bede was there, answering questions and giving away information about the lions. A man spoke and suddenly Marcus felt ill. It was a voice he would never forget. Sturov!

What they heard made him feel sicker. The black magician was boasting he had permission for a cull of lion cubs. 'My permit is for Saturday.'

There was something particularly slimy about his tone that made Marcus recoil and withdraw his attention but the shaman held the younger man's arm fiercely so that he was forced to listen. The discussion moved on and they seemed to forget Bede, who slouched immobile on his chair, ignored. They were discussing international agreements about the killing of whales and dolphins. And in ten minutes they had pooled their evil power to find ways of manipulating quotas and making a farce of the honest world. Marcus's revulsion was being replaced by anger, red-hot fire like a volcano inside him.

Sturov had a peculiar smirk on his face. He was telling them of his plans to support the use of sonar radiation in the ocean, which would kill the dolphins and whales and weaken all ocean life. That would make food scarce and people dependent. He could do it in such a way that would make governments turn to him for guidance. The evil man turned and walked arrogantly towards the windows. He was so close Marcus could see his eyeballs.

Quick as a flash the shaman pulled him back. 'Hurry.'

They melted back to the gate where the shaman talked to the dogs, who stood up one by one to release their captive. The guard opened his eyes and looked around in horror and disbelief. 'Let us out of the gates!' ordered the shaman. The trembling guard, fearing for his job, his life and possibly his sanity, did so.

As they roared away up the hill the dogs started barking in frenzy, people were spilling out of the house and all the lights went on. Marcus drove recklessly fast.

What could he tell Joanna about the white lion cub? What could he say to Monica about her nephew? And what was to be done about Bede? Marcus was in an agony of horror. His solace was that Zoranda, Edward and the unknown Master were arriving tomorrow. The sooner they knew of Sturov's plans, the better.

He did not yet know what was unfolding back at the safari lodge.

Chapter 29

When Marcus slipped out on his mission to follow Bede, Joanna felt unexpectedly nervous. She sat in the lounge talking to another guest but she was aware that part of her was with her partner and the sangoma, out on a dark and possibly dangerous quest. She was sure that Sturov was involved in Bede's odd disappearance. It was a strange feeling and she found it hard to concentrate on what the elderly man was telling her.

Monica was behind the bar, serving drinks and talking far too much. Her voice was high and shrill and Joanna realised suddenly that she had been drinking. She knew that the woman rarely drank alcohol and it was going to her head. Was she trying to drown her fears about Bede? What did she think he was up to? Joanna's stomach churned with anxiety. She tried to put it out of her mind. She'd get a book and go to bed early.

But as she excused herself and rose, there was a sound of glass smashing and Monica held up her bleeding hand. 'Joanna!' she called, slurring slightly. 'Will you help me with this? Come to my room. I've got a bandage there.'

'Of course.' Joanna smiled falsely. There was nothing she wanted to do less. Monica motioned to their student helper to take over the bar and, with her hand wrapped in a bloodstained tissue, allowed Joanna to guide her across the garden to their bungalow.

Her husband was asleep. 'Peter always goes to bed early,' she explained, as Joanna washed the cut and bandaged the gash, not very expertly. Monica's hand was like a claw. She had never realised before how very thin she was.

'Have a drink?'

'No thanks. I was going to bed early. It'll be all right. Get a good night's sleep, Monica.'

'Joanna, I've got to talk to you.' Her voice sounded urgent and desperate and her hands were trembling as she poured another gin. 'I can't stand it any longer.' To the girl's consternation, the older woman's face crumpled and tears poured down her cheeks. 'It's too much to bear.' She started to rock. 'I've got to tell someone. He's out there tonight and he might be killed and he'll never know.'

'Bede?'

'Yes, of course, Bede.'

Joanna had a horrible feeling she did not want to hear what was about to be said. She put her hand on Monica's bony arm. 'Don't you think you should go to bed? You'll feel better in the morning.'

Monica pushed her hand away savagely. 'You don't understand.' Her voice had a touch of hysteria. 'No one understands. Bede's in danger and he's my son.'

'Your son!' Joanna tried to keep the astonishment out of her voice. 'Bede's your son?'

'Yes, and he's going to get hurt and I can't do anything

to help him.' Her breathing was ragged and a sob choked her. 'It's killing me. And I daren't tell him. It's all so terrible. What shall I do?'

Joanna shook her head.

Monica gulped her drink and poured another. Her body was trembling. 'Can I tell you what happened? I've got to talk to someone.'

'What about Peter?'

'No. He knows, of course, but we never mention it.'

'So your sister brought Bede up and he thinks you're his aunt?'

'Yes. I was only seventeen. In those days . . .' She raised her hands in a gesture of despair and helplessness. 'My father was a tyrant. I was terrified of him. We all were. Everyone thought he was genial and charming but if he'd ever found out he'd have killed me.'

'Your father didn't know about the baby?'

'No, you see it wasn't just a baby. It was a black baby. In those days . . .' Those helpless words again. 'When I was at school I fell in love with one of the trackers. He was gorgeous, big brown eyes, short curly hair and a wonderful body. He was funny too and he knew every-thing about the bush. I looked up to him, thought he was wonderful. I used to dream of him at night. Of course he was older and he had a wife and child. But they all do. They all have lots of women. It doesn't mean anything but I was different. I was special. He said so.' Her eyes were feverish, holding an anguish Joanna had never seen before.

The girl nodded, thinking, How naïve can you get.

Monica picked up the judgement instantly. 'You think I'm stupid. But he loved me. He really did. We made love whenever we could meet. That might have been foolish but it was magic.'

'And you became pregnant?'

'Well, no.' Bede's mother started shaking with sobs and could not speak, so Joanna sat awkwardly waiting. She put a hand of comfort on her emaciated shoulder and wondered if Edward knew. Then she asked herself why she felt so embarrassed. Perhaps it was the degree of raw emotion and pain emanating from the woman.

Monica blew her nose and continued, 'No. Not then. His wife found out and threatened to tell my father. Rocky would have lost his job and he couldn't do that. So he said he wouldn't see me again. Ever.' She sobbed again. 'Oh, Rocky! Rocky!' and banged her fists on her head, rocking and swaying as long-blocked teenage emotions burst out. 'I loved him. I've never stopped loving him.'

Joanna glanced nervously at the bedroom door, hoping Peter didn't wake and hear. But Monica, wallowing in the drunken luxury of murky emotions, continued to wail. 'I called Bede after him, Bede Richard, even though he wasn't his child.'

'Not his child,' Joanna repeated softly.

Monica finished her drink and looked as if she would rise to pour another but Joanna put a hand firmly on hers. 'You've had enough!' She wondered if she could get her to bed.

'It wasn't Rocky's child,' she repeated. 'No. You don't understand. I was distraught when he said it was over. I wanted to kill myself. I didn't want to live without him. His friend was nice to me. He tried to comfort me and, well . . .'

'You got pregnant?'

She nodded. 'It only happened once. I was terrified but you couldn't get an abortion in those days. I pretended to myself he was Rocky's baby, a love child, and that made it all right, but he wasn't.' She clenched and unclenched her fists in anguish. 'I had to tell my mother. She was devastated. Said she'd never trust me again. Called me a prostitute. It was dreadful. I wouldn't tell her whose child it was. She snooped around though and decided it was Rocky's. She got him sacked. Then she told my father she was taking me to England for my health. We went to stay with my sister Pauline and her husband, and my mother kept writing to my father that I wasn't well enough to come back yet. Pauline and Jack agreed to adopt him. They said they were worried for my sanity if he was taken away and my mother said, "Blood is blood." I had to let him go. They made me. My baby. My son. I always knew he'd come back one day. One day he'll know I'm his mother.'

'Yes, of course,' said Joanna soothingly.

'And my father never knew. Never knew Bede was my son and not hers. And we all swore we'd never tell anyone.'

'No one knew?' murmured the girl.

'No one. And my sister wouldn't talk about it. My mother told her not to. She said Bede was her child. But she had Edward. She had a son of her own.'

Monica's voice was rising hysterically again and Joanna offered to get her coffee, but then the mother remembered that Bede was in danger and was shaken by another paroxysm of fear and grief. It also reminded Joanna where Marcus was, but she steeled herself to forget. She focused on soothing her drunken companion, talking gently to her for some time and persuading her to drink water. At last Monica hiccupped a few times and her anguish diminished as alcohol blurred the edges of memory and pain.

Eventually, in order not to disturb Peter, Joanna persuaded Monica to lie on the sofa, covered her in blankets and held her hand until she fell asleep.

At last, very tired, she tiptoed out into the dark night and crossed the garden, thinking about Monica's heartbreak and the effect of over twenty years of buried pain. She wondered about Bede's reaction if he found out and sensed that it was more likely to be when he found out, unless his mother got some help. She also considered Edward's response when he discovered his adopted brother was his cousin, assuming he had not realised. Most of all she fervently hoped she would not be involved any further.

When she opened the door to her room she sat on the bed and thought about Marcus. The fear that she had put out of her mind over the last two hours surfaced. Horrible visions of him in danger or being hurt flashed into her mind. At last she took herself in hand. No, no, Joanna, she said to herself. This won't help him. She made a clear picture of him returning cheerful and well. 'Please come home soon,' she said aloud.

Chapter 30

This time Helen enjoyed the early morning taxi ride to the Giza plateau. Sitting in the back, with Zoranda and Tony, she had time to notice the minarets, hear the calls to prayers and watch beggars and traders about their business. She loved the clear-cut white buildings, the dusty palm trees that fronted them and the general air of spaciousness. As they rose up to the desert plateau, the sun perched like an orange ball on the horizon before it powered its way into the day. She had no idea that Zoranda had accompanied her specifically to protect her. He was concerned that the scar in her aura was not fully healed and hoped his presence would dissolve anything astral or physical that came towards her.

When Zoranda started on his own spiritual journey as a young man, his teacher, an earthy Yorkshireman, had told him that you can put constant protection round yourself but the only true safety is inner purity. What the man had actually said was, 'You can protect your home till the cows come home but, if you've got rotten meat in a room, rats will find a way to get in. If you don't want rats, mice or spiders in your house keep your cupboards clean and your corners dusted. And that applies to your inner, young man.'

On another occasion he had told his young disciple, 'If you're living a murky life, you ain't got a light and the forces of darkness aren't interested in you. But if you decide to be spiritual and your light grows, then you'll be bombarded. You'll be visible to the darkness and they'll make sure all your weakest areas are challenged as they try to stop your light from growing. Always remember moths flutter round a flame.' The youthful Zoranda had taken it all on board and assiduously examined his inner demons ever since. He discovered early in his mission that suppression only shoves things in cupboards to go bad, which lets in physical problems as well as psychic attack. So he endeavoured to examine himself and his attitudes daily. He also became aware that it is impossible to be one hundred per cent pure while inhabiting a human body. Everyone has fear, guilt, anger or something dark within them from this life or another and we come to Earth School to learn about it. That's why it is unwise to judge yourself or another.

The master in Zoranda knew that Helen had her human foibles as well as anyone. Yet her light was very bright and she was clearly visible to the forces who would like to stop her. He was only too aware that, because the awakening and enlightenment of many souls depended on the successful completion of her book, the forces of evil would do anything they could to stop her.

As the taxi mounted the plateau they could see the pyramids in a row, thrusting out of the grey desert, one of the miracles of the galaxy. The driver stopped in the car park while Helen and Tony stared at the huge, imposing edifices. Zoranda had indicated to them that they would not be going inside today. 'I know you'll want to experience the King's Chamber but if you don't mind you can come back on your own, while I'm in South Africa.' Helen was not too disappointed. She confessed to herself that she felt slightly nervous at the thought of going into the claustrophobic chamber, especially as she had heard plenty of strange stories from her friends.

She was wearing a large floppy hat, new sunglasses that hid her face and a big scarf over her bare arms. She did not want to be recognised by anyone who might have seen the television footage.

Together the three of them scrambled over the uneven, stony ground to a vantage point where, exposed to the blazing sun, they perched on an uncomfortable rock and examined the three vast pyramids in silence. At last Zoranda enquired, 'What do you feel? What impressions do you get?'

'I feel I'm connecting to the stars, as if I could enter another world,' replied Helen.

He smiled at her. 'And you, Tony?'

'Well, not quite so fanciful as Helen but it certainly feels surreal, and just a bit hot.' That was his attempt at a joke and they ignored it.

'Just take yourself back to ancient times,' the big man said. 'On top of the Great Pyramid was an enormous solar crystal which hovered above the pinnacle, suspended in the cosmic energies rising from it. It radiated such light that it lit up the entire area and was an unimaginably clear beacon.'

They were silent, contemplating such a concept.

Zoranda shaded his eyes and looked up at the great stone pile. 'Many things have been written about the pyramids and many of them are true but all are limited,' he told them. 'Yes, they were great storehouses of ancient Atlantean wisdom, placed here so that they would survive the fall of Atlantis and the flood. They were not tombs, though a Pharaoh was buried there. He ascended, which is why there is no trace of his body, only dust.'

'Isn't the ancient wisdom of Thoth Hermes meant to be in there?' asked Helen.

'Ancient Egyptian texts state that Thoth Hermes came to Earth to teach humanity. Then he rose again to the stars, going back to his home and leaving behind his teachings with their celestial secrets. These are the emerald tablets, the secret books of Thoth, which will some day be decoded and are said to be hidden within the Queen's Chamber.'

'Are they?'

Zoranda looked at her. 'I don't know.' And when Helen looked surprised, he laughed gently and reminded her that there were many things he did not know and many things that were not to be known while in a human body.

'So why were the pyramids built?' Tony asked curiously.

'They are ascension chambers and entry portals. The pyramid is a symbol of ascension. Let me explain. When the Sphinx and the pyramids were being built, the pyramids were lined up to the stars so that Pharaoh's body would ascend through the shaft. Because of his light and the great ceremonies and invocations around his death, he would also take the spirits of others with him. So spirits of the dead who were awaiting a return home would gather round the portal anticipating this impetus to propel them to their destination.'

'Where was their destination?' asked Tony, curious.

'From this portal it was Sirius or Orion. Imagine that the path to both of them intersects in the pyramid. It's also a two-way road, like a crossroads with traffic lights. At certain times the shafts are open for ascension and at other times for descension or perhaps it would be better to call it the reception of incoming souls. The pyramids are portals between the two planets.'

'Are there other ways for spirits to get home?' Helen wanted to know.

'Yes, there are other ways.'

'Do they only go back home when they ascend?'

'Oh no. Many religions and cultures talk about different levels of heaven and that's not what this is about. It is not about one person being better than another but being different from each other. They go back for more training or another task. It was just that when a Pharaoh ascended the energy was like a tidal wave, sweeping them back more quickly.'

'So what about incoming souls?'

'Souls to be born gather there waiting for a birth body. Incidentally a soul coming from Orion or Sirius attaches to the mother a moment before it is conceived. Souls from other places attach at different times.'

'That's interesting,' said Helen. 'I've often wondered about that.'

'So the beings from Orion and Sirius are very linked?'

'In some ways. As you know, their purpose, training and experience is quite different. Those who train in Sirius are cerebral people. They are thinkers and instigators, teaching us and alerting us to what is really happening in the world. Right now their higher purpose is to show people there is a better way than capitalism, while those who have trained in Orion before coming here are bringing enlightenment.'

'Am I right in thinking that the Egyptians didn't really rate Orion? All their literature seems to be about Sirius?'

'You are right, Tony. Sirius was the star whose rising formed the basis of their entire calendar, and Orion, who preceded it, was looked on as Sirius's advance man.'

'Strange,' said Helen.

'In later Atlantis a vast proportion of those in incarnation came from Sirius, which is why the technological advances were so awesome, but the spiritual light went out. Now there are balanced numbers incarnating from Sirius and from Orion.'

'And other planets, surely?'

'From many places in this universe and others. Many people who appear brain-damaged or physically impaired are totally perfect in spiritual terms. All are experiencing this plane in the way they need to.'

'Thank goodness the crystal and indigo children are coming in now to bring enlightenment. Joanna told us that they came from Orion,' said Helen.

'Indeed,' nodded Zoranda and Helen got the impression once more that he knew so much more than he ever revealed.

The taxi driver drove them down to the Sphinx and here Helen felt more nervous of being recognised. But she need not have worried. No one took a second glance at the middle-aged holiday maker with her husband and friend as they approached the sacred statue with its watchful eyes. At last they walked through the temple by the statue and stood looking across the gap at the great animal aloft on its plinth.

'The Sphinx used to be painted red,' Zoranda told them quietly.

'Red!' Helen was startled.

'That was a colour beloved of the people in the early times.'

'When was it built?'

Zoranda hesitated briefly. 'It has always been there but was not visible to man until the twelfth century BC, that is fourteen thousand years ago.'

Helen wished he would not always talk in riddles but, when she contemplated them, the meaning of his words often became clear.

'So it was painted red?' prompted Tony. 'That seems an odd colour for a statue.'

'Remember it was the guardian of the planet and had sacred warrior energy. Also it was built at the start of the Leonine Age which was to bring out the qualities of courage, beauty and love. The Sphinx when it had one hundred per cent of its power sent out such pure and powerful light that it stopped invaders as they approached.' He paused as if considering whether to continue. When he spoke again his voice seemed deeper. 'You may be aware that on Mars there are sites which exactly match the pyramids, the Sphinx, and many other sacred places such as Avebury, Stonehenge, Silbury Hill and Glastonbury Tor?'

Helen said she thought she had heard that somewhere. 'Isn't the face on Mars really the Sphinx?'

'Indeed.'

'So who built them on Mars?' asked Tony.

'First let me say this. Just as there are aliens who want to help our planet, there are also aggressors. The main aggressors are the Annanuki. They feed on our minerals and also on our lower astral energy. The more fear they can engender, the more they can suck our energy to feed themselves. People like Sturov serve the Annanuki, which is why he has such power. They feed his vanity and he stirs up food for them.'

'That's horrible.' Helen shuddered.

'It is,' agreed Zoranda. 'It was the Annunuki who designed the city on Mars and the replica sites. The work itself was done by many galactic tribes.'

'Surely Avebury, Stonehenge and the other portals weren't built by dark aliens?' Helen looked pale as she asked the question. 'I've always felt they were wonderful places.'

Zoranda agreed. 'They are! The sacred sites on Earth were built by the good for the good. They were created by extraterrestrials working for light. Later they were mirrored by the Evil Ones on Mars as a means of access to damage the Earth. This is still going on and it can be prevented by the portals being used as was originally intended.'

Helen felt shaken. 'Are people from Mars incarnated now?' she wanted to know.

'A lot of the aggressors in the world today have a link with Mars and are shark people. Sharks and shark people are from Mars and many were incarnated in Atlantis. Warmongers are direct descendants or relatives of direct descendants of Mars shark people.'

Helen wished she had never asked the question and wanted to change the subject. She was particularly fond of Avebury, the great stone circle in the West Country, so she asked about the road that had been built through it.

Zoranda sighed. 'The road has damaged its energy. The decision to build it through the sacred site was influenced by the Annunuki, who worked through ones such as Sturov. The circle was originally formed so that each stone in the circle generated its energy to every other stone in the circle. The road has chopped the power of the circle in two, sheering its influence.'

'Does Avebury connect to a particular star?' asked Helen.

Zoranda smiled indulgently at the way she loved to know the details. 'In the galactic web the power of Avebury is attuned to Mercury,' he responded.

'What was its original purpose?'

'There are two different energies. The southern circle is a reception area for space ships from everywhere. It is a welcome port. The other half is now dormant and needs energy. Its purpose is liberation, to free man's ability to communicate. But broken as it is, it is stifling our possibility of true connection.'

'Can we do anything to help?'

'Visualise the circle whole and tell everyone to do this.'

They nodded.

Helen said, 'I had a special feeling at Bradbury Ring, in Dorset. Is that a portal?'

'Oh yes. It is a portal for healers from Neptune. They heal the spirit. If you feel in low spirits it is a good place to go.'

'Right!'

'We've got completely off the subject of Mars,' Tony reminded them.

Zoranda agreed. 'The Martians, the shark people, control the intergalactic army and Mars was a highly respected warrior training school. Their higher purpose was to be commanders, warriors for the truth and protectors of the galaxy. But when beings from Mars went bad, they became aggressive, controlling and acquisitive.

'When Mars eventually imploded because of massive negativity, it could no longer protect Earth. That's when the Annunuki took advantage and built the city and other monuments to mirror our sacred sites. They could then beam a discordant frequency into our power points. It has contributed considerably to the lowering of the vibration of Earth.'

Helen and Tony were staring at him open-mouthed. 'That's terrible,' mouthed Helen.

'Worrying,' added Tony. And they were all lost in thought for a few minutes, gazing at the Sphinx.

'So the best thing we can do is to keep visualising the sacred sites clear and light again.'

'Exactly how does the Sphinx store the akashic records?' Even though she was wearing a large hat and sunglasses Helen was screwing up her face against the sun.

'Remind me,' said Tony patiently. 'What are the akashic records?'

'The records of everything that has ever happened to anyone and anything on Earth,' said Helen promptly.

'Yes,' said Zoranda. 'The Sphinx contains the Hall of Records, the akash. They are under, in and through the Sphinx. They are not physical but they can be read by people with the gift. They can be read as though in a library. Therefore *man* has called them the Hall of Records. The Pharaohs called it that because they could read it and,' he added softly, 'when we return to purity and Atlantis rises again everyone will be able to access it. Then all will be transparent and no one will be able to hide anything or keep any secrets. The white lion has incarnated in order to open hearts and accelerate this process, for only closed hearts keep secrets.'

They all continued to stare at the enigmatic statue, containing so much knowledge. Zoranda said, 'Under it is an initiation chamber and the pyramids were used for initiation ceremonies.' He added, 'When you write your book, Helen, I want you to include the connection between Atlantis, the Sphinx and the dolphins. Very soon you will have a bigger picture to describe to people.'

'Wow!' she breathed and her spine tingled in anticipation. 'There's so much to discover.'

'More than you have any idea of yet,' Zoranda assured her and Helen felt as if she were floating in joy. Life was exciting, interesting and there was more to come.

Zoranda excused himself as he saw one of the brothers from the Great White Lodge arrive to take him to an appointment. He felt he could safely leave Helen now as she would be returning to the safety of the lodge in a few minutes. Unfortunately the powers of evil grasped those few minutes to deal a blow.

Before they left, Tony and Helen wandered round the stalls, holding hands and feeling like honeymooners. As Helen was deciding whether to purchase an onyx statue of the Sphinx or another crystal pyramid, the mind of an empty-headed youth was taken over by the force of darkness. Quite oblivious that he was being used as an agent of Sturov, he hurtled into Helen and sent her flying. She landed on her shoulder and an agonising, sickening, all-consuming pain rushed through it. Tony helped her up. One look at her white, drawn face told him it was serious.

'Do you think it's broken?' he asked her gravely.

'I don't know,' she replied, holding her shoulder and fighting an overwhelming desire to cry. 'If it is, what about the book! How will I write it? Oh no. Why now? Now just as the white lion is to be born! What am I going to do?'

Chapter 31

The three wise men, representing the light, arrived at the safari lodge that afternoon: the Master, who Marcus and Joanna had never met but instantly respected; Zoranda, who they had admired for many years; and Edward, who they knew and liked as a friend. All three were pulsing and shimmering with energy in anticipation of the birth of the white cub. Yet Marcus sensed an underlying apprehension as if they knew of the evil afoot. Nevertheless the presence of the great ones lit Joanna and Marcus up and filled them with excitement. Tomorrow! The cub would be born tomorrow! They could hardly wait.

The trio were able to reassure Joanna that her mother's shoulder was not broken. 'But it's very badly bruised and she's having to rest for a while. She can't write at the moment,' Zoranda told her.

'Oh, poor Mum! She'll hate that. Just when she was stuck into collating notes and getting her ideas together for the book.'

'She's taken it pretty philosophically. Better than I expected. And Tony has been really supportive. We left them sitting at the table with her giving instructions and him sorting her notes out!'

They laughed and Joanna had a vivid picture of her

mother, desperately frustrated and trying to be sweet and patient. 'Oh, I shouldn't laugh. It's so awful. Just when everything was going so well for her.' She remembered that moment which seemed so long ago when she caught a leaf and thought things were going too well. Her life had instantly changed. 'Why did it have to happen to Mum now?' she groaned.

'I suspect she was slightly ungrounded as she was so excited. That's when accidents happen,' replied Zoranda sympathetically, refraining to mention the rent in her aura which had needed more time to heal and which had allowed entry to a violent force.

Edward said, 'It will serve her highest good, I am sure. Everything, however horrible, ultimately serves us.'

'You're right, Edward. The dark always serves the light so some good will come out of it, even if it only forces her to rest.'

'I wonder if one of the hidden reasons could be to enable Tony to co-operate more with her work on the book?' Joanna wondered aloud. 'If he has to help her, it will bring them together.'

'I think you're right,' Marcus agreed. 'And your mum is so special, she'll make the best of it.'

'I know,' agreed his girlfriend with a smile. She liked the mutual respect and affection that had grown between her mother and Marcus. 'I just wish I was there to help her.'

Edward added, 'She was tracing the map of Africa every day, drawing the gold line of enlightenment down it and placing the crystals on the sacred power points.

Now she can't do that so they've laid it out and she and Tony are visualising the web of light being healed there. She is sure the angels are working with them.'

Joanna was pleased. Her mother had a special connection with angels, so she was sure a healing was taking place. She must remember to put the crystals on a map of Africa and do her part, she thought. The more people who did this, the sooner the web of light would be repaired and the world would be a better place.

As she saw Monica appear with a tray of cold drinks, she thanked the three men again and Marcus arranged to meet them in the lounge when they had showered and unpacked.

As soon as the newcomers joined him and Joanna in the lounge, Marcus told them of the events of the night before at the Black Rhino Lodge. They listened with grim attention to Sturov's plans. Marcus felt terrible as he related the details of Bede's complicity, for Edward went ashen as he realised his brother's perfidy. When he had finished they all prayed for the protection of the cub when it was born. Then the Master and Zoranda left them, presumably to discuss the situation.

Joanna went off to find her book, though she was so filled with excitement and dread that she could not concentrate. That left Edward alone with Marcus. Bede's brother looked directly into Marcus's eyes, a gaze the latter would not quickly forget. 'At Uluru you were given the gift of looking into people's souls. Have you done that with Bede?' he questioned.

Marcus confessed that he had not. 'I don't really do it very often. I don't think about it,' he justified himself apologetically.

'Do you think it would be appropriate now?' Edward suggested quietly and totally without judgement.

Marcus nodded, thinking how much his friend had changed and evolved since he last saw him. He closed his eyes and asked for permission to look into Bede's soul. Permission was granted, for immediately he saw a corridor of doors and on twelve doors were written the word, 'Betrayal'. He could see that in four lives Bede had been betrayed and in eight he had betrayed someone or a cause. There was a wall of pain, hurt, guilt and darkness in his soul, which was surfacing to be expressed. Marcus also saw a chasm of abandonment. He was shown incarnations when Bede had been abandoned or felt alone, leaving his heart filled with unexpressed rage and grief.

Marcus told Edward what he had seen and the latter replied thoughtfully, 'We have a choice. He is an instrument of the dark forces. We can either make sure he can do no more damage by psychically imprisoning him, which will reinforce and activate his feelings of isolation, anger and abandonment. Or we can shine light into his soul so that he no longer wants to do harm. Then we would have to trust that together we can make him feel belonging.'

'You're so wise, Edward,' said Marcus. 'Do you believe we can put enough light into him to change his soul journey?'

'Probably not on our own. If it were that easy, light-workers would have healed the souls of all dark people long ago. But I imagine a being so pure that it has been chosen to carry the cosmic Christ energy could do so.'

'The white lion!' Marcus suddenly felt really hopeful. 'Let's keep holding your brother in the light and trust that the energy the cub brings in can help him.' A thrill tingled through him from head to toe. 'The cub will be born tomorrow.'

The following evening as usual Bede was driving the safari vehicle. There was a palpable air of excitement as the party set off into the extraordinary pink sunset, which was rapidly becoming grey as night fell. The only movement was a pair of storks flapping belatedly home. Other than that everything seemed to be wrapped in a cocoon of silent anticipation.

Drake was in his customary position as lookout. Behind him sat Zoranda, the Master and Edward and in the row of seats at the back were Marcus, Joanna and Monica. As they reached the road a figure stood waiting, still as a statue. It was the lion shaman. He did not indicate that he wanted a lift but they stopped and he climbed in beside Bede.

The comet was bright in the sky and seemed to stand still over the Timbavati. Tonight was the night. They all believed that the white lion cub had been born and they would find it. The sangoma with his unerring instinct indicated the direction with a movement of his hand and they wound and twisted through the bush.

Marcus looked at Bede's big hands on the wheel. They were quite firm. He seemed composed, though his jaw was tense. No one had mentioned last night. Nor had there been anything in his words or manner to indicate where he had been and with whom. What can be going on in his mind? wondered Marcus. Then he remembered the conversation he had earlier with Edward and made a conscious effort to visualise love and light pouring into Bede.

Joanna's heart was thumping as if it would burst. She peered in all directions at tall, dry grass and grey trees. At each twist and turn she was sure they would come across the pride of lions. She prayed with all her might that they would find them. And suddenly there they were. Three lionesses with seven cubs and one was pure white. He sat between his mother's paws, eyes open, watching them, his little rounded ears pricked.

Bede turned the engine off and they all stared. Everything went silent. The cicadas had stopped whining. The birds were still. Not a leaf rustled. Even the elephants seemed to have stopped their forage for food. And they noticed animals who never went near lions sitting quietly in the long grass, waiting.

The little white fluffy animal scrambled on tottery legs to root for his mother's teat and for a moment seemed like any new-born babe. When he had taken his fill, he lay on his back, paws in the air and rolled in ecstasy. Then he looked up at them and light shone from his eyes. Joanna received a message loud and clear into her third eye. 'Love loves itself.' She realised instantly that the little creature knew he was divine and all new-born babies still know they are divine. Love is one with God. Because it is not separate from anyone it can never hurt another, for it would be harming itself. Then she realised that love is able to respond to the needs of all creation, to the needs of plants and animals and everything, including itself.

She had barely digested this when another impulse burst into her mind. 'Love has many faces.' The words came to her: 'Love can be in the compassion of the mother as well as in the discipline of the father. It can be in the devotion of a lover or carer. It can be in the action of death, where one dies to set their family free. Love is selfless intention. Never judge another, for you may judge a face of love.'

Joanna absorbed the messages in silence. She did not know how long they remained there. She sent thanks to the universe, to the powers-that-be and most of all to the white lion cub for being born and for letting them see him. She had no doubt that they had a divine dispensation to be there at that moment.

She tried to send telepathic messages to the lioness. 'Leave the Timbavati. Go now. Your cub is in danger. Please leave as soon as you can. Bad men are coming to hurt your cub. Please go.' She felt exhausted with the effort of sending such an intense message so repeatedly. Then she realised that the mother cat chosen for the task of birthing this special infant probably knew already and she relaxed. She had done what she could. A soft warm feeling entered her heart and she felt enfolded in peace.

As she drank in the tableau in front of her she was aware of a white glow around the scene.

Edward, Zoranda and the Master had travelled a long way to pay their respects and bring the homage of the Great Brotherhoods of Light. The Master had seen many awesome sights in his life but the pure white light, which radiated in all directions from the tiny creature in front of him, was the most ineffable of all. Edward and Zoranda too, both spiritually and psychically open, were aware of the bright light emanating from the cub, bathing them and the entire area in its radiance. They sat quietly offering gratitude to the powers-that-be.

As the lion shaman became aware of the purity of the light pouring through the tiny animal, he felt as if his heart were pierced with a dagger of joy. This was beyond his wildest imaginings. Tears fell down his cheeks as he saluted the innocent creature and received a blessing in return.

The others saw nothing other than a small fluffy white lion with a beautiful expression on his face. They were nevertheless unconsciously touched by his essence.

It is not possible to be within the aura of a Christed being without your soul being influenced. When they arrived home again at the lodge they sat without speaking, looking at the stars, lost in gratitude, love and awe. Bede was happier than Marcus had ever seen him. His eyes were shining and he was smiling, as if he had abandoned all his defences. He even sang them an African song. It was only later when a lion roared in the distance that he suddenly frowned. His face set in tense lines and he scowled and disappeared without a word. Marcus and Edward watched him in surprise and disquiet.

Before they went to bed Edward asked Marcus to look once more into Bede's soul. He and Joanna sat on the end of their bed as Marcus closed his eyes. This time he saw that a pink light was pouring out of all but one of the doors marked 'Betrayal'. That one remained closed and locked. And the chasm of abandonment was filled with gold light. Just one hard black rock sat under the surface. Just one.

'What a difference,' he commented to Edward. 'It's as if Bede is a different soul.'

'Good. Let's hope the white lion cub grows up to spread that light to people throughout Africa.'

But, remembering that Bede still had a closed door and a stone locked in his soul, Marcus remained wary of him, which proved just as well.

At the other end of the hotel the Master, Zoranda and Edward met in the Master's chalet. They felt deep disquiet, for they could feel waves of evil being directed towards the cub by Sturov and the dark forces. They lit candles and invoked extra protection for the lion cub. Then they extended their auras to surround it. Satisfied at last that it would be safe that night, they retired.

It was too hot to sleep and Joanna and Marcus were much too excited to settle down. They discussed the white cub and his extraordinary messages for a long time. After a sticky, restless couple of hours Joanna announced she was going to get up and run a cool bath. 'Good idea. I'll join you,' agreed Marcus and they crawled out from the mosquito netting, which made the bed even more stifling. Marcus found his magna light and set it on the bathroom floor. The bath, old-fashioned and capacious, was set on a plinth, so you had to climb up steps to reach it. For a long time they luxuriated in the cool water and talked in low voices.

Suddenly they were alerted by a shuffling sound, followed by a strange roar. At the same instant Joanna smelled it. 'Fire!' she shouted, jumping up in panic. She grabbed a towel as smoke poured into the bathroom. Marcus smashed the window and pushed her out. It took seconds. They ran. Moments later a huge ball of orange and blue flames exploded and engulfed their chalet. Then the glowing tongues were licking the next one.

'Fire,' screamed Joanna unnecessarily, for already panic-stricken figures were emerging from the chalets and running in all directions, coughing in the acrid smoke. The babble of sound, screams and shouts were muted by the roar of the flames.

In the midst of the chaos Bede had appeared and was organising a chain of buckets. Drake was dousing the rapidly spreading fire with an inadequate hose. 'It could run through the whole area. It's tinder dry,' snapped Peter, who had joined the mêlée.

'Lucky there's no wind!' Marcus shouted back. 'The fire's moving away from the main buildings.'

Monica, looking distraught, was wringing her hands and giving orders. 'Make sure all the guests are up. Be ready to evacuate the servants if the fire moves towards the village,' she shouted to her husband. 'This is our worst nightmare,' she screamed to Marcus and her voice was staccato and shrill. 'It's just what they were saying would happen when the white lion was born.' Even as she spoke an entire chalet exploded loudly in flames while they grabbed buckets of water and passed them down the chain.

Someone had given Joanna a T-shirt and shorts, for their chalet was a charred ruin, while Marcus had tied his towel firmly round his waist. They could feel the heat on their faces. 'Talk to the salamanders,' shouted Joanna to her partner and he nodded, trying in vain to tune into the elementals in the midst of the chaos and shock.

In the flickering orange glow, he could see Zoranda, the Master and Edward, who had been sleeping at the far end of the hotel, hurrying towards the fire. The shaman emerged from the shadows and crossed over to the trio. All four consulted briefly. Then the three Magi clustered together and Marcus could sense that they were making an invocation. He had never seen such intense concentration emanate from them before. The shaman moved some distance away and started to dance wildly, uttering shrieks and calls into the night. Their focus was identical, their method very different.

Then something surreal and extraordinary happened. Within minutes a glowering black cloud formed above them, blotting out the stars. Big, sharp raindrops started to fall. Seconds later the heavens opened and a deluge, like a bucket of water pouring over them, extinguished the fire.

People were saying that the fire was caused by the birth of the lion and it was a bad omen. They were milling round cursing the cub. At the same time everyone knew that the magical rain was spirit intervention, especially as it had fallen only over the area of the fire. It was freaky.

Bede was gabbling about the pure white lion cub, so wondrous that it caused animals to lose their fear and approach it. Confusion and gossip, like intertwined snakes, contorted everyone's perception and allowed rumour to run riot.

But Joanna and Marcus knew that the fire had been started deliberately. They had been targeted and they were lucky to be alive. Joanna felt as if she were shrinking in her skin, faint and sick as she stared at their burned-out chalet. 'Who did it?' she asked Marcus and Edward. 'And how did it start?'

Monica's voice shrilled, 'They're saying it was started deliberately. But why would anyone do such a thing?' She was walking towards them.

'Someone tried to kill us.' Marcus's voice sounded harsh.

'Maybe he wanted people to believe the birth of the white cub would bring trouble!'

'But it's crazy. Who'd want that?'

Monica stopped in her tracks and looked at them, her eyes wide with horror as she picked up their instant thoughts. 'Bede! No!' she exclaimed and, turning, hurried away.

'She's right,' said Marcus, not wanting to believe it. 'Surely it wasn't Bede? He's Edward's brother. He's been telling everyone about the wonder of the white lion cub.' But he felt heavy and sick with doubt.

It took the rest of the night to clear up the mess and find beds for those whose chalets had gone up in the blaze. Thankfully no one was hurt but nothing could douse the strange feeling in the air. Joanna felt as if she were in some sort of dream. 'How did they get through our psychic protection?' she asked Edward.

He was pale too. The suspicions about his brother, which had been voiced, concerned him too deeply to allow him to be detached. He touched her arm gently. 'I suspect we were all focusing our energy and power on sending protection to the cub.'

Joanna nodded. 'I forgot to put my protection up last night. I just concentrated on the lion. Oh, I'm so stupid.'

'No. It's natural. But it is important to remember yourself,' replied Edward. 'And you were looked after. Something made you get up in the night and have a bath. If you'd been in bed, it would have been a different story.'

A long shudder ripped through Joanna's body, starting in her stomach and blocking her throat.

Edward was concerned about her. 'Are you all right, Joanna?'

'Not really but I'll be okay. Marcus is fetching me some water. You go to bed. You look done in too.'

Edward was thankful. He felt exhausted. And he did not want to talk about Bede. He could not face the suspicions that were creeping into his mind. Not yet anyway.

Later that night, as they lay, sleep still eluding them, in a different bed, Marcus said to Joanna, 'Maybe Sturov paid Bede to start the fire and, having taken the money, he had to do it.'

'You could be right. Sturov would want to create maximum confusion and doubt. That's what darkness feeds on. He must have had some hold on him.'

Neither of them paused to wonder why they were trying to find excuses for Bede, who, they were certain, had just tried to kill them. But it's a defence mechanism to try to rationalise chaos. It's a way of controlling the fear.

'It couldn't have been an accident, could it? The gas light falling over or something?'

'No, it wasn't on. That's why I turned on the torch.'

Joanna sighed.

'No,' Marcus told her grimly. 'Petrol was deliberately spilled to start the fire. Though with everything as dry as a tinderbox, it didn't need anything much to get it going.'

Joanna shivered. In the vastness of Africa she felt very vulnerable.

Marcus put an arm round her. 'Jo, we've got to think clearly. In a few hours the cull starts and there's nothing more we can do, so let's send out light for the protection of the cubs, especially the white one.'

'And we'll put protection round ourselves, this time,' she added. 'Remember, love loves itself!'

So in the dark before dawn, they sat on the bed and asked the universe to protect the baby white lion and themselves. Tomorrow it might all be over.

Chapter 32

In the morning a smell of smoke, muddy earth and fear hung over the lodge. The blackened area behind the hotel was a sobering sight, a reminder of human powerlessness against the elements. People for miles around had seen the fire and all night the phone had been ringing. Monica was sharp, strung up with adrenaline and bore hollow rings of exhaustion round her eyes. There was a feeling of menace in the air and the animals everywhere seemed more nervous than usual. Yet underlying the fear there was an extraordinary buzz, for the birth of the white lion cub was being hailed with wonder and the timely and strategic rainstorm as a miracle.

All the trackers in the area had been brought in to take part in the shoot and Bede, of course, was among them. There would be no safaris later that day as those licensed to kill would be sweeping through the area with their rifles. No one understood the order from the authorities and there was a general sense that it was wrong, especially as the rumour was circulating that the holder of the licence to cull intended to target the white cub. Feelings were running high, some for and some against.

Bede told Marcus that he would try to protect the white lion but he could not meet his eyes. Joanna overheard him telling other trackers that the white lion cub was special and they should shoot to miss. All the same she felt sick with apprehension. Icy shivers ran down her back as they stood in the dark, cold early morning watching the safari vehicles roar off to meet those from other game lodges. Surely the powers of the universe would not let them snuff out the emissary of light? But she knew that this was a decision of man not spirit.

After breakfast she and Marcus lay on a chaise-longue under an umbrella trying to read but they couldn't concentrate. One or other of them was constantly getting up to find out if there was any news. Edward, Zoranda and the Master sat in the lounge, quietly talking. Though they did not appear concerned, they were good at keeping their feelings under control. It was a very long morning.

At eleven o'clock they heard the sound of engines as the safari vehicles returned. Instantly they were running towards the reception area and out to the drive. Drake, on the lookout seat, held up a fist jubilantly when he saw them. He was grinning broadly. Bede too was laughing manically as if a weight was off his shoulders. 'We couldn't find him,' he shouted. He told them that two cubs of one lioness had been shot. One of them had a deformed paw and would have died anyway. Apart from these the entire area seemed devoid of lions and there had been no sign of the white cub.

'Must all have gone over the border,' announced Drake with evident satisfaction. 'It's as if they knew.'

Marcus and Joanna silently sent up a prayer for the soul

of the dead cubs and a thousand prayers of gratitude for the deliverance of the white cub.

Joanna felt the vice-like tension draining from her whole body. 'It's like the end of something big,' she said to the shaman.

He laughed, flashing his white teeth. 'It's only the beginning. You mark my words, there's more yet. A great deal more.'

In the late afternoon Joanna and Marcus, accompanied by the three guests from Egypt, explored the bush. Drake drove with a new tracker on the lookout, for Bede had not turned up, to Joanna's relief. It was magic as usual to see the wildlife. A kudu bull watched them from a clearing before he ran away, giraffes, zebras, buffalo and every variety of monkey and deer decided to show themselves to the guests. Joanna had a strange feeling that this was connected to the birth of the white lion cub. Were they thanking them for trying to help?

Before night fell they drove directly to the quartz hill where they had laid out the symbol a few short days ago. They could see it was intact and spoors showed that three young lions had been lying in the centre of the symbol. They took this as a sign and Marcus could not contain his delight. He kept repeating, 'That's amazing.' The Master invited the two trackers to join them in a short ceremony within the symbol and they agreed somewhat bashfully. As they chanted, walked round the circle clockwise to wind up the energy and invoked the light of the universe, the shadows deepened and the stars above blazed. When the ritual was finished, they sat on some of the big crystals within the circle. Marcus had trodden in some lion dung and he laughed as he wiped his shoe. 'Perhaps they came into the symbol to say it is possible now to heal Africa.'

'And its connections with the galaxies,' added Zoranda, craning his neck to see the whole sweep of stars.

'There's Orion's belt,' said Edward, pointing.

'And Sirius,' indicated Zoranda, stretching his arm out towards the bright star.

'There's the Pleiades.'

'I wonder what they have to tell us?' asked Marcus.

'More than we have any concept of while in a human body,' Zoranda reminded him.

'All the same,' Joanna persisted. 'If the portals were open during Atlantis and the initiates were in contact with the galactic Masters, we must still be connected even though we don't realise it.'

'True,' agreed the Master, and they all drew closer, sensing he was about to tell them something important. He began slowly, 'As you know everything is a microcosm of a macrocosm. Most people realise when they look at the night sky that there is something important and beyond comprehension out in the vastness. In the early times of Atlantis when the energy was pure, the gateways were indeed open to the galaxies beyond. At that time there were twelve portals, each linking to a star system or galaxy. When Atlantis fell, twelve soul groups departed to places prepared for them in advance and each group took with them the esoteric secrets of one of these connections. They each held part of the great wisdom of the early times.'

'The lion shaman also told us there were twelve tribes who left Atlantis with the secrets,' put in Joanna.

'Good! I gather he explained to you how the Dogon people still keep the gateway to Sirius open for everyone on Earth?'

They nodded and Marcus added, 'He said they are enlightened ones who are dedicated to their task and also that they are fish people.'

'Yes, they are,' confirmed Zoranda.

'The lions guard the gateway to Orion,' the Master told them. They looked surprised and he added, 'You see we humans tend to think we are the only enlightened beings who inhabit this planet. That is far from the case.'

'Is that why the white lion was chosen to carry the flame of enlightenment right now?' asked Drake, the first time he had spoken.

'He is one of the few beings pure enough to contain the light of the cosmic Christ within his energy system,' agreed the Master, nodding.

'You mentioned the twelve soul groups. You don't include the lions in that, do you?'

'No. The cat people from Orion are scattered wherever enlightenment is needed.'

'So where did the twelve soul groups go that left Atlantis?' Joanna persisted. 'I know they were Mayan and Aztec and Inca, but who else?'

'I guess some Native American tribes hold the knowledge, and Tibetans,' ventured Marcus.

'Egypt of course,' said Edward.

'Oh, yes and what about the Kahunas?'

The Master smiled. 'Yes. Any more?'

'What about China and Japan?'

He shook his head. 'No, the other groups originally went to Babylonia, Greece, Mesopotamia and two more.' He paused to remember which of the twelve ancient races he had missed.

'Maori and Innuit,' supplied Zoranda.

'That's it. Thank you.' He continued, 'We have already mentioned the Dogons, who travelled from Atlantis to Egypt and then down to West Africa, bringing their connection to Sirius with them, so that they could keep it open, active and growing. Other people and tribes from different planets are doing similar work and have moved and spread round the world. Look at the Druids and the way they look after the portals and stone circles in the magical mystical lands of Wales and Cornwall and elsewhere in Europe.

'At present there are seven of these soul groups that operate within human understanding. Our world is as it is because of these seven. We are told that in future another five cultures will bring in information.' He paused while they digested this information before he addressed Marcus and Joanna directly: 'Of course, the dolphins hold the key to the whole jigsaw.'

They stared at each other, rendered unusually speechless, so that Edward was able to ask, 'What about the Pleiades? Every ancient culture talks about visits from the Pleiadeans or a connection with them.'

The Master responded, 'During Atlantis the Pleiadeans taught the initiates about navigation.' He noticed that they looked surprised. 'Take yourself back to a time before people knew how to navigate. Introduce the principles of navigation and see how the world has changed. That is what the Pleiadeans brought down for Atlantis and the world.'

'So they taught them about the movement of the stars and the way the Earth moves?' queried Marcus.

'Exactly and much more. About the movement of tides, the wind, the effect of the moon. They opened the world up for the Atlanteans and taught them many of the mysteries of the cosmos.'

'And the Greeks keep the link open to the Pleiades?' checked Edward.

'The esoteric branches of the Greek culture do that,' agreed the Master. 'Let me clarify this. In Atlantean times all portals were open and the priests and high priests had access to the wisdom of the universe. Since then each enlightened culture or esoteric branch of a religion has kept the portals to a particular galaxy open and is holder of that specific sacred information. None will have all. It is a jigsaw and anyone who thinks they can get eleven pieces and guesses the twelfth will get it wrong. Many have done this and caused chaos on Earth.'

He looked at Marcus and Joanna again. 'Soon you will meet the angel dolphins, the beings who hold the key to all the information.'

'Angel dolphins!' Joanna almost screeched. 'We're going to swim with them at Christmas!'

Zoranda continued, ignoring her, 'In Egypt Helen will also access the key. Together you can unlock something important for the enlightenment of humanity. The white lion has incarnated now in order to enable this to happen. He is the catalyst that will send enough light into the web of light to reactivate the portals and enable ancient wisdom to be released.'

There was a long, deep silence, broken by the hoot of an African owl and a strange howl in the darkness.

Then Zoranda spoke again and a thrill ran through Joanna's body as she realised he was about to reveal something tremendously important.

Chapter 33

Zoranda looked at Edward, Marcus and Joanna in turn, appraising their readiness to receive the information he was about to impart. 'I want to talk to you about another link in the web of light. Those who illuminate the web from the seventh heaven. The unicorns.'

'Unicorns!' Joanna could not keep back the exclamation of surprise and delight.

'As you may be aware the angelic forces are gathering around our planet now to help with our ascension?'

They nodded, breathlessly awaiting his next words.

'The unicorns are from heaven. They are seventh-dimensional beings and of the angelic kingdom, just as angel dolphins are. They are part of the web of light round our planet.' He paused as he often did when he was gathering his thoughts. 'They are now approaching people who are ready to carry their pure light.'

Joanna fervently hoped one would come to her but she did not know if she was truly ready. Zoranda smiled and she flushed, knowing he had picked up her thought.

Then he continued, 'Their purpose is to trigger the innocence of the divine self, that essence we had the moment we became a divine spark.'

'Trigger our true essence!' Joanna's eyes were shining.

Zoranda nodded. 'They embrace the qualities of purity, magic, healing and grace and have come to teach us dignity, pride in ourselves, self-worth and honour.'

'How do they do that?' asked Marcus, curious about these mythical creatures. He wondered if they were incarnate in Atlantis.

'Let's start at the beginning. Horses come from one of the stars of Sirius, called Lakuma, which has ascended.'

'And a unicorn is a horse that has ascended? Of course it is.' Joanna answered her own question.

'Yes. All horses originate from Lakuma. Because the planet's ascended frequency is beyond our range of accessibility, we can't see it. Horses incarnate on Earth to learn and teach just as humans do. They reincarnate progressively to learn the lessons of this planet until they become white horses. Then they earn the opportunity to ascend into the seventh heaven and become unicorns.'

'Do they ever come back in physical form? I thought angels never had a body?' Joanna wanted to know.

'Angels never take a body, at least only occasionally as an angel dolphin. It may be deemed necessary soon for some unicorns to incarnate. They will live as pure white horses, in a body of flesh, with an incredible dignity and light. People will sense it and respond to them with honour, kindness and grace. Humans haven't treated horses well but in some ways that has accelerated their ascension because they faced their challenges with love. You see they come to Earth to see if they can maintain the qualities of dignity, courage and self-worth in the face of the unkindness of humanity. Earth still bears karma, of course.'

His listeners nodded, thinking of the way animals were ill treated and meat was considered as a commodity not a sacred gift.

'Unicorns are of the element air and their connection with incarnated horses helps them to link to Earth. We must remember that every time someone sends love to a horse it helps that animal's journey to ascension. Being unkind to a horse or any creature holds the whole species back.'

'Do the unicorns go to planets other than ours?' Marcus enquired.

'They do work with other planets round Sirius but at present their concentration is on Earth because of the incredible changes taking place here. I said they symbolise hope. Why do you think so many girls love horses? It is the young feminine energy linking into hope.'

Edward spoke for the first time since unicorns were mentioned. 'So white horses symbolise purity and preparation for ascension, just as the white lion and other white animals do?'

'Yes.'

'And the unicorn's horn?'

'The horn from its third eye is an energy just as angels' wings are. It is like a laser and beams pure light into people and situations. You may think of it as a magic wand.'

'How do people who can't see or sense unicorns connect to them?' Marcus asked and Joanna smiled at his typically pragmatic question.

'When you think of unicorns look for a star in the heavenly sky and one will twinkle and speak to you. That will be a unicorn connection. Or think of a stream of light with stars shimmering through it and you will have a link to a unicorn. That twinkling stream is like the magic emanating from Merlin's wand.'

Joanna stirred and he answered her unspoken question. 'Yes, Merlin is connected to unicorns too because of their mystery and power of transformation.'

'Can you say a bit more about the magic?' Edward asked.

'Magic means hope and unexpected things that happen beyond our expectation and comprehension. The unicorns touch souls. Just thinking about one wakens energy within you and starts to connect you to their energy so that great changes take place. A stream of light shimmering with stars enters your aura and magic starts to come to you. All innocent and pure people can connect to this quality of the unicorns.'

'Thank you,' said Edward and Joanna noticed he had tears in his eyes.

'I know this is a silly question,' Joanna said, 'but do they grant wishes?'

'They can indeed grant wishes to the pure of heart and innocent children.'

'You mentioned healing?' Marcus reminded him.

'Yes, unicorns can heal. Any being of the seventh dimension can do so but the ascended horses can heal the soul just as dolphins do. They bring grace. The stream of light filled with stars that flashes into someone's soul when they make the connection actually dissolves some of the darkness within the soul. You know, when someone has a wondrous vision for helping the world the unicorns come and add their light to that person.'

'Do they?' Marcus was startled.

Joanna was struck with a thought. 'Do you mean unicorns can influence us like the Christ consciousness and angels?'

'Indeed. Their energy can come into people when they are ready, just like the Christ consciousness. People are not necessarily born with unicorn energy but it can enter and live through them later in life. It is so special it enables people to act with pride and dignity in terrible situations.'

'Can you give us an example?'

'In your quiet time, think of people who have done things for the world and have developed an air of composure and dignity. They may well carry unicorn energy.'

'Like who?' Joanna persisted.

'Nelson Mandela was first inhabited by unicorn energy when he was in prison. The energy is so special that people sense it in him. It is powerful in its purity, so it comes for a while then retreats, then it comes in stronger and retreats until it can come in fully.'

'Like the tide?'

'Exactly.'

Chapter 34

While Joanna was on the phone, Tony had been scribbling away trying to note down everything his step-daughter was saying. She was jubilant that the cub had not been seen since the night he was born, yet Tony sensed a tension about her, which surprised him. Joanna had underplayed the fire, mentioning it but not that it had been deliberately started in their chalet. She did not want to worry her mother nor did she want to energise the darkness by talking about it. She and Marcus just wanted to get out of the danger zone fast.

Helen, nursing her heavily bruised shoulder and cursing that she could not write, asked a torrent of questions, which Tony relayed and Joanna did her best to answer. 'Did she ask Zoranda about the Bermuda Triangle?' Helen demanded unexpectedly. 'I'm sure that has something to do with Atlantis, doesn't it?'

Tony repeated the question.

'I don't know. I never thought about it,' replied her daughter. 'You'll be able to ask him yourself soon. They left the Timbavati this morning, so they should be back in Cairo this evening.'

'Will they?' Tony was surprised. 'Good! I didn't realise

it was so soon. If that's all you want me to write down, I'll hand you to your mother.'

Helen grabbed the receiver. 'They're coming back today? Great. I have lots to ask them.'

'I bet you have,' murmured her husband, but he was smiling.

She made a face at him and said to Joanna, 'So where are you? Are you still at the safari lodge?'

Her daughter thought about the burned-out chalet and shuddered. The fire had been a catalyst in their decision to leave the Timbavati so quickly. Luckily, apart from loose change, their wallets and passports had been in the hotel safe. Perhaps the angels had looked after that too. She shut the memory out of her mind.

'No. We're in a hotel in Jo'burg on our way back to England.' Until now Joanna had not told her mother about Marcus's proposed job in South Africa, mainly because they wanted to make sure it was definitely happening. Now that everything was confirmed, she gave her the news.

So Joanna and Marcus would be in South Africa for a year, mused Helen. She would miss them but she was delighted for them. 'That's wonderful! It'll be a great experience for you. And,' she added lightly, 'we'll be over for a holiday!'

'I hope so,' replied Joanna, grinning. She wondered how long her mother would wait.

'So when does Marcus start work?'

'After Christmas. We've decided to come back to

England first and let the flat.' She hesitated. 'Perhaps we could put a few things in Tony's garage?'

Helen replied that she was sure it would be fine but not to overdo it. She realised, not for the first time, that they should sell both their houses and buy one together for their new life as a married couple.

'Thanks, that's great. We're going to Hawaii to swim with the dolphins before we come back to South Africa.' She updated her mother about the angel dolphins and was gratified by Helen's excitement. 'Do you and Tony fancy coming too?'

'We can't,' replied her mother. 'I'd love to but it's our turn to have the old folk for Christmas. What a pity! I wonder what you'll learn from the angel dolphins?'

'I can't wait to find out!' exclaimed Joanna.

Helen and Tony were delighted to see the three wise men back at the Great White Lodge. Even though Joanna had told them in exhaustive detail about the white lion cub on the phone, they were eager to hear it all again first hand, especially the messages about love that Joanna had received from the white cub. Zoranda and Edward obliged them the following morning after the early morning meditation.

'Could I ask you about the white cub's aura? Could you see that it was special?' Helen wanted to know when they had finished.

Both men nodded. Zoranda motioned Edward to speak first. 'I saw a pure white light radiating from him in all directions. It's the brightest and purest aura I have ever seen and seemed to extend a mile or even more.'

He looked at his mentor, who confirmed that he had seen the same thing. Zoranda added, 'There were tier upon tier of Ascended Masters, avatars and angels around him. I have personally never experienced anything like it.'

Helen's eyes shone. 'It really is bringing in the Christ light, isn't it?'

They nodded and all their auras lit up with an orange flame of hope.

After breakfast Helen asked Zoranda about the Bermuda Triangle. 'Does it have something to do with Atlantis?'

Zoranda chuckled at her eagerness. 'Yes, it is connected with Atlantis.'

'I thought so.'

'The Cathedral of the Sacred Heights, sometimes known as the Temple of Poseidon, housed the great crystal of Atlantis, which was the central powerhouse for the continent. At the end, when the flood waters settled, the great crystal lay under the ocean in the centre of the area now known as the Bermuda Triangle. The crystal opened a universal gateway which is still activated by certain galactic conditions at times when the intergalactic masters need to use that portal.'

'I see.'

Lines of concentration furrowed her third eye and Zoranda wanted to say, 'Relax and you will know for yourself,' but he refrained.

'So am I right on this? When a person or object enters the portal while it is activated, they move into a different dimension, which is why they dematerialise.'

'Exactly.'

'What is it a portal to?'

'You are not ready to understand that yet.'

Helen nodded, though she was disappointed. 'So only people who are ready to move through that portal would be there at a time when it is open?'

'Of course. You know nothing like that happens by chance. Only souls who are called to be there for that experience would be in the area at the moment the portal opens.'

'It's incredible,' said Helen, not for the first time. 'We live in such an amazing world.'

'And we haven't even touched a thousandth of the sacred mysteries of the universe,' Zoranda reminded her.

'I know and that makes it even more amazing. I just feel so privileged to have learned what I have done so far.'

'Now that we've talked about the Bermuda Triangle, I must reluctantly talk about the fall of Atlantis. I don't like to energise the darkness but your book won't be complete without the information. Just don't dwell on it, please.'

'Okay. So if everything was so pure and they could use the power of their minds to create whatever they wanted and they only wanted what was for the highest good, why did it change? Sorry, that was rather a convoluted sentence. But they had everything they could possibly want,' said Helen.

'I understand what you mean and I'll try to explain. Angels are messengers. Where there is light there are light angels and only light angels. Agreed?'

'Yes.' Helen nodded, wondering what he was getting at.

He continued, 'Remember the pure energy of early Atlantis was used by the initiates with wisdom and integrity for the highest collective good. Atlantis in its purist forms had no dark angels. However, at the pinnacle of purity one priest thought he would use the energy for his personal use. That thought allowed a dark angel into Atlantis. Then one by one they arrived.' Zoranda surrendered to a philosophical contemplation for a few quiet minutes, then went on, 'All was pure until greed reared its head and an angel of dark whispered. It is a chicken and egg situation. Which happens first, the dark thought coming into an untainted person or a dark angel whispering to someone?'

He looked at Helen and she shrugged. 'I don't know.'

Zoranda let out a breath. 'Anyway, eventually a few greedy people realised that this pure energy could be shaped and used personally. Then ordinary people learned to access it without integrity. In good Atlantis, the knowledge, information and technology used wisely made it a wonderful place. Greed and desire for control destroyed it and allowed the angels of dark to turn the minds of men.

'You know, where there is dark, there are dark angels. When there are planetary problems angels of dark surround the warmongers. They talk to egos gone wild, who listen to the dark whisperings and the spiral descends. That is what happened in Atlantis. It was a slippery slide to destruction.'

Helen sighed.

'So in pure Atlantis, they used sonar and crystal power with mind control for their energy requirements. The pyramids were painted white with golden tops and had a crystal floating above them to generate light. Crystals were also charged with blue light and used to light up cities. They were activated for laser surgery. And, of course, airships were powered by crystals. Lines of energy were set at different levels, so that small planes moved near the ground and huge bus planes were higher.'

Helen listened, entranced.

'After the technological revolution, nuclear power was utilised. By then the power of crystals was misused to control. They were implanted into people, rather as some politicians are mooting silicone chip implants now.'

'That's frightening.' Helen frowned and the big man nodded in agreement.

'All that had been used for good was inverted and used to taint and control. Laser beams that had been used to heal were used as guns for destruction. Animals who had been friends were trained to kill the enemy and the natural power lines were broken and distorted.'

'We'll mend them,' Helen assured him and Zoranda smiled at her determination and confidence.

Chapter 35

She was sitting alone in the shade when a fresh-faced young brother approached and handed Helen the next instalment from the Scroll. She was not expecting anything more so soon and looked at it with the usual feeling of anticipation and expectation, mingled with guilt that there was no one to share it.

A note with it said that this section was stand-alone and in different script from the previous pages. Evidently it had originally been elaborately decorated with gold and blue edging. The scribe had noted that he had been asked to design this page to show the future world how Atlantis had descended from the pure white peak of high spiritual life to the muddy depths of degradation. He intimated that when it was time for Atlantis to rise again, the Scroll would be revealed to remind people that it was possible to retrace these steps up the mountain to the summit.

Intense curiosity now accompanied her excitement as she started to read and discovered that it was a rough summary of much of the information that had already been revealed.

Nature

During the great and glorious golden years of Atlantis the people loved nature. Their spiritual lives were aligned to the natural world, for they respected its rhythms and needs. They planted according to the moon at the appropriate time for each plant. They communicated with plants, placed specifically programmed crystal among them, played music and studied their divine properties.

They understood that certain herbs contain a geometric structure, which will seek out the same geometric structure within the body if eaten. It will then heal and regenerate that area.

As the consciousness lowered, the people no longer honoured nature or observed the rituals . They cut down trees indiscriminately and polluted water and air. When nature rebelled they fought it and tried to change it.

We are one. To contradict nature is to harm your own body.

In order that pure Atlantis may rise again honour nature again.

Religion

During the great and glorious golden years of Atlantis highly trained priests served the people with kindness and wisdom and were always revered and respected, for they had genuine connection with the angelic and elemental kingdoms.

The people worshipped in nature, creating stone circles at sacred power points, frequently over streams and natural springs. They carefully chose rocks with special characteristics or healing powers, picking stones, which were slightly concave on one side, so that circles became sound chambers. These could be used to heal and raise consciousness. Rocks were angled to point to specific stars in order to harness their energy or access the help of the extraterrestrials.

At full moon or other celebration times the people would walk the ley lines to the stone circles, then dance round them, winding up the energy. Families would chant ancient stories as they did so. In this way they connected the spiritual points on the web of light.

Kindness, love and wisdom were highly honoured qualities.

Alas, as the spiritual energy decreased the people worshipped indoors in increasingly elaborate temples.

Priests claimed power over the people by falsely claiming that they communicated with ancestors and demons and threatened the people with the wrath of these invisible forces. As a result superstition increased. When something had a positive outcome it was repeated until dogma resulted.

Highly trained Magi had vast occult power, which some of them used to frighten and control the people. A huge wave of negativity flowed round the continent.

In order that pure Atlantis may rise again, worship in the natural world and use the power of the spiritual world with wisdom to help, heal and support each other.

Social and Family Life

During the great and glorious golden years of Atlantis family life was nurtured and respected. If a couple wished to marry, a highly trained priest examined their spiritual development to check that they were compatible. Children were welcomed.

Families sang and danced sacred songs together, which cemented family closeness. They had many pets, which were considered part of the household.

Days were spent in a relaxed, contemplative way, communing with nature and telling stories. People loved to spend time in the countryside, communicating telepathically with other dimensions. They sought beauty and created it around them.

The people lived moral, loving, upright lives with integrity and contentment.

In the purest times there were no criminals. Gradually more people turned to crime and the wise priests tried to help them rather than punish them. The criminal was anaesthetised by magnetism and, by the use of crystal rays, blood was sent to the part of the brain responsible for the deviation. A healer then raised the criminal's consciousness by telepathically reprogramming his beliefs.

As people lost their spiritual and psychic connection they became greedy and ambitious. Because they were not in tune with nature they had to work harder to reap their harvest and became busy, self-centred and discontented.

As discontent set in people sought material and

sensual gratification. Loud parties, orgies, feasts pro-
liferated and moral turpitude festered. As a nation they
sought to control others and, with morality deterio-
rating at home, the army became inhumane and
merciless. Soldiers treated prisoners appallingly.
Criminals were shackled and imprisoned.

Before attacking a country the commanders used
black magic techniques to gain power over the people
they wanted to conquer. With the back-up of their
extraordinary weapons technology, Atlantis became an
acquisitive empire.

*In order that pure Atlantis may rise again relax and
review your life. Choose to love and serve with integrity
and wisdom.*

Government

During the great and glorious golden years of Atlantis
priest kings ruled with wisdom and genuine desire to
serve. They promoted co-operation, a sense of community, family life and justice. They took decisions and
used their power for the highest good. In return the
people sent them light.

As the purity diminished Atlantean kings sacrificed
animals before meetings, drank wine mixed with animal
blood and tried to control the people. The rulers were
feared and hated. They turned people into slaves or
soldiers, by placing conditioning boxes on their backs
and remotely controlling them.

In order that pure Atlantis may rise again promote harmony, co-operation and community. Make choices for the highest good and empower everyone.

The Universe

During the great and glorious golden years of Atlantis the people were spiritual and psychic. They lived in openness and honesty, communicating with the angels, elementals and extraterrestrials. Because they kept the portals to the other galaxies and stars open, Earth was an integral part of the galactic community.

As the frequency of the people diminished and their psychic and spiritual powers closed down, they could no longer communicate with the wise beings of the universe. As a result Earth became an isolated backwater, resisting and fearing help from those they termed aliens.

In order that pure Atlantis may rise again develop your spiritual and psychic powers. Communicate with angels of light, elementals and extraterrestrials. Become part of the galactic community again.

Animals

During the great and glorious golden years of Atlantis all the people were vegetarian. They loved animals and birds and lived freely among them. Animals worked with the people, trusted and helped them.

Later, people killed animals, ate meat, then sacrificed them and drank their blood. The people enjoyed gory bullfights, and spectacular horse and elephant racing.

After that they controlled animals with fear and used them for fighting, training them to attack the enemy.

In order that pure Atlantis may rise again honour and respect birds and animals. Help them to trust humans again.

Education

During the great and glorious golden years of Atlantis children were taught in a relaxed way for their highest good. Their memory, artistic ability and creativity were developed.

As the energy lowered, children were taught to read and write, study astronomy and mathematics. The social aspect of storytelling deteriorated and the right-brain connection to spirit gradually closed down.

In order that pure Atlantis may rise again develop your own creativity and artistic ability. Open up to spirit again. And honour the creativity in others.

Simplicity

During the great and glorious golden years of Atlantis everything was simple. People lived quiet, honest lives.

Dress was a plain robe, only adorned for spiritual enhancement.

Buildings were natural, with elegant lines and built harmoniously according to sacred geometry.

The people accepted that they had all that they needed.

As the high consciousness diminished people became more devious and personal appearance became more important. People wore elaborate clothing with flamboyant or intricate jewellery.

Buildings became complicated and often inlaid with gems.

People sought more knowledge, while science and technology replaced spirituality. The end came through decadence and too much knowledge. They had too much of everything and misused it.

In order that pure Atlantis may rise again simplify your dress, your home and your life. Be satisfied.

Helen put the piece of paper down and Tony found her much later, deep in contemplation.

Chapter 36

Banks of crimson poinsettias against the azure sky of the big island of Hawaii shouted vitality and happiness as an exuberant Joanna and Marcus floated round the coast road to their hotel in their hire car.

'Oh, it's beautiful.' Joanna's face was alight as she watched a host of small brightly coloured birds flutter in front of them. She touched the soft petals of the orchid and lily lei, which Marcus had bought for her and placed round her neck when they arrived on the island. As she smelled the exotic perfume she felt a spurt of joyous anticipation. This was going to be an amazing two weeks!

An e-mail received from Monica had reassured them that the lioness had not returned to the Timbavati with the white cub. Trackers thought they had crossed the borders and disappeared. No news is good news, she said. Marcus and Joanna felt free to relax.

Their first task was to buy a snorkel, mask and flippers, and they were convulsed with laughter as they pranced around in the shop trying on different gear. 'This had better be worth it,' snorted Joanna. 'You look like an alien.'

Marcus retaliated. 'And I didn't know my girlfriend was a frog.'

'Wait till you see me in the water!' responded Joanna, giggling. 'I've never used flippers before. Goodness knows what'll happen.'

But three hours later, after they had lingered over an ice cream, chosen some postcards and watched with their hearts in their mouths as young boys surfed the huge curling waves perilously close to the rocks, they were floating on the blue waters in front of the hotel. They followed each other through the reef, entranced by the myriad coloured fish: yellow ones with black stripes, blue with violet patchwork, green with orange splashes and a profusion of different shapes and sizes.

And then Joanna glanced sideways to see a big turtle paddling along beside her. She spluttered as she took in a mouthful of salty water while trying to shout to Marcus. 'Marcus, a turtle,' she called and he turned to join her. They swam along with it until it reached the rocks. Then they stood on the reef, avoiding black sea urchins and watched while the huge shelled creature let the waves nudge it on to the exposed reef and it tried again and again to clamber on to the rock. It was frequently knocked into the water and patiently, laboriously endeavoured once more. At last they left it to its struggle and snorkelled back to the beach, where another turtle had dragged itself up the sand to rest. This was such a familiar sight that people ignored it. Only one small boy squatted nearby, big-eyed and watchful, clearly fascinated by the huge shell and stubby spread-eagled limbs of the crustacean.

Marcus shaded his eyes and looked out over the

expanse of blue-silver water. 'No sign of dolphins but we'll find them tomorrow.'

'Of course we will,' Joanna replied as she stood on one leg, struggling to get her flipper off. 'We'll swim with them in the morning.'

And Joanna was right. In the morning they drove to another beach, reputedly a dolphin bay. They arrived so early that the shore was deserted except for a man with long grey hair, who looked like one of the ageing hippies who blend into the island culture. He was sitting on a wall watching the ocean. 'They're here,' he announced, 'over there.' They assumed he meant the dolphins. He pointed but they could see no sign of movement. 'In a minute they'll come in this direction,' he assured them. 'Just be patient.'

He proceeded to give them a lecture on how to behave with the dolphins, how best to enter the water in flippers, that they must never leave their buddy out there and how long to stay in the water. As tourists they listened carefully, though most of it was common sense. Then he reminded them, 'The dolphins know you're here. Even before you enter the water they'll have scanned your energy fields and will know all about you.'

Joanna and Marcus looked at each other.

'Ah!' the man remarked and pointed. They saw only fermenting water, the aftermath of a splash, then peaceful sea. But moments later, following the direction of his arm, they could not miss the dozen or so dolphins leaping and curving in graceful synchronicity out of the water.

'Let's go in,' said Marcus eagerly, but the local cautioned against it. 'They're too far out. You've got to swim there and back, remember. Wait a bit.'

They did as he advised and ten minutes later clambered over the rocks and pebbles to the waterline. Joanna was glad she had listened to his instructions about putting on your flippers and then walking into the ocean backwards. The waves were rougher than she realised and there was quite an undertow. Once in, however, they set off in the direction of the dolphins. There were two other couples heading out at the same time. All four looked experienced dolphin swimmers and the holidaymakers were content to let them lead the way.

Joanna was just beginning to feel the dolphins were ignoring her when Marcus motioned with his hand and she saw a school of perhaps ten swimming right under them. She could hear their sonar and tried to tune in but neither sensed nor received anything. She felt disappointed.

Suddenly a spinner dolphin leaped up into the air and spun like a whirlwind, shaking droplets in all directions. 'Wow, did you see that?' Marcus called, giving her the thumbs up. And the spinner dolphin responded by performing several more times.

Some time later Joanna shivered and complained, 'I'm cold.'

'Another few minutes,' pleaded Marcus and she obliged. Her reward was to see several more dolphins swimming under and round them and they accompanied them part of the way back to the shore.

'That was wonderful,' she said to Marcus when they finally beached, 'but they didn't communicate with me.'

'Tomorrow is another day,' he pointed out. 'Let's have breakfast at the Coffee Shack.'

And the following morning, despite visiting the volcano which dominates the island and spending half the night watching red-hot lava flowing into the sea in a fascinating drama of flame and steam, they were up early to swim with the dolphins.

This time they could see the dolphins in the bay when they arrived, for they were much nearer the shore. Disappointingly, several swimmers were already approaching them. Marcus and Joanna hastily donned masks and flippers, before negotiating the waves backwards into the sea. As before, the dolphins ignored them for a time. Then the graceful creatures delighted them by swimming under and around them for some time until, suddenly and without warning, the entire pod rocketed off across the bay. Marcus was ready to chase after them with all the other swimmers but Joanna had a different idea.

'Why don't we float and call them to us,' she suggested. 'If they want to come they will.'

'Okay, we'll wait here.'

They lay on the sea, faces down watching the depths below, and telepathically invited the dolphins to come to them. It seemed like a long wait. Then a pod of six mothers with two very small babies swam right under them. Joanna held her breath with excitement. The group swam in a circle and under them again. This time one of the babies turned upside down, fastened itself on to one of its mother's teats and started to suck. When they disappeared out of sight the couple swam slowly back to the beach, feeling honoured and privileged.

Later, Joanna said, 'It felt as if they were telling us they trusted us.'

And Marcus agreed.

'I don't think they were angel dolphins though, do you?'

'No. Probably not. I think we'll know when we see angel dolphins.'

And he was right. But they had some time to wait before they appeared.

They had planned a two-night trip to a Buddhist monastery and set off the following morning, bowling down the coast road, through forests and villages, stopping on whim to explore or find a snack. When they left the coast and drove inland towards the hills they were startled how quickly the weather changed from sunshine to cool misty rain. In places the track to the monastery had been temporarily rebuilt after it had been washed away by floods and in others it looked decidedly precarious. The monastery was a wooden building, nestling among the great broad-leaved trees in the tropical rainforest. The temple, with its curved roof, looked as if it had stepped out of Thailand and only the drip of rainwater and sodden prayer flags indicated otherwise.

That evening in the temple they listened to the lamas chanting. A profound sense of peace and harmony enfolded them, as if they were wrapped in angel wings. They slept that night in the simple building attached to the temple, listening to the rain dripping.

It was the following morning while they sat in silence when the chanting had finished, that Joanna had a sense of the dolphins calling. First she could hear the clicking of their sonar and then a clear stream of consciousness poured in. 'To enter our world you must surrender your will and let go of preconceptions. Do not call us with desire but rather with your spiritual voice. The angel dolphins guard the treasures of the planet but they will not come to you when others are round you.'

After that communication Joanna sat for a long time, hoping for more, but nothing came.

As soon as they left the temple she told Marcus what she had received and they discussed what best to do. Clearly they must find somewhere they could be alone if the angel dolphins were to approach them.

To escape the rain they drove down to the coast again and walked along the black volcanic sands and rocky shore. Here they watched more turtles coming up on to the shore to lay their eggs and rest for some time before returning to the sea.

Again that evening after listening to the magical chanting of the Buddhist monks and feeling the vibration of peace shimmer through her, Joanna sat, lost in another world. Suddenly a picture of a huge dolphin appeared in her third eye. 'I am the Great Dolphin of Sirius. All dolphins have messages for you and can help you transmute your past and prepare for a different future. All can give you knowledge. However only the angel dolphins can offer you spiritual wisdom.' And abruptly the communication ceased. This was not how Joanna expected to connect with the dolphins and she did not know whether to be disappointed or ecstatic.

They returned to their hotel by the reef the following morning and chilled out by the pool all afternoon. Tomorrow they were to go on a dolphin boat trip and hoped to see whales. Big Bertha owned the boat and she was a delightful but formidable lady. She was large as her nickname suggested, with several spare tyres round her middle, huge muscly arms, a booming voice and wild hair. She was also extremely knowledgeable about Hawaii and the sea world and within seconds she knew the capability of all her passengers. Joanna intuitively trusted her and they chatted for some time. Within fifteen minutes, dolphins surrounded the boat, some leaping, some spinning, some racing along beside them, and there were always a few at the front enjoying the bow wave.

Big Bertha shared several dolphin stories with them, but when they saw a whale spouting in the distance conversation ceased while they watched for another. 'The dolphins love the whales,' she told Joanna. 'Whenever the big ones come past, the dolphins accompany them as far as they can on their journey. They have a really good relationship. There is a special link between whales and dolphins.'

Joanna knew that was an important piece of information but as yet she did not know why.

'Why don't you go talk to Maybelle,' suggested Big Bertha to Joanna after a while. 'The dolphins have helped her big-time and she comes to Hawaii every Christmas to take a dolphin trip with me. Ask her the story. She's right up there in the bow.'

'Thanks, I will,' replied Joanna and climbed up the ladder to the front. Several people were sitting up there and they squeezed up amiably to make room for her.

'See the dolphins,' one of them said, indicating that she look down, and there were four, travelling in the bow wave, looking as if they were laughing with exhilaration. From time to time one would move out, giving another the chance to take its place.

'Big Bertha told me to ask for Maybelle,' she remarked.

A thin lady with a New York accent and frizzy grey hair replied cheerily, 'That's me. I guess she wanted me to tell you about my MS.'

'I don't know,' Joanna replied, feeling that was rather personal. 'She just said to talk to Maybelle.'

'Right, well, I had MS. It was real bad and I was in a wheelchair. They said I could expect remissions but it got steadily worse.'

Joanna nodded sympathetically.

Maybelle continued, 'I'll tell you my story. My daddy was the most charming, attractive, handsome guy you could imagine. I just loved him to death. But he had no sense of reality. He was a conman and I heard him tell so many different stories I never knew what was true. How he remembered all the lies he told people I have no idea. As a child I didn't know if he was going to tell someone he was a brain surgeon or a naval hero or a millionaire. And I still don't know what he really did for a living, if he did anything. When I was thirteen he lost a whole lot of money gambling. My mother didn't know this till later. But he was skint. So what does he do? He goes out, hires a limo and throws a party, puts it all on credit, tells everyone he has made a heap of dough. Then he disappears. Just vanishes. It turns out he has a pile of debts. Worse still, he has another family, a wife and two children in Virginia.'

Joanna wanted to ask which marriage was bigamous but instead she said, 'That must have been terrible.'

'Yeah, well, my life had no foundation. It was like living in an earthquake zone.'

'Did you see him again?'

'Yep. He turned up three years later full of apologies, said he'd finished with the other woman and my mom took him back. A year later he fakes his death. Presumed drowned. We went through hell but my brother bumped into him in London years later.'

Maybelle looked at Joanna. 'So you can guess I wasn't high on trust. And I married a man I couldn't trust.' She sighed.

Joanna wondered where the dolphins came in but Maybelle was on another tack.

'You may know that there is a big underlying emotional content in most cases of MS?'

Joanna shook her head. 'Not really. I'm afraid I don't know a lot about it.'

'That's okay. Well, it's like this. A memory is just a

picture, which you hold in your conscious mind. But if that memory has an emotional charge that you don't like, you use a lot of energy trying to cope with it or even to suppress it into your unconscious.'

'Yes, I see that,' agreed Joanna.

'I know now that I was using all my energy dealing with the emotions attached to the memories, so my body was getting sicker and sicker.' She looked at Joanna. 'That's where the dolphins come in.'

'Ah!'

'A friend brought me to Hawaii and I managed to get into the water in a great rubber ring. The dolphins surrounded me, but I don't think it would have mattered if they hadn't. What they do is use their frequency to wipe out the electrical charge attached to the difficult emotions.'

'I see!'

Maybelle nodded. 'You understand? That night after my first time in the water with the dolphins, I had a vivid dream.'

'Go on.' By now Joanna was sitting forward, listening intently to the woman's words.

'I dreamed I was living on an earthquake. The ground constantly moved all round me and it felt very unsafe. I managed to make my way to the edge of the water and a dolphin swam to me. He said, "Time to move away from the familiar but frightening." And I got on to his back. He took me to another land where there was solid rock foundation.' She met Joanna's eyes. 'And when I woke I knew I was on my way to recovery. It hasn't always been easy but my physical body is much stronger and my life is no longer on shaky ground. I believe the dolphins wiped out the electrical charges of the emotions with their sonar, and healed the memories. I couldn't even talk about it before and now I can.'

'How long ago was that?'

'Five years ago and I've been back every year to say thank you and to maintain the connection.'

'What a story!' exclaimed Joanna. 'Thank you so much for telling me.' And she looked with new eyes at the dolphins, spinning, leaping and dancing all round the boat.

Two days later they were to meet the angel dolphins.

Chapter 37

The sun was golden, happy and hot, the ocean azure, unfathomable and cool. Joanna and Marcus sat on rough rocks forming a cliff and watched the blue infinity of the sea. Two men in wet suits had caught a gleaming silver fish and were proudly carrying it to their car. A bird swooped down and plucked an offering from the water. Joanna closed her eyes and leaned against Marcus. She felt warm and drowsy and lulled by the sound of the waves. Just as she was about to fall asleep, he leaped to life.

'Look, whales!' he exclaimed.

She opened her eyes and the ocean as far as the eye could see was spouting fountains of water. Whales everywhere. One flipped its huge tail and then another. They watched for a long time, sometimes exclaiming and pointing, sometimes silent.

Joanna said, 'I feel we should find a cove where we can swim.' So they wandered hand in hand along the coast path until they could scramble over rocks down to a soft sandy bay, entirely deserted. There were no humans, dogs or dolphins. They donned their flippers and masks and lay in the deliciously cool sea without expectation. Within minutes there were dolphins all round them, their sleek silver-blue bodies shining in the sunlight. As the humans copied their movements, the dolphins played with them until Joanna was cold and tired and went back to the shore.

She sat on a rock at the edge of the water and could hear the sonar in her head. A stream of consciousness from the dolphins came to her, leaving her stunned.

'We, the angel dolphins, greet you. We are few in number but we are spiritually protected and can never be harmed by man. However we must warn you that those dolphins who hold the knowledge and technology of Atlantis can be killed by man and need to be protected.

'We angel dolphins have the same purity of energy as the angels of light. We are angels in incarnation and from the angelic hierarchy. We hold the complete spectrum of information from Atlantis. It is time to bring the information back to Earth.

'There are energies out there that are searching for the information from Atlantis and don't know where it is held.

'You ask about the whales. We will tell you.

'Imagine the knowledge we angel dolphins hold is like the crown jewels. The jewels need to be protected and the whales form the army, which protects the information we hold. If necessary they can carry the sacred wisdom for us. They are the last line of defence before people can get directly to us, the angel dolphins.'

I wonder where whales come from, thought Joanna, and why they are on Earth?

Directly came the reply to her thought. 'Whales come

from a long way away. They are from an asteroid you are unaware of in this universe. Their purpose is to protect the glorious information of Atlantis and ultimately to learn about it and take it back to their home.'

I see, thought Joanna.

And before she had time to formulate another question, the voice continued, 'Here is another story for you to help you understand the importance of the whales and angel dolphins. Imagine one man has control of information about the atom bomb. We choose the analogy of the atom bomb to represent the sacred and dangerous information held by the dolphins. The dolphins are carrying the atom bomb and are protected by the army. If necessary the army, in this case the whales, can take on the atom bomb. When the whales are fewer, the dolphins are more at risk of the information being stolen by the force of evil.'

Oh, my God! thought Joanna.

'Sturov is influencing weak, evil and ambitious men to allow sonar under the seas, which interferes with us. He is trying to distort fishing quotas. And many other things you cannot conceive of.'

Joanna shivered even though the sun was hot on her body. She could see Marcus still snorkelling round the rocks at the edge of the cove. Do turtles and sharks play a part in this?

'Oh, yes. Turtles are like the resistance fighters in a war. They are the underground movement and are working unseen to keep the dolphins safe. They are so small they are underestimated. They are from the planet Neptune.'

Really! Joanna was startled.

'Indeed,' continued the stream of information. 'Sharks are aggressive. They are the front-line troops, protecting the information from Atlantis, which is held by the angel dolphins. They come from Mars.'

Have I got this right? Joanna checked. The angel dolphins carry the spiritual knowledge of Atlantis, which is vitally important in order for pure Atlantis to rise again. The pure angels of Atlantis have incarnated into certain dolphin bodies so that they can hold the information on Earth, without anyone suspecting where it is. The whales, turtles and sharks have incarnated to protect the information and finally to learn about it themselves.

'Yes.'

And the dolphin angels hold all the pieces of the jigsaw? They hold all the knowledge from Atlantis and wish to return it all to humanity now?

'Only some of it for now.' There was a sense of urgency in the next communication. 'If humans knew right now what the angel dolphins know you would destroy not just Earth but the galaxy.'

Joanna sat watching the sea, brooding about human folly. At last she sent out the thought wave: Is there a link between dolphins, Sirius and the Sphinx?

'The Sphinx is the god of the knowledge held by the dolphins. If the dolphins were to deliver to the Sphinx the knowledge they possess the puzzle of Earth would be complete. That is the riddle of the Sphinx. The Sphinx can at any time call them in but it waits and it watches.

It is the conductor of the orchestra, watching, waiting, telling which bit to do what.'

I see. At least I think I do. Is there anything more I need to know?

'The white lion is the keeper of a sacred energy, which can help humanity now. In order for the power to return to the Sphinx, the white lion must fulfil what he came to do. He's here to open the hearts of people everywhere to prepare them to receive more spiritual understanding.'

We'll do our best.

She watched the dolphins leaping gracefully out to sea and a few minutes later Marcus came out of the water to join her.

Chapter 38

It was sixteen months since Joanna and Marcus had visited Hawaii. Time had flown so fast for them in South Africa that their holiday seemed like a distant dream and so did the information that Joanna had received from the dolphins. She had told her mother, of course, who had persuaded her to write everything down. She had done so in a hurry, while packing up the flat and arranging everything for the next step of their lives.

Despite their intentions of visiting the Timbavati again while they were in South Africa they had not gone back, though they had been in constant contact with Monica and Bede. The main reason was that the white lion cub and his mother had disappeared. Since the night of the cull, they had vanished and there had been not a single sighting. At first Marcus and Joanna worried about them. They felt they ought to be doing something, but what?

Then Zoranda phoned to say that the Great White Brotherhood was looking after the cub. 'He's safe, where Sturov can't get to him,' he reassured them. 'He's free, growing up in the wild and will be protected until he's ready to undertake his mission.'

They both felt an overpowering sense of relief and relegated the cub to a corner of their minds, while they enjoyed their new life.

One morning they received an e-mail from Monica informing them that people had seen the white cub, who had grown into a magnificent young lion and that extraordinary stories were circulating about him. Apparently refugees from Mozambique would cut through the game reserve even though it was prohibited and provide easy pickings for lions. Many had been killed. One night a predatory lion had savaged and eaten a child, one member of a refugee family. The father, aunt and a child had climbed a tree to escape. The lion, hunger slightly assuaged, had sat under the tree, waiting for them to fall out or descend. Before sunrise the white lion had appeared. According to the story he had marched up to the man-eating lion, who slunk away into the bush. The white lion then sat under the tree but now the terrified and grieving family felt an extraordinary sense of peace and love spread over them. They felt he had come to protect them. The white lion waited until a ranger's vehicle appeared and, seeming to recognise that the ranger could rescue the humans, he melted away.

Joanna and Marcus were amazed at the story and wondered how much was truth and how much journalistic embellishment. But they were overjoyed to have news of the sacred lion again. 'We must go to the Timbavati to see him. It sounds as if he's started his mission,' Joanna exclaimed.

'Yes!' agreed Marcus. 'It does, doesn't it! Perhaps he will give you another message.'

'I hope so. Oh, I do hope so!' she agreed.

It was about this time that Bede started to think in earnest about tracing his real mother. He had never wanted to know anything about her, partly out of a sense of loyalty to his adoptive mother, but ever since he had seen the little white cub his roots had been on his mind. He knew he had been born in England and presumably his birth would be registered there, so that was the starting point for his search. As secretive as ever, he mentioned it to no one but phoned his mother to say he planned a visit in March, before the busy Easter season began. She was ecstatic at the thought of seeing him again, little guessing his intention.

Back in England, Helen was beavering away at her book, which she had decided to make into a novel. Zoranda, who had returned to Kumeka House and was always willing to help her, made it clear that the information it contained would greatly assist the white lion in his mission to spread Christ consciousness and heal the web of light. He impressed on her that the book was vitally important and this spurred her on.

Marcus and Joanna had flown home to England for Christmas, which revived all the memories of their previous year in Hawaii, and they told Helen and Tony yet again of the messages from the dolphins and how wonderful it was to swim with them. They constantly found themselves talking about the white lion, which was hardly surprising as there were an increasing number of reports in the international press about him and mysteries and miracles that surrounded his presence. One American paper was the first to report a very strange story. A gazelle had died in childbirth, whereupon the white lion had appeared and licked the baby until it stood up. Followed by the long-legged baby, the lion then walked slowly into a herd of gazelles, which as everyone knows is impossible. According to the trackers who were said to have seen the incident, it happened. Something even more bizarre then took place. The white lion took the little shaky creature to a mother whose baby had died. He waited until she allowed the little one to suckle, then walked away. This possibly apocryphal story went round the world by e-mail and people were beginning to realise there was something extraordinary happening in Africa.

Joanna and Marcus arranged for Helen and Tony to visit South Africa for Easter where they would all vacation at the safari lodge and hopefully would see the great white star beast himself.

'I'd love that,' said Helen, with rapture in her voice.

Edward spoke to his brother Bede a few times on the phone. He had been a changed person since the escape of the sacred cub, descending into gloom for a short time after the fire but becoming noticeably friendly and cheerful since the white lion had returned to the Timbavati. Edward never mentioned the fire, except to ask about the progress of the rebuilding, which was now complete. The chip on Bede's shoulder had evidently healed and during one of their calls he mentioned to Edward that he was visiting their parents in England in March, though he did not mention the purpose of the trip.

Edward was surprised to find that Bede talked constantly about the white lion and felt it an honour to be in his presence. He told Edward that the lion possessed healing qualities. Apparently one of the animal's favourite spots was on a rocky outcrop where he could literally be king of all he surveyed. A blind man was taken to sit on the rock when the lion was not there and his sight was restored. He and his family believed this was the influence of the great cat.

A disturbed young woman, whose family were at their wit's end, was given a photograph of the white lion to hold. She put it above her bed and after that she felt better, behaved normally and slept like a lamb. They were convinced that the white lion was helping her.

As the stream of stories found their way into news-papers and magazines about the sacred white beast, tourists arrived in droves in the hope of catching a glimpse of him. Many with illnesses believed that they would be healed if they saw him and their faith seemed to be justified.

In March Bede flew to England to stay with his adoptive parents for a two-week holiday.

One grey and dismal morning, without telling them or

anyone else his intentions, he took a train to London and crossed the city to the public records office. His quest proved simpler than he had expected, for the moment he saw his birth certificate the realisation dawned. Monica is my *mother*, not my aunt.

She gave me away to be brought up in England! Shock reverberated through him. Then anger. A maelstrom of emotion flooded through him as he travelled back on the train. He clenched and unclenched his fists and beat one against his hand. Other passengers on the train watched him nervously but he was oblivious.

The last locked door in his soul, which had been loosened by the light radiated by the white lion, had burst open. The rage and darkness suppressed behind it were ready to be released. He stormed into the house where his parents were quietly going about their business.

'How could you? Monica's my mother, isn't she?' he shouted.

His parents rose in alarm and sought protection by standing side by side. Bede started beating the wall with his fists and his parents were desperately alarmed.

'Bede!' His mother called his name as she used to when he had temper tantrums as a toddler. He was inconsolable then and she could not get through to him now.

'Why didn't you tell me before?'

'We promised your grandmother we'd never tell anyone.'

'But I'm not just anyone. It's my life! And she's dead!'

They nodded. The ghost of the grandmother still hung

over them, as did that of the grandfather who never knew Bede was his blood grandson.

The furious man shouted that he had been taken from his roots, that he had always felt different. His bitterness, rage and blame knew no bounds. A foul torrent of invective flooded from his mouth. The well-meaning couple who had done their best to love and nurture him despite his moods and darkness were hurt to the depths of their souls. His mother tried to explain, endeavoured to give him a gentler perspective but he packed and left the house. They were never to see him again.

The distressed and horrified parents phoned Edward, their blood son, to explain at last that Aunt Monica was Bede's mother and that he and Bede were cousins not adopted siblings.

Edward felt a tremor of shock flow through him as dozens of strange things fell into place. The way Aunt Monica looked at Bede. The way his mother did not want Bede to go to South Africa. She thought she might lose him, of course. But when it was Edward's turn to go she did not mind, for he was unquestionably hers. A million little whispers made sense. And why had he never realised? He, the psychic, could not even probe his own family secret. He reminded himself that was common. It is always more difficult to see your own life. Typically he blamed himself. If he'd been aware perhaps he could have done something to ease the situation. Most important of all he felt deeply troubled about Bede's state of mind. He had heard that his brother was furiously angry with

Monica for rejecting him as a baby. What would he do? Edward was well aware of Bede's black rages and he hoped Monica was safe.

Monica's reaction to the news when her brother-in-law phoned her was very different. She felt exultant, triumphant even. At last Bede would know she was his mother. She ignored her brother-in-law's warnings that Bede was furious with her. Nothing could dim her excitement.

Chapter 39

Just before Easter Joanna and Marcus met Helen and Tony in Johannesburg and they flew together to Hoedspruit airport, where someone from the safari lodge would collect them. Monica herself came to meet them, which was a special surprise as she was so busy. They did not know that she was hugging her incredible secret: her son knew she was his mother and soon she would be able to acknowledge him! But they could see she was tingling and glowing like a woman in love. She was absolutely delighted to see Marcus and Joanna again and pleased to welcome Helen and Tony.

The trees wore green clothing now, though the giraffes still poked their curious heads above them and monkeys peered from the leaves and swung on bare branches. It was a beautiful trip back to the lodge, but they were shaken to see how much frailer and thinner Monica's husband Peter was looking.

Not even this could take away their sense of excitement at the prospect of seeing the sacred white lion. For Joanna and Marcus it was to be sooner than they anticipated.

They were lying in the safety of their bed that night, both wide awake, listening to the strange mysterious sounds of the bush in the distance and discussing the white lion.

'The cub looked so full of innocent delight when he sent the first message, "Love loves itself," ' remarked Joanna. 'And it's true babies know they're lovable because they're still connected to the divine. And everyone's essence is love, so when you know this you can't harm anyone because you are hurting yourself.'

Marcus smiled in the dark, for he had heard this several times. He added, 'So love is responsible to everyone. By that I mean able to respond to everyone's needs.'

'True, but we are not responsible for anyone because if we take responsibility for someone else we impinge on their free will.'

'I agree.' After a pause for reflection, he prompted, 'And love has many faces.'

'It's true. We think love is about being sweet and nice but it's not. It's about being clear and honest and acting for the highest good.' She snuggled into his arms and he kissed her hair. Then suddenly she stiffened and lifted her head slightly as if listening to something. 'He's here,' she whispered, sounding both tremulous and excited. 'He's calling me. The white lion's calling me.'

Marcus did not need to ask how or why. Throwing back the cover and the mosquito net he leaped from the bed. Joanna was but a second behind him. It was dark in the chalet but they groped their way to the window and opened the shutter.

The moon was not yet full but it was light enough to see that a young lion was waiting outside their room. He stood with his head held high, every inch a king, proud, regal and pure white. They gasped involuntarily. Marcus made as if to open the door of the chalet but Joanna held him back. 'No!' she whispered. 'He may carry the Christ light but he is still a lion.'

'You're right.' Reluctantly Marcus returned to the window where their view was impeded by netting. 'Ask him what he wants.'

Joanna was trying to still her mind to connect with him. She was in no doubt that he had sought them out with a purpose. Seconds later a white light beamed into her third eye and a message, which she knew came from the lion, filtered into her consciousness.

'Greetings, Beloved One. Thank you for returning. Time is of the essence and I ask you to pass this on. My message is love. Remember that love holds the key. Love can always find a solution.' This was followed by a deep silence as thoughts of co-operation and pictures of people and nations working together for the highest good flooded her mind. The pictures withdrew and she was just about to relax when the white light flowed back in with the words, 'You can't give love away.' Then came a warm glowing feeling of being loved unconditionally. She closed her eyes and basked in it. She felt as if she were being held in angel's wings.

When she opened her eyes Marcus was watching her. She told him about the lion's first message and added, 'Then the second one was, "You can't give love away." You can't give it away because it always comes back to you. It's free and you can't buy it. It's also everywhere and is absolutely unconditional, so there are no strings attached to genuine love. It is totally abundant but you have to open up to receive it.'

Marcus absorbed the power of the messages in silence. The moonlight glinting on Joanna's face gave her a mystical glow and Marcus was thinking how beautiful she looked when the lion lifted his head. The movement caught their attention and the great cat gazed straight at Joanna. Even Marcus could sense the energy emanating from him towards her and she received the essence of it clearly.

'Love walks with its feet on Earth and its head in the heavens.'

The girl was immediately reminded of the avatar, Sai Baba's words: 'Hands that help are holier than hands that pray.'

Yes, she thought. It's about being sensible and practical so that you keep the balance, and always staying connected to the divine. It also means honouring everything on the Earth, for it is all part of the Source. She nodded slightly to herself, and the lion, scrutinising her as if checking her energy, nodded too. She sensed there was more to come and she was not mistaken. As she cleared her mind, a wave of light entered her third eye. 'Love is greater than the sum of its parts,' flowed in. She thought of families, communities, schools and all co-operative activities, where there is a common vision and saw how they could achieve, where individuals could not.

Again a burst of love entered her heart and she felt as if she were one with the lion, one with everything. She was in ecstasy. When she opened her eyes, the lion had vanished, disturbed by someone shining a torch out of their window.

She stared blankly at the spot where the lion had stood moments earlier. Then she turned to Marcus and shared his message. 'I'd better write it all down,' she said slowly, as if trying to bring herself back from her experience. He lit the old-fashioned gas lamps that graced their cabin and found her journal for her. After seeing the new-born cub, she had written:

1 **Love loves itself.** Love knows it is God and there is no separation, so it can never hurt another. Love is able to respond to the needs of all plants and animals, to all of creation.
2 **Love has many faces.** Love can be in the compassion of the mother as well as in the discipline of the father. It can be in the devotion of a lover or carer. It can be in the action of death, where one dies to set their family free. Love is selfless intention. Never judge another, for you may judge a face of love.

She scrabbled in her bag for a Biro and scribbled intently.

3 **Love holds the key. Love can always find a solution.** When people let go of self and co-operate for the highest good all can be resolved. Earth can be a planet of love.
4 **You can't give love away.** It always comes back to you. It is free and abundant. Unconditional love is detached from outcome. You must open up to receive it.

5 **Love walks with its feet on Earth and its head in the heavens.** Be sensible and practical, for love is service. At the same time remain in tune with the highest purpose and divine will.

6 **Love is greater than the sum of its parts.** When love works with love the light created is greater than if each was working separately.

They talked half the night, energised by the white lion seeking Joanna out and even more by his message.

'We'll have to tell Mum. She can record his message in her book. That's the best way of spreading it out quickly.'

Marcus agreed.

Yet their enthusiasm was diminished by the sacred beast's first communication. 'Time is of the essence.' Did this mean that the people on Earth needed to hear his message, or that he did not have long to live?

Joanna repeated several times, 'He had more to say. I know he did. The torch you saw must have disturbed him.'

Marcus nodded. 'Yes, it did. And we'll look for him tomorrow. One thing's certain. If he wants to communicate with you, Joanna, he'll come to find you!'

Chapter 40

The following morning Monica's mood fluctuated moment by moment. Today she was to meet Bede at the airport. One second she was dancing on air that he knew she was his mother. She pictured him hugging her and being delighted. She saw herself proudly standing with her hand on his arm saying, 'This is my son.' And then she would remember her brother-in-law's warning about Bede's rage and her world would crumble into uneasy disquiet. Her hands would become clammy with anxiety and her stomach flutter.

She had told Peter about the child before their marriage but, by mutual consent, he was rarely mentioned. They had no children of their own and Peter was already ill when it was mooted that Bede come to stay with them. He acquiesced without demur, surmising the boy's presence would bring happiness to his wife in a way that he could not. He knew he was dying, so why should he deny Monica a chance of joy. He could only guess from her reaction how much the child meant to her but, even then, the subject was never discussed in detail. Peter did not want to plumb the depth of his own feelings, but he supported his wife in his own way by letting her talk endlessly about Bede. It was exhausting him though, and draining his already low vital force.

Monica went alone to meet her son at the airport. She was strung up like a puppet and a nerve was twitching by her eye but she had put on a dress and lipstick, as if she were going to meet a lover rather than a son. She was late and Bede was already waiting with his luggage outside the tiny airport. Her heart thumped as she pulled up beside him, smiling a wide red smile.

'Lovely to see you,' she called and, jumping down, ran towards him to fling her arms around him. But he stood frozen, his arms by his sides, until she dropped hers; then he pushed her roughly away.

She blanched. 'Bede?'

His black eyes were filled with rage. 'Hello, Mother!' His tone was deeply sarcastic. 'So the black child you sent to the far side of the world comes back to haunt you!'

'No! It wasn't like that, Bede. Listen.' Tears were running down her cheeks and people were looking at her curiously.

'Get in,' Bede said coldly, opening the passenger door for her to enter. He slammed the door behind her and sat in the driving seat, his hands big and firm on the steering wheel. He felt powerful, in control. The world had hurt him and he wanted to hurt this woman who had given birth to him and abandoned him in a distant land. Now he poured his anger over his birth mother, just as he had done with his adopted parents. 'I belong here. And you sent me away.'

'I built this place up for you, hoping some day it would be yours,' she protested. But nothing placated him.

By the time they reached the lodge, Monica was hurt, bewildered and sobbing. All her castles in the air had crumbled into dust. She could not see a future.

Bede jumped out with his bags and strode to his room, leaving her to mop herself up before she faced the guests.

Helen was in the little shop at reception looking at post-cards when the phone rang in the office next door. Peter was looking after it but when he saw Bede leaping from the car and marching to his room, looking like a bomb about to explode, he hurried out to find his wife. In his hurry to comfort Monica, he left the office door open, so Helen heard the message coming through loud and clear on the answerphone. 'Message for Bede. I've got a job for you. Phone this number.' Helen recognised the voice. It was one she would never, ever forget. An icy lump plunged into the pit of her stomach. Sturov! Now that the cub was out of the protection of the Great White Brotherhood, the evil one was back on the scene.

Her legs felt woolly and her voice cracked as she called to Marcus out of the window. 'Quick! Come here. Listen to this.'

None of them knew that Sturov and a party of his henchmen were once more staying at the Black Rhino Lodge. The evil man was becoming increasingly disturbed by the influence of the white lion. People were changing their perceptions and their lives when they saw or even

heard of him. The lion could disrupt his plans and machinations and he was not having it. Already in the few
months since the lion's reappearance pharmaceutical
profits had dropped. The media had unwittingly helped in
this, despite Sturov's dark influence and efforts to stop it.

It started on the day a programme about the white lion
was broadcast in America. People had seen his beautiful,
proud and dignified face on the screen and the love
pouring from his eyes overwhelmed them. Men, women
and children found themselves crying, even politicians
and hard businessmen. Their tears were catalysts for
change and healing. The programme was repeated all
over the world. Endless articles and books were
produced. White lion mouse mats, pictures, coasters,
T-shirts and every conceivable product were sold and, in
every case, Christ consciousness poured from those eyes.

As the hearts of humanity opened people started
talking of co-operation and caring. Dishonest businessmen felt a need to be honest. Hard-nosed journalists
with questionable morals embraced integrity so that trust
in the press was growing. Violent men yearned for tranquillity. Even political leaders had been touched and were
seeking wise solutions to world hunger and poverty. That
would inevitably lead to peace and the decline of the
trade in arms. The youth of the world seemed to be
finding an ideal, a vision to live by and were eschewing
drugs.

Even more disgusting to Sturov, people were taking
responsibility for their lives and their health. There was
a move to demand organic food and an end to genetically

modified products. With the opening of hearts, the immune systems of sick people were already becoming stronger so that long-term debilitating diseases, especially those with an emotional content such as AIDS and cancer, multiple sclerosis and Parkinson's, were being overcome.

In Africa wise leaders were emerging, who were persuading the people to throw off the yoke of corruption and violence. The people themselves were generating a programme of building works, and schools were mushrooming to teach children and adults alike about harmony, healing and forgiveness. It was extraordinary. Unbelievable. It seemed as if an energy was rolling across the planet, changing the order of things. The power-hungry Sturov was outraged and fearful. The edifice of his life, built on a foundation of scheming and corruption, was collapsing.

All this in less than a year!

He marched round snarling at everyone and barking orders. That white lion must die. He was constantly watched by adoring tourists so his disposal must be legal. His influence must end now.

The dark forces have advantages the light-workers do not possess. By use of bribery and corruption, a little extortion, quite a lot of blackmail and even a touch of light torture, he had obtained a shooting licence for Friday. He had a licence to kill one lion and he knew which one he intended it to be. Nothing would stop him this time. And the fact that it was legal gave him a twisted sense of satisfaction. He laughed aloud.

As soon as the licence was safely in his hands he phoned the hotel and left a message for Bede at reception. That was the message Helen heard. Sturov knew that Marcus, Joanna and Helen were staying at the safari lodge and his eyes glinted with humourless mirth. This would spoil their equanimity! Bede would be his tracker and would set up the white lion for the kill.

When Helen told Marcus that Sturov had phoned Bede, his face set in rigid lines. She had never seen his lips so tight and angry but he did not look shocked.

'This isn't a surprise to you?' she surmised. 'But why Bede and how does he know Sturov?'

Marcus had never told Helen about Bede's visit to the Black Rhino Lodge or what happened that night. Now he did so. At the same time he filled her in on the fire and their suspicions. 'There was no evidence and no one was charged but I'm sure it was him,' he told her, then added with some embarrassment, 'It was probably stupid but I thought he'd changed after the cub escaped the cull. But he tried to kill us with the fire.' As he remembered that night, Marcus's face paled.

Helen was not sure whether it was a response to fear or anger. She herself was reeling with shock, having had no idea Marcus and Joanna had been in such danger. A feeling of rage and revulsion towards Bede spread through her and she was thinking some particularly nasty thoughts about him when she realised that Marcus was still talking.

'I've tried so hard to believe it wasn't him and since the

white lion came back he's different again. He's always talking about him and I hoped against hope that the lion had healed his heart.'

Helen pulled herself together. 'Maybe he has. Extraordinary things have happened since he returned,' she replied gently, as ever wondering at Marcus's capacity for understanding and forgiveness, while she battled with thoughts of revenge. 'But why didn't you tell me before? You just said there had been a cull and that the white lion cub wasn't hurt and there was a fire at the lodge. I didn't know three chalets were burned down.'

'You were in Egypt on your honeymoon and it didn't seem fair to worry you, especially as Bede seemed so different after the birth of the cub. So Joanna and I decided not to trouble you. But there's more.' He told her how he had looked into Bede's soul and how the light of the sacred cat had changed him. 'When I last looked, just before the fire, there was one door closed and only one small hard black rock left but it was enough to make him try murder.'

'Maybe that's dissolved now,' suggested Helen, without conviction. But she did not believe so. Not for a moment.

At that time they did not know about the shooting licence. They could only speculate about the job Sturov wanted Bede to do. Whatever it was, they knew the white lion was in great peril.

Their hearts heavy, Marcus and Helen walked slowly to the dining room for lunch. Joanna and Tony were already there with several other guests so they did not have an opportunity to tell them the terrible news that Sturov was trying to contact Bede.

By now all the guests knew that Bede had arrived back from England and had stormed off to his room, leaving Monica in tears. It does not take long for information like that to fly to all ears. Peter was in their room with her and it was left to a student who was helping out to keep the guests happy. But nothing could clear the weird pall of anger and grief that was hanging over the lodge that lunchtime, like a haunting spectre. And the fact that Helen and Marcus were silent and withdrawn, while Joanna and Tony were wondering what had transpired, did not help.

Later that afternoon, Drake told them he had heard that an American syndicate had a licence to kill one lion.

Marcus and Joanna stared at each other and at Helen and Tony in horror. They knew who was behind it. Sturov! And which lion he wanted to kill! So that was the job Sturov had for Bede! Would he be bought by the darkness or would he help them save the lion?

'When?' demanded Marcus.

'Friday.'

'That's tomorrow!'

Chapter 41

No one saw Bede that day. Peter said that he had taken the answerphone message to his room. He had knocked but there was no reply, so he had pushed it under his door.

Joanna looked at Marcus as if to say, 'Has he gone to Sturov?' But they did not tell Monica. She was already distraught.

When Monica heard about the licence to shoot a lion, at first she crumpled. Like everyone, she knew that the killers would go for the white lion. 'A white lion fetches a premium,' she explained. Then it seemed as if the news galvanised her into action. And activity took her mind off Bede. She phoned everyone she knew but a dozen calls left her and everyone else frustrated and exhausted. Officialdom said a licence for a shoot had been obtained and nothing could be done to change that.

'Look into Bede's soul again, Marcus,' begged Joanna.

'How would it help?' he demanded. But Joanna and Helen persuaded him that it might afford information, which would enable them to aid him. And that would assist the white lion.

Once again he meditated and asked for permission from Bede's higher self to see into his soul. Once again it was granted. This time he saw that the last door, which had been firmly shut, held back feelings of abandonment in this life. The door had now been blasted open by white light, which swirled round in his soul. This allowed the torrent of bitterness locked behind the door to pour out. It was causing havoc and destruction. Because he was not in touch with his higher self, he was unable to discipline or order the chaos of his emotions. 'There is also a hard rock, which was there before and which is smaller but still preventing him from understanding other people's feelings. The influence of the white light is powerful, but has not yet completed its task,' Marcus told them.

'Or his soul is giving him free will and has ordered his guides and angels to stand back while he takes his own decisions,' suggested Helen.

'Either way, I don't feel we can reach him now,' said Marcus, with an expression of concern.

'We can ask the angels to help him,' reminded Joanna.

'Yes, we can do that. It always helps,' agreed Marcus, pacing restlessly. 'I wish we could go out to find the lion now and warn him off!'

'Don't even think about it in the dark,' replied Helen. 'If he wants to he will come to you.'

'I do hope he does,' Marcus responded fervently.

They were all up long before sunrise on the following morning, Good Friday. They wanted to see the white lion one more time and try to persuade him to leave the area before the killers arrived. Drake arrived to report that there was no sign of Bede. Monica went white when she heard that but, holding herself on a tight emotional rein, drove the safari vehicle herself.

The white lion had a favourite haunt on a rocky outcrop where he could be king of all he surveyed. They prayed he would be there.

'Send him messages, Joanna,' her mother kept saying.

'I am. All night I've been telling him to leave but I have a feeling he's still here.'

'He left before the cull,' said Marcus, trying to raise their hopes. 'Perhaps he'll go this time too.' But they all had an overwhelming feeling of doom. Things felt different now.

Even Tony, usually like a rock, felt the atmosphere of gloom and despondency. He took Helen's hand and held it tight.

The white lion was sitting on the ledge, silhouetted against the sun as it rose. In other circumstances it would have been an overwhelmingly wonderful picture. Now they only felt anguish. They drove as close as they could to the edge of the clearing under the rock. Joanna sent the cosmic creature messages and they shouted to try to disturb him but he sat there, with a sphinx-like smile, head up and eyes slanted, seemingly unaware and unruffled. At last they realised their efforts were in vain.

'I'm getting out to try and chase him away,' said Marcus at last, starting to climb down, but they pulled him back.

'No!' commanded Monica. 'He's a wild creature.'

'No!' shouted Helen. 'He knows exactly what he's doing.'

'No!' screamed Joanna, clinging to his arm. 'Don't be stupid.'

Tony tapped him on the shoulder and said quietly, 'Fate has a hand here, Marcus. Let it be.'

Marcus sat back and took a deep breath, the duality of the situation striking him. The white lion, wild beast and star king of Christ consciousness! Every creature on Earth was simultaneously subject to the laws of the jungle and the laws of spirit.

The great beast turned his head to look at them and opened his mouth with what appeared to be a laugh. Joanna took a deep breath. A burst of energy hit her third eye. 'Love has nothing to hide.' She received an understanding that love knows everything and nothing can be hidden from it. It is clear and innocent so it never keeps secrets. For this reason it reveals all.

'He knows all that is happening and he's teaching us his sacred truths right to the last,' she gulped.

Marcus squeezed her hand and pointed to the great beast, which was looking at Joanna over the distance as if willing her to give him attention. 'He wants to give you something more,' Marcus said softly. 'Listen.'

She calmed herself immediately and made her mind receptive. She thought the animal smiled as she received, 'Love is a rainbow.' For a moment she felt confused as she wondered what that could mean but a flow of wisdom followed. 'A rainbow indicates eternal hope,

343

optimism, good fortune. However dark a storm, love waits to show itself. It is the grace when the challenge has been faced.'

She had scarcely shared the communication and was preparing herself to receive more when a vehicle full of pale-faced Japanese tourists with flashy cameras arrived on the scene but they took their photos and left quickly. Joanna wanted to scream with frustration and horror. Icy fingers of dread were running up and down her back. She could see the lines of tension etched on her mother's face and knew she felt the same. Marcus had a great knot in his stomach and even Tony had a chest so tight he could hardly breathe. Monica's entire body was racked with pain and her eyes were huge and staring. No one knew how Drake on the lookout was feeling.

The sacred white beast looked unperturbed. He shook his head slightly, then communicated to Joanna. 'Love is the power.' For a moment she felt paralysed with the immensity of the statement. And then the message flooded through her that love dissolves hate and fear and cannot be corrupted or coerced. It has total integrity. She understood immediately that anger, fear and guilt originate in a feeling of powerlessness. When you embrace love you have everything. She knew then that the lion was choosing his fate.

At last came the moment they dreaded. An opulent safari truck appeared, gleaming new and clean. Sturov sat behind the driver with a gross couple, evidently Americans. They pulled up in the clearing and the evil man turned his head slowly towards their vehicle, a gloating smile on his face.

But their eyes were all on the man in the driver's seat. It was Bede! Looking neither to right nor left, he indicated the lion to the visitors with his hand. The man squinted at it through thick glasses and beamed with delight.

In a flurry of desperation Monica stood up and screamed, 'Bede! No! Bede!' at the top of her voice. The sound pierced them all, shattering their auras. Joanna felt her insides contract.

With a sudden movement Bede leaped out of the vehicle. He jerked towards them and pointed the rifle at Monica. His eyes were red. Sweat poured off him and his vicious expression spelled murder.

Monica gasped loudly. Then the tableau froze. The world stood still. For a moment there was an intense silence. The lion observed.

At last the American in his new khaki hunting clothes and snappy hat, safe in his seat on the vehicle, whimpered. The sound seemed to reach Bede, who gave his mother a dark, contemptuous look. Afterwards Marcus could have sworn he spat. Then, as if nothing had happened, Bede turned towards the hunter. He reached out a solicitous hand and carefully helped the portly man down. The American smiled with relief that the weird charade was over and delight that he would have his expensive moment of glory after all. Bede handed him a rifle.

The man was elderly and slightly unsteady, Helen observed, as though he never left his computer screen for exercise.

The white lion watched him and stood up too. He yawned carelessly. Then he padded slowly and majestically down from the rock and across the clearing. The anonymous American looked nervous as the beautiful white creature approached, with quiet dignity. Then the great cat, holding his head high and proud, halted and waited.

Bede, the Judas, helped the tourist to hold the rifle correctly and aim. The white lion watched and seemed to smile. Bede indicated the killer should pull the trigger.

Everyone was totally silent, holding their collective breath, one party in agony, the other in triumph. Then the shots rang out. Blood spattered all over the lion's chest and the noble beast fell.

'Well shot!' called Sturov loudly to the man, as if he had courageously hunted a wild and dangerous beast. 'A fine trophy.'

The American looked delighted. He took his hat off and bowed to the shocked audience as if acknowledging their accolade. They knew he was unaware of what he had done. He was a young soul, a vehicle for Sturov's dark will.

As the pure white lion died Joanna received into her third eye: 'Love is the dark side of the moon.' The message was that darkness serves love. So much remains unknown while in a human body that we can but scratch the surface of the great mystery of Earth. Most of all she had a conviction that the lion's life had not been in vain and his death was but a beginning. It felt almost too much to bear.

Monica crumpled into her seat like a rag doll and started to sob, Marcus felt heavy as stone and Helen retched over the side of their vehicle, while Tony patted her back. Bede sauntered over to inspect the lion. He indicated that he was dead and it was safe to approach. The hunter gave him an envelope. Then Bede showed him where to place his foot on the dead beast for the best possible photographs.

That was too much for Drake. He jumped down from the lookout, moved Monica along the seat and started the engine. In silence he drove them back to the lodge.

When they were all sitting in the lounge Joanna told Marcus, her mother and Tony what the white lion had communicated.

1 Love loves itself.

2 Love has many faces.

3 Love holds the key. Love can always find a solution.

4 You can't give love away.

5 Love walks with its feet on Earth and its head in the heavens.

6 Love is greater than the sum of its parts.

In a slightly shaky hand she added:

7   **Love has nothing to hide.** Love knows everything and nothing can be hidden from it. Because it is totally innocent it reveals all and never keeps secrets.

8   **Love is a rainbow.** From love springs eternal hope and optimism, which is eventually rewarded by good fortune, which is good karma. Love constantly looks for the rainbow, which inevitably appears after a storm.

9   **Love is the power.** It dissolves hate and fear. Anger, fear, guilt and all dark emotions come from a feeling of being powerless to get love. Because love has total integrity it cannot be coerced, manipulated or corrupted.

10 **Love is the dark side of the moon.** Life in a human body is full of unknowns and we can but scratch the surface. But remember darkness ultimately serves love.

That evening the four visitors returned and placed a cross and flowers on the spot where the white lion had fallen. As the news had spread of his death, others had been to the place of the massacre and left flowers too. It was an extraordinary and poignant scene. The sunset that night was the most beautiful and flamboyant they had ever seen. And yet it could not lift their hearts, which were inexpressibly heavy. They felt a light had gone out. They stayed for ten minutes, then left.

Bede did not return. Monica cried and screamed all night, feeling something dreadful had happened to him. For her sake Peter called in all the favours he could and everyone searched for the missing man. One of his fellow trackers reported that he had seen Bede after the shooting. 'He looked wild, crying that he couldn't live with himself. He said he'd put out the Light of the World. Then he ran off.' They did not dare tell Monica their worst fears.

Early the following morning Drake came to the lodge with the news Bede had been found hanging on a tree. Monica was bereft. She had only been his true mother for a few days and she had lost him. She kept wandering into the bush in such a distraught state that the doctor sedated her.

Peter collapsed with exhaustion and it was left to Marcus to phone Edward to tell him the terrible news. He caught the next flight from Cairo and was with them by Sunday lunchtime. He also arranged for his parents to fly out from London for the funeral but they would not arrive until the following day.

That night Drake drove them to the quartz hill, where they had created the symbol. There were five of them: Helen, Tony, Joanna, Marcus and Edward. The tracker followed behind with the rifle.

An eerie silence cloaked the area. Not a creature moved. Not a bird sang. The world seemed in mourning.

As they approached the clearing they saw what at first seemed to be an upright log of wood in the centre of the symbol. It turned out to be the sangoma, completely still. He had heard about the death of the white lion and, shocked but not surprised, had come here to pay his respects.

'From Orion he came. To Orion he will return,' he said.

'And will the Christ energy return to the cosmos?' asked Joanna.

'Not all of it. Some will live on through the white lion's memory. He has done what he came to do. His influence has been felt everywhere. The impetus of what he has started will continue for generations and he will be remembered for his death as much as for his life.'

Joanna was glad of that. She was reminded of a crucifixion two thousand years ago that still influenced the world. She told the sangoma of the lion's communications about his message for Earth. 'It's all about love,' she added. 'Mum's going to put the message in the book she's writing.'

He nodded. 'Tell me please.'

The girl knew it by heart. She almost chanted, as she repeated what the lion had communicated.

The wise man had tears in his eyes. 'If only the whole world could hear that.' He turned to Helen. 'Your book will touch many. You are doing your part well in spreading the message.'

She glowed with pleasure. 'The lion has done so much good even in his short life,' she responded. 'Already love has started to change the world.'

'What about Africa? Is the work of the white lion enough to heal the tear in the web of light over this continent?' asked Marcus.

The sangoma frowned for a moment and they found their hearts sinking. Then he spoke in measured tones. 'The work has started. Hearts are opening and souls are healing. That will liberate the people and heal the web. There is more to do but truth and integrity must accelerate as people remember the white lion.'

They all found themselves nodding in relief and gratitude.

'He'll continue to touch the hearts of many. He'll never truly die,' added the sangoma sagely. Then he continued softly, 'The true purpose of the Sphinx and the pyramids is to hold the information for the ascension of the planet until the time is right to release it. They contain records of a formula for world government, which will allow all on Earth to live in peace, harmony, economic growth and abundance. But there must be a level of love on the planet before this can be released. The white lion has brought in the wind of change, which is allowing love to spread. The dolphins and unicorns are already touching people and accelerating a rise in consciousness. Soon the Sphinx will come into its power again and a world of love and peace will be created. Then the world government can emerge for the highest good of all.'

They sat in the circle sending the white lion thanks for coming into their lives and asking for a blessing on humanity. They were invoking angels to help the world, when a blanket of peace spread gently over them. A beautiful fragrance surrounded them. As one they looked up and there, like a cloud stretched across the vast sky, was the spirit of the white lion. They all saw it, even Tony.

'His spirit will never die,' said Joanna exultantly. And spontaneously they started to chant the sacred ohm, their hearts feeling lighter.

'That'll be an extraordinary ending for your book, Mum,' Joanna said to Helen as they walked back to their transport. 'We literally saw his spirit rise up before us. We saw him ascend. Tell the world that and his message of love and you will raise the consciousness of so many people.'

'Yes, so many sacred mysteries, the white lion, the Sphinx and pyramids, the dolphins, the angels, the unicorns and the stars all linked in love, trying to help the planet,' agreed Helen.

'They create a wonderful web of light round us,' added the sangoma. 'And we can add our light to strengthen it. Your book will continue the work of the white lion so that his message will live on.'

'That's what it's all about,' exclaimed Helen. 'We can all do our part to illuminate the web of light.'

Bibliography

Andrews, Shirley, *Atlantis: Insights from a Lost Civilization* (Llewellyn Publications)

Bauval, Robert, *The Orion Mystery* (Random House)

Cori, Patricia, *Atlantis Rising* (Authors Choice Press)

Lewis, H. Spencer, *The Mystical Life of Jesus* (The Rosicrucian Press)

Quan Yin, Amorah, *Pleiadian Perspectives on Human Evolution* (Bear and Co)

Randall-Stevens, H.C., *Atlantis to the Latter Days* (The Order of the Knights Templars of Aquarius)

Temple, Robert, *The Sirian Mystery* (St Martin's Press)

Tucker, Linda, *Children of the Sun God* (Earthyear Books)

HODDER
MOBIUS

Transform your life
with Hodder Mobius

For the latest information on the best in
Spirituality, Self-Help,
Health & Wellbeing and Parenting,

visit our website
www.hoddermobius.com